Secrets and Lords

JUSTINE ELYOT

mischief

Mischief
An imprint of HarperCollins*Publishers*
77–85 Fulham Palace Road,
Hammersmith, London W6 8JB

www.mischiefbooks.com

A Paperback Original 2013

First published in Great Britain in ebook format by
HarperCollins*Publishers* 2012

A catalogue record for this book is
available from the British Library

ISBN-13: 9780007553396

Find out more about HarperCollins and the environment at
www.harpercollins.co.uk/green

CONTENTS

CONTENTS

Chapter One

Edie Crossland pulled another bramble from her skirt, then put her bloodied finger to her mouth, looking up with dismay at the gathering clouds. Her feet were sore and she'd had enough of it.

It was not that Edie was unused to walking. Her footprints were sunk into the paving stones of Bloomsbury and Holborn many times over, mixed with millions of others. But the London streets hardly compared with this new terrain. The grass verge of the road was bumpy and thick with weeds, and sometimes it disappeared so that Edie was forced back on to the narrow track that led out of Kingsreach from the station.

She could have been sitting up on the box of a pony and trap sent from the Hall, making this trip in relative comfort, carpet bag stowed safely at her feet. But she had not wanted her first view of Deverell Hall to be contaminated by the inane chatter of some fellow servant. So she had deliberately omitted to send them advance warning of the train she would be on, as she had been asked to do. When questioned, she would shrug and assume the letter was lost in the post. These things happen.

Words she did not particularly care to dwell on, given the context in which she had last heard them. The nagging, dark feelings overcame her again and she stopped for a moment, swallowing the bitter taste that came to her mouth.

As if in answer to a silent prayer for distraction from the misery of a stroll that now felt like a death march, there came a distant roar, like an approaching swarm of bees, from somewhere behind her. It was not thunder, although that looked likely, nor could it be attributed to any of the livestock in the surrounding fields. She was far enough away from the railway now to rule out a train.

It grew louder and louder and all she could do was look over her shoulder, transfixed with a vague fear that seemed to go hand-in-hand with her earlier brooding. Her legs weakened just as a gleaming silver fender appeared at the bend of the road, then the cream-coloured body of a motor car. It zoomed past her, expelling great gaseous clouds that made her splutter in their wake.

Of course, she thought with relief, they must have such things in the countryside too. But she had not seen one near the station or anywhere on the streets of Kingsreach until now. It must be heading for Deverell Hall. But to whom did it belong? Maybe to … But no. That was unlikely.

A fat drop of rain landed on her back. She had not thought to bring an umbrella. Sighing, she lowered her head, with its meagre protection of a cheap straw hat, and began to hurry, cursing the fashion for narrow skirts as she shuffled along.

* * *

A further half an hour passed before Edie's first glimpse of Deverell Hall, and by then she was so thoroughly drenched and utterly miserable that a fairy palace would scarcely have impressed her.

The turrets were bare outlines against the black sky, every finer detail obscured by the driving rain. Edie perceived a great many windows and a prospect that would normally have delighted her. The road led downwards amidst lush green woodland until the landscape opened up, neatly planned and bordered, and the pale ribbon of driveway brought the eye to the stately entrance of the house. She saw fountains at the head of the drive and a hint of some formal gardens to the left side of the building. It was very much as she'd imagined and yet somehow less real.

'It's because of the weather,' she told herself. 'I never thought of it in the rain.' In her imagination, Deverell Hall was impervious to the elements.

The sighting gave additional impetus to her journey, although she was fading with weariness, wetness and

3

hunger now. She dragged her aching feet onwards, under the arching trees, for another half a mile.

As she emerged, another blast of engine noise made her jump to the side of the driveway, just in time to be splashed to the knee by the same cream-coloured car. Its driver, a dark-haired man in an expensive coat, cigarette in the corner of his mouth, did not pause even to look at her as he hurtled onwards and away from the estate.

She half-turned after him to remonstrate, but was surprised to see another car coming in the opposite direction, towards her. This one was less flashy, sleeker and quieter. All the same, it made a harsh coughing sound as it slowed down and came to a halt behind her.

A fair-haired man in a uniform wound down the window and stuck his head out.

'You the new girl?' he asked.

She nodded, too wet and cold to speak.

His stunningly blue eyes crinkled sympathetically at the edges.

'You're pretty much there, but hop in anyway. I'll take you the rest of the way in style.'

She hesitated, tightening her slippery grip on her bag handle.

'Come on,' he insisted. 'Don't stand there like a statue.' He opened the passenger door.

The first flash of lightning over the roof of Deverell Hall made her mind up for her. She scampered over to the other side of the car and climbed carefully inside and pulled the door shut. 'I'm going to get the leather all wet.'

The man laughed, a glint in his eye. 'It's seen a lot worse.' He put out a hand skinned in a tan driving glove. 'Ted Kempe,' he said. 'His Lordship's chauffeur. Delighted to make your acquaintance.'

'Edie,' she said, putting her own hand in his larger one, enjoying the warmth of the small squeeze he gave her fingers. 'Edie ... Prior.' Close one, she thought. She had almost forgotten her new name.

'That's right,' he said, unnerving her for a moment, sounding as if he was in the know about her and her situation. 'I heard Mrs Munn mention you at breakfast. The new housemaid.'

'Yes. And quite a house. There must be a legion of us.'

'You've never been here before?'

'No, I was interviewed up in London.'

'Oh, a London girl, eh? You didn't fancy getting a job up there then? Most of us here are local.'

'I ... needed a change of air,' said Edie, feeling leagues out of her depth. She looked away from the shrewd blue gaze of her new colleague, but only succeeded in looking straight into the reflection of his face in the window. He watched her and, for an uncomfortably long moment, said nothing.

'We all need those from time to time,' he said eventually. 'Well, Edie, you'll be wanting to get out of those wet things. Better get you to the house.'

The way his look lingered over her after the mention of 'wet things' made the back of Edie's neck prickle.

He was thinking of her peeling down her clinging damp stockings, unbuttoning the water-stained blouse. Her underwear was silk, not suitable for a servant girl, but she had not quite been able to bear the thought of wearing coarser fabrics next to her skin. Not yet.

No sooner was that thought in her mind than it was succeeded by other, even more disreputable imaginings. How would it feel to have the chauffeur's leather-gloved hands on her, disrobing her, moving slowly and smoothly over the curves of her body?

Stop it. Just stop it.

Mercifully, he put his foot on the accelerator and drove, his attention diverted to the road.

'I don't know what your last place was like but you'll find the servants' hall here a very tight-knit bunch,' he said. 'A bit like a secret society. It's hard to get in, but, when you're accepted, you become a member of the family.'

'Oh dear, that sounds rather intimidating. I suppose I shall be sized up. I hope I'm not found wanting.'

He gave her a sideways smirk.

'Can't imagine why you would be,' he said gallantly. 'Never mind the others, but keep the right side of Mrs Munn. She's the power behind the Deverell throne. If she doesn't take to you, you'll never prosper here.'

'Gosh, you really aren't inspiring me with confidence, you know.'

He drew up at the huge front steps, pulled the handbrake and turned to her, frowning in confusion.

'You sure you aren't some kind of governess or something? I've never heard a parlourmaid talk like you do.'

Edie held her carpet bag tighter. 'And how's that?' she asked with a nervous laugh. She had to watch her little quirks and mannerisms of speech. If possible, she must pare her conversation down to the bare minimum necessary for communication.

'Ladylike,' he said. 'Are all the London slaveys like you?'

'No, not at all. Well, perhaps some of them.'

He smiled. 'I might consider moving to London, then.'

Edie's wet clothes suddenly felt too tight, especially around the chest, and her toes curled inside her boots. He was flirting with her. And he was rather attractive, even if he was only a chauffeur.

'Oh,' she said, tongue-tied, looking all around her for extra luggage that did not exist. 'Well. Thank you for the, for, you know, driving me.'

'A pleasure,' he said. 'No, don't open the door yourself. You'll do me out of a job.'

He got out into the rain and ran around the front of the car to the passenger side.

Edie, toting her carpet bag, put her feet out of the door, preparing to stand.

'Now remember, Miss Prior,' he said, leaning down and speaking softly, 'if you ever need a friend in this place, Ted Kempe's your man. Do you promise you'll remember it?'

She nodded. 'I promise.'

'One more word,' he said, looking over his shoulder as if he expected a legion of eavesdroppers to have materialised from the sheets of rain all around. 'Watch Sir Charles. Don't let him ...' He shook his head. 'Just watch him, all right? Servants' entrance is round the back.'

Edie had almost made the ridiculous mistake of walking up the front steps.

'I'd see you inside, but His Lordship's ordered the car up to take him into Kingsreach. Good thing he sits in the back – you've left the passenger side all wet.'

She shot Ted one last breathless nod and a smile, then ran around the side of the building, looking for the way in.

It took a long time to find, given the vastness of the edifice. Edie looked in at every window on her way round, but saw only empty room after empty room until she arrived at the rear of the house. A kitchen garden lay a few hundred yards off, beyond a low wall. Surely the kitchen must be close to that.

She scrambled along a gravel path, desperate now to be out of the rain. A crash of thunder accompanied her descent into a basement area that belched heat up the stairs she squelched down. In the corner a large door stood invitingly open.

Shelter, at last. She stood with her back to the wall, blinking raindrops out of her eyes. Once they were gone she realised she was not alone in the room. The clatter of steel and crockery that filled the room stopped instantly. Two girls, their faces crimson from their endeavours within the hot room, and neither of them much above fourteen, stood against a huge Belfast sink, staring at her.

'Are you the new girl?' one of them asked.

Edie nodded.

'Filthy weather,' she said, hugging herself.

'Mrs Munn thought you weren't coming. You never wrote. She's been cursing your name all morning,' said the stouter of the two girls.

'You'd better go and find her,' added her companion.

'How shall I do that?'

Both girls shrugged and turned back to their washing up.

Tight-knit, that was what Ted had said. Meaning 'unfriendly' apparently.

Here, in this dark scullery, Edie's splendid plan did not seem so splendid any more. It had seemed so easy when she had huddled with Patrick and his sisters, evening after evening, discussing and fine-tuning. Now that she stood here, in Deverell Hall, it had immediately assumed a new character with an objective that appeared insurmountable. Failure seemed so likely that she thought about leaving then and there.

A red-faced woman in a dusty cap and apron appeared in the inner doorway and brandished a rolling pin at her. 'Whatever have we got here? A drowned rat from the garden?'

'I'm Edie Prior, the new parlourmaid.'

'Well, what are you doing skulking in here with these two ne'er-do-wells, then? Mrs Munn's got no hair left, she's torn that much of it out over you. Come on.'

Edie hurried after her, through a cavern of a kitchen that seemed to swarm with bodies rushing this way and that, and out into a cool, tiled hallway.

'I'm Mrs Fingall, the cook,' said the woman. 'You'll want to keep civil with me, because I'm the one as feeds you.'

'Oh, I hope I'm always civil,' said Edie.

The cook stopped and stared at her, hands on hips. 'You jolly well do, do yer?' she said. She knocked on a door. 'Mrs Munn's office,' she said confidentially.

Edie was relieved to be out of the heat and clash of the kitchen, which she had found unnerving. All the same, perhaps she had just left the frying pans – literally – for the fire.

'Come in.' The voice was low and calm, giving the lie to what everyone had said about the occupant tearing out her hair.

'Miss Prior, the new parlourmaid,' said Mrs Fingall, jabbing her in with two fingers between her ribs.

10

An angular woman sat at a desk, poring over a ledger. She looked up at Edie, expressionless.

'Thank you, Mrs Fingall. Would you fetch Jenny, please?'

Edie wondered why she had never considered the reality of the role she had thrown herself into. She had to converse with people, convince them of her background in domestic service. The best she could do was mimic her friend Josie McCullen, who worked as a daily girl in a house in Pimlico. She had shown Edie how to black-lead a grate and polish silver, but how to be another person … that was a rarer skill.

'Why did you not write?' asked Mrs Munn. 'I'd have sent Wilkins to meet you with the trap.'

'Oh, did you not receive my letter?' muttered Edie, finding the barefaced lying more difficult than she had expected.

'No, I did not. You were interviewed by Mrs Quinlan from the London residence?'

'Yes.'

'I suppose you were hoping for a job in Belgrave Square.'

'I am perfectly happy to work here.' As an afterthought, she added, 'ma'am', finding the word so odd that she had to suppress an embarrassed smile.

Mrs Munn was right, though – Edie had assumed that her application to work for the Deverell family would result in a place in their London residence. The fact that the only opening was at Deverell Hall had been the first snag in the plan. It was only thirty miles from London, but it seemed that a huge ocean stood between Edie and her familiar urban world.

Mrs Munn picked up a piece of paper and sneered at it.

Edie, recognising the character her friend's mother had written for her, felt her heart skip.

'Your last place seems to be a respectable house, if not one of the best in society. You will find the scale of things here somewhat different. It may alarm you at first, but if you keep a cool head and attend to your duties first and foremost, you will soon settle.'

A timid knock at the door interrupted Mrs Munn's flow.

'One last thing,' she said, before bidding the knocker enter. 'There must be no communication beyond that which is strictly necessary between you and the gentlemen of the house. Do you understand me? None whatsoever.'

'Of course, ma'am. By "gentlemen of the house", do you mean ...?'

'His Lordship's sons. The elder in particular.'

'I see.'

Mrs Munn raised her eyebrow. 'I hope you do.' She looked past Edie at the door. 'Come in, Jenny.'

Jenny was a mouse in human form and parlourmaid's black-and-whites. She hid in a corner while Mrs Munn instructed her to show Edie her room and help her with her uniform prior to a grand tour of the house.

The servants' staircase seemed to go up and up for ever. Conversation – a desultory affair – died out after the first flight and, from then on, nothing was heard but puffing and the echo of boots on stone.

'You're a London girl, then?' said Jenny, once they were at the very top of the building, in a low-ceilinged, dark room containing four beds and little else.

'Yes,' said Edie, moving instinctively towards the window, against which the rain beat so dismally that little could be seen outside.

'Most of us here are from Kingsreach and hereabouts. We've grown up on Deverell land. You don't know anything about us.'

Edie turned to the plain little creature, surprised at the edge of resentment in her voice.

'We're all of us in the same boat, aren't we?' she said. 'Service. What does it matter where we learned to wax a floor, so long as we wax it well?'

Jenny shrugged and pointed to some folded clothes on the bed furthest from the door. 'Uniform,' she said. 'Hope it fits. You've got a lovely figure.'

'Thanks,' said Edie. She tried a smile, but the wistful look on the girl's face caused it to misfire.

'He'll have an eye for you,' said Jenny.

'An eye for me? Who will?'

13

'Charlie Deverell. He tries it on with all the pretty maids.'

'Well, he won't try it on with me,' said Edie stoutly, moving behind a screen and unbuttoning her blouse.

'Yes, he will. You're ever so pretty. Even prettier than Susie Leonard, and she had to leave in disgrace when he got her into trouble.'

'Heavens!' Edie's fingers paused on the faux-pearl buttons. This must be what Mrs Munn was driving at before.

'He denies it was him, but everyone knows it was. Susie didn't even have a sweetheart. And I've seen her with the baby – got his eyes, she has, and his dark hair.'

Dark hair. The man driving the car.

'Well, I'm no fool and no flash Harry is going to seduce me,' said Edie briskly. She allowed room for a little pause, removing her skirt in the silence, before changing the subject. 'What do you think of Lady Deverell? She's new to the house, isn't she?'

'Not so new. Been here a year now.'

'Is she nice?'

'My ma always says if you can't speak well of someone, don't speak of them at all.'

Edie laughed uncomfortably, her face flushing hot.

'She's awfully glamorous, though, isn't she?' she said, putting the black dress on. It was a little tight under the bust but, apart from that, a snug fit. 'I saw her on the stage in London, in one of Mr Bernard Shaw's plays. She was quite magnetic.'

Jenny sat down on the side of one of the beds.

'London,' she said, as if intoning a magic spell. 'I'd so love to visit the theatre one day. I mean, I've seen the Kingsreach Players, everyone has, but the proper theatre. All red and gold, with balconies and plaster cherubs. That'd be smashing.'

'Well, I suppose you will one day,' said Edie, trying to steer the conversation back to her preferred subject. 'But Ruby Redford won't be treading the boards.'

'Hush, you're not to call her that! It's Your Ladyship and Lady Deverell now. She hates anyone mentioning her past. She's a bit sensitive about it. Well, more than a bit. You're best off forgetting it, if you've seen her on stage. Not that you'll get to speak to her much. She don't have much to say to the servants.'

'Really? I thought she might be a good mistress to have – since she's closer to, to our class than most of the gentry.'

'The opposite. Everyone says the first Lady Deverell was a real smasher, kind and sweet. She gave extra half-holidays when the weather was nice sometimes, and she always asked after your family. This one don't even acknowledge you. Like I say, she's funny about her past. She thinks talking to us like we're people shows her up, I reckon. But we all know that that's the mark of a someone who ain't a real lady. But I mustn't talk like this.'

A flicker of fear had crossed Jenny's pale face.

'Not when I don't know you. You won't repeat any of this, will you? Do you promise? Not to a soul?'

'Of course not. What has passed between us is in strict confidence. You may be sure I will observe it.'

'Gaw, you London girls talk proper, don't you?' Jenny's momentary anxiety had turned to a curious admiration.

'Oh, not really, I studied my mistress and her daughters at my last place and tried to imitate them. It's a habit. I expect I shall grow out of it here.'

Jenny stood again, seeing that Edie had tied her apron and pinned on her cap.

'Well, might be for the best,' she said. 'You'll get teased for it downstairs. Come on. I'm to help you find your feet today. What would you like to see first?'

'Well, I hardly know. Should we do a wing at a time?'

'Good idea. Let's start with the West Wing.'

They sallied forth, black-and-white neatness in duplicate, to the servants' staircase.

'The West Wing's used for visitors and children. We spend less time on it, especially since there aren't any Deverell children just at the moment. The ground-floor rooms aren't used at all.'

The West Wing was indeed, though splendid, a little neglected; its carpets threadbare and its wainscots dusty in places. The unused downstairs apartments were empty of furniture – huge, high-ceilinged bunkers with ornate plaster mouldings and pictures behind dust sheets.

16

Edie found it quite sinister and was glad to cross the courtyard to the East Wing, which contained the family rooms.

On the upper floor, the younger son and daughter of the house kept their suites.

'This is Sir Thomas's rooms,' said Jenny, briefly opening a door into a neat and unusually plain chamber. 'We needn't go in.'

'Who is Sir Thomas?'

'Lord, you really don't know nothing, do you? He's the younger son. He joined the Army and did very well for himself at first, but after getting shot in the war, he wanted out. Lord Deverell had to buy him out, even though he was injured. Walks with a limp now, always will.'

'Does he have another occupation now?'

'No, nothing.' Jenny shook her head. 'He can't settle. They say Lord Deverell's at his wits' end with him.'

'What is he like?'

'Well, I don't know him, really. He keeps himself to himself. Spends a lot of time at the races, or out with the dogs.'

They reached the next door.

'Whose rooms are these?'

'Lady Mary's, but I wouldn't be opening them if I didn't know she'd gone out. She gets wild if anyone disturbs her in her room.'

Jenny opened them with a furtive, mysterious air then stepped a little way into the light, airy chamber. Everything seemed to sparkle in there. Edie thought, with a sickening pang, of her room at home in London. She had the same cut-glass scent bottle on her dresser. The silver-backed hairbrush looked familiar too, even if Edie's was not monogrammed like Lady Mary's. Fresh cut flowers stood on the bedside table and the chest of drawers, and a tangle of stockings and scarves were strewn all over the bed.

'I suppose she was trying to decide what to wear tonight,' said Jenny with a laugh. 'She's fearful fussy. Ask Louise, her maid. She leads her a merry dance, she does.'

'A hard taskmistress?'

Jenny whispered, 'A spoiled little madam,' and then put a hand to her mouth, giggling guiltily.

'What is happening tonight?'

'Didn't Mrs Munn say? A big dinner, some visitors from London. I don't know who they are but I think they're supposed to be important.'

Another surge of panic rose through Edie's stomach.

'Will I have to serve them?'

'I shouldn't think so, not your first day.'

She exhaled gratefully.

'I wonder if Lady Mary will announce an engagement soon,' Jenny prattled on. 'They say she's got ever so many admirers in London. But, like I said, she's fussy.'

'Neither of the sons are married?'

Jenny sighed. 'No, and it don't look likely neither. One's a womaniser and the other's a recluse. Come on, shall we go downstairs?'

The windows were bigger on the floor below and the fittings notably more elaborate.

'Sir Charles's rooms,' whispered Jenny, her hand on an antique gold door handle.

'Should we?' Edie was suddenly nervous. 'What if he's in there?'

'He went to town,' she said. 'With Lady Mary. Come on.'

'There could be a woman in there.'

Jenny let out a peal of merry laughter. 'You ain't met him yet and you've got the measure of him already. Come on.'

She opened the door.

No woman was hidden behind it. The rooms were magnificent, crimson and gold, but the style was decidedly masculine and his valet had not yet cleared away his shaving things from the basin in the little bathroom. Edie felt possessed by a sense of the man who used these rooms; the scent of his cologne, mixed with a faint aroma of smoke, crept into her and took up residence in the corners of her consciousness. A dressing gown hung carelessly on a bedpost and his slippers were in the middle of the floor.

19

'Who is his valet?' Edie wondered aloud. 'Should he not have tidied these things?' She was proud of herself for remembering that aristocratic men all had valets. Although the social circles she moved in at home were mixed, they rarely involved lords and ladies.

'He is between valets at the moment,' said Jenny. 'His last one resigned a few days ago. He is sharing with Sir Thomas until they can hire a replacement.'

'Why did the last one resign?'

Jenny pinched her lips and shook her head.

'I don't know.'

But Edie thought that Jenny was concealing some further knowledge.

Moving towards the other side of the room, Edie saw a book on Sir Charles's bedside table and was consumed with curiosity to know what kind of thing this man enjoyed reading.

'Oh!' she said, picking it up. '*The Moon and Sixpence*. I have read this.'

'Put that down,' exclaimed Jenny, rushing over. 'Don't touch a thing.'

'We shouldn't be in here, should we?'

'No,' she admitted. 'Come on.'

She dragged Edie out by her elbow, but Edie was already wondering to what extent Sir Charles might identify with the book's hero, his namesake, a man who abandons his established life to pursue an impossible dream.

'His Lordship,' she said, flapping her hand at another door without opening it, following up a moment later with 'Her Ladyship'.

'Oh, can we not go in?'

'Her Ladyship is *in*. No, we cannot.'

'I would so like to see her rooms.'

'Well, you can't. So there. Come on, let's go to the ground floor. Like reading, do you?'

She opened a smaller door at the end of the corridor. It led on to a large gallery, looking down into a treasure trove of bookcases.

'Oh, a library! Oh, this is huge. How wonderful.'

It occurred to Edie that perhaps she should not be displaying such raptures in her role as a housemaid. But surely housemaids might like to look at a book or two now and again?

'Do a lot of reading, do you?' asked Jenny, leading her down the steps to the main room. 'You can't have been very busy in your last place.'

'Oh, I was, but I read on my days off, you know.'

'Must have been nice for your family.'

'They didn't mind.'

Edie barely registered Jenny's disparaging tone, too engrossed in the endless spines of gold-embossed leather that lay behind the glass doors of each cabinet.

'At least they had the shelves turned into cupboards,' said Jenny with a sniff. 'I hated dusting all those perishing things. Lord Deverell thought we were going to ruin them just by touching them so he locks them away now.'

'He is a keen scholar?'

'No, not really. I suppose they're worth a few bob, that's all.'

Edie shook her head. The idea of valuing books for their monetary worth was quite beyond her. At home, in her room, her books lay in piles, higgledy-piggledy, with dog-eared pages and dusty jackets, but they were the landscape of her life, to be kept round about her, not shut away in cages.

She was reluctant to leave this wonderland, but they had to move on regardless, to a breakfast room in modern pinks and pale greens, then a comfortable sitting room and a brace of cold gilt state rooms, until they were at the central part of the house.

The splendour of these rooms left even Edie open-mouthed – as huge as the British Museum galleries and several times more ornate. She craned her neck up at pricelessly painted ceilings and then let her eye move downwards to works of Tudor and Stuart art, interspersed with gold leaf twining all over everything. The impression was sometimes sumptuous, sometimes intimidating. It was nothing like a home. How did people conduct their daily business in rooms like these? Reception rooms opened on to more reception rooms; then there were morning, drawing, breakfast and dining rooms, each with a different colour scheme and each groaning with antiques that would need careful dusting and cleaning, over and over again.

Seeing everything with a maid's eye, Edie came to resent all the magnificence, much as her artistic senses were impressed. But really, who needed all this?

Out of the wings, Edie and Jenny now ran across several of their colleagues, all working hard to get the grandest rooms of the house into a fit condition to receive guests. Flowers were being arranged, feather dusters wielded and, in the dining room, a French polisher attended to a scratch on the table.

'They'll cover it with a cloth,' whispered Jenny, whisking Edie past. 'But Tilly Gresham got in terrible trouble for it all the same.'

A tall, thin, fastidious-looking man in a dark suit and white gloves appeared to be directing the carrying up- and down-stairs of a number of ornamental urns.

'Jenny,' he said. 'Is this the new girl?'

'Yes, Mr Stanhope, Edie Prior.'

'Pleased to meet you, Miss Prior.'

'Likewise,' said Edie, unsure whether or not to curtsey. She decided against it.

'Well, I'm sure you have work to do,' said Stanhope after an awkward pause. 'On such a day as this. And if not, I'll be asking Mrs Munn why not.'

'Don't mind him,' muttered Jenny, leading them to the

back stairs. 'He gets himself a bit worked up when there's a big do. He's the butler, if you didn't know.'

They descended to the depths of the house once more, where Jenny collected a trug of cleaning materials before showing Edie to the room where Mrs Munn had ordered them to work.

They passed along endless yards of corridor, under the baleful eyes of the Deverell ancestry, up and down the back stairs and through that busy, bustling series of reception rooms before arriving at the well-named Green Drawing Room.

It was very green, and very golden, and very velvety and very cold – in style rather than temperature. Everything in it was heavy and sharp-cornered. When Edie considered her family drawing room in Bloomsbury, with its cheerful patterns and fringed shawls all over the place, it could not have been more remote.

'Do people come in here to relax?' she asked, looking over a two-hundred-year-old spinet in the corner of the room.

'People hardly come in here at all,' said Jenny vaguely, sorting through rags and polishes. 'It's not much used. Here, I'll wax the wooden furniture and you can polish the mirror there.'

Edie accepted a rag and a tub of metal polish and made a start on the heavy ormolu-framed square mirror that stood over an unused fireplace.

They worked silently and diligently until Edie was drawn to the window by the sound of a car drawing up in the drive. She would not have admitted it to herself, but she was hoping for a glimpse of Ted.

The car was not the one she had ridden in earlier, though. It was that same sleek, cream-coloured monster that had twice passed her on the road.

The rain had abated and its driver got out on to wet gravel, looking up at the house windows as he did so. Edie took a swift step back, her heart pounding. Why did she not want to be seen? Because this must be Charles, the rake of the Deverell's, and she had no wish to draw his attention to her.

He was pristine in a pinstriped blazer over light-coloured waistcoat, shirt and trousers. His dark hair was immaculately cut and he was clean-shaven. He didn't wear a hat, and Edie approved of this, for she had no taste for the current fashion for straw boaters on men.

His eye was soon drawn away from the house, and he went to the passenger side to open it for a young woman.

'Who is that?' asked Edie, and Jenny came to look over her shoulder.

'Lady Mary. Oh, don't look. Sir Charles will see you.'

'She is fearfully lovely.'

'Yes. Come away.'

But a creeping fascination had overcome Edie, who noted that Mary was exceptionally fashionable and

25

glamorous in a calf-length beige skirt, a lace-collared blouse and a loose belted jacket. Her hat was low on her brow over dark, shiny bobbed hair and she wore three long strands of pearls.

Jenny tried to tug her away but to no avail. Edie watched Charles take Mary's arm to help her up the steps, then – disaster! He looked directly at her window. Her throat tightened and she tried to move away but she felt held there by the keen penetration of his gaze. It only lasted a moment, before Lady Mary slapped him on the elbow, as if in reproof, and he turned back to her, laughing.

But a moment was enough. Edie had been noticed, and now she felt like a marked woman.

Chapter Two

Her stomach in knots, she returned reluctantly to her mirror. The surround was devilishly full of sharp points and curlicues and polishing it was a more arduous task than she had imagined.

'Lady Mary, the spoiled beauty. Shouldn't she be in London for the season?' she asked, resuming her labours.

'So many questions,' said Jenny briskly, putting the polish back in the trug. 'Oh, lor'. Oh, dear me, no.'

Edie looked around, putting her materials down on the mantelpiece as a stricken-faced Jenny drew nearer.

'What is it?'

'You don't never use polish on the ormolu. Didn't you know that? It damages it. You can only dust that down.'

'Oh, I had no idea,' said Edie, her hands flying to cover her mouth.

Josie McCullen had never mentioned ormolu. Only silver and plain brass. Oh, there were so many gaps in her domestic education. She would be making huge mistakes all the livelong day.

Jenny sighed. 'It's probably all right,' she said. 'But that polish strips the gilt away. The most you can do is dab it with meths and a soft cloth, and then only when you can see some corrosion. Let me look a bit closer. Oh. Oh, dear.'

A tiny scrap of one of the curlicues had dulled, a tarnished patch amidst the bright gilt.

'We'll have to tell Mrs Munn,' Jenny decided. 'She'll know how to fix it.'

Mrs Munn did know how to fix it – or, at least, she knew a restorer who did – but she still pursed her lips and tapped her fingers against the mantel in the servants' dining hall when the maids made their confession.

'It'll have to come out of your wages,' she told Edie. 'I can't imagine how you could be so careless. What kind of place have you come from, where they had no ormolu in the house?'

'I'm sorry,' repeated Edie, feeling like a spot of grease on the floor at Mrs Munn's feet. 'I only had charge of the silver and brass at Mrs Winchester's.'

'Perhaps we should keep you to the corridors and anterooms,' mused the housekeeper. 'But if I can't use you where I see fit, then what's the good of having you?'

'Please, I promise to do better,' pleaded Edie, close to tears.

'Come on, have a heart, it's her first day.'

The male voice from the doorway belonged to Ted Kempe.

'I'll thank you to keep your opinions to yourself, Kempe,' snapped Mrs Munn. 'This matter does not relate to motor cars, or any other area to which you can be expected to contribute.'

Ted shrugged. 'We've all made mistakes, the first few days of a new place. Haven't you, Mrs Munn?'

'Yes, and I was properly corrected,' she hissed, clearly unappreciative of the chauffeur's attempts to pour oil on the troubled waters. 'And thankful for it. You may go, Edie, and I will expect a substantial improvement on this performance tomorrow.'

'Thank you, Mrs Munn,' whispered Edie, and she ran from the servants' hall, regardless of the fact that it was almost dinnertime, and into the darkening kitchen garden where she sat herself down on a low wall and burst into tears.

This was all a crazy, ridiculous mistake.

She would pack her bags, go back to London, back to papa and back to her circle of friends. Service was perfectly horrid and so was Deverell Hall and so was everything.

Except Ted Kempe. He was not horrid. He was kind and handsome, and he approached her now from the scullery door, uniform cap in hand, smile of rueful sympathy on face.

'Hey, you'll be missing your supper,' he hailed her, coming closer and perching at her side. 'That won't do.'

'Oh, please, leave me be. I'm not fit for company and I can't bear to go in there and have all those eyes on me, knowing what a useless creature I am.'

'Don't be daft. They don't think that at all. Here. Dry your eyes. I'm sure you don't need to blow your nose, a ladylike person such as yourself but …'

He handed her a handkerchief and she giggled woefully.

'Actually, I do,' she said. 'But I won't, not in front of a gentleman.'

'First time I've been called that,' he said, beaming brightly. 'I'll treasure it.'

'Well, you are, you know. Thank you for standing up for me in there. You didn't need to do it.'

'Mrs Munn needs reining in a bit sometimes, that's all. She breathes fire on everyone and everything, not realising that, half the time, it just ain't needed. You don't need the same amount of flames for a paper tissue as you do for a bloomin' oak tree.'

Edie laughed again. 'Am I a paper tissue then?'

'More like a paper rose,' he said gallantly.

'Oh, give over,' she said, rather proud of herself for replicating one of Josie McCullen's favourite expressions.

'So, are you coming in? Get yourself some food, it'll cheer you up. Steak and kidney pudding tonight, one of Fingall's specials.'

Edie tried a few moments more of token resistance but ultimately she could not resist Ted's blend of charm and solicitude. She followed him back into the house just as the first spots of new rain fell on already sodden ground.

* * *

'I have my reservations about this.' Mrs Munn hardly needed to voice the words; her face said them for her. 'But Carrie really isn't well enough to serve at table tonight. I don't have anybody else. I'm counting on you.'

'Thank you, I won't let you down,' Edie assured her, though she hoped she wouldn't be asked to swear on her life.

Dinner in the servants' hall had been surprisingly heartening, most of the staff having secret sympathetic smiles for her for her misfortune in getting on Mrs Munn's bad side so soon. Nobody asked any awkward questions and only a couple of the girls looked askance at her when she came out with an overly London turn of phrase.

She had been sent on an errand after tea, a kind of test of her knowledge of the house's geography. Unfortunately she had failed.

The first footman, Giles, had found her wandering about in the East Wing, wringing her hands as she passed the same door for a third time.

'Hey,' he said, appearing from behind a door – one of the family bedrooms, if she wasn't mistaken. 'What are you doing here?'

'I don't know where I am,' she said helplessly. 'I'm sorry.'

'Let me show you back to the basement. Too many stairs in this place, that's the problem. Don't worry. I was the same when I started here.'

'How long have you been here?' she asked, following him along yards and yards of crimson carpet patterned with gold fleurs-de-lys.

'Couple of years,' he said vaguely. 'Straight after I demobbed.'

'Gosh, were you in the trenches?'

'Yes.'

'It's a bit different to that here.'

He turned around and gave her a very odd smile.

'Yes. In some ways,' he said.

No more was spoken until they reached the kitchen.

But now Edie was in best black-and-whites, listening to Mrs Munn's pep talk on how to behave when serving dinner guests.

She felt like breaking in and telling the woman that she'd been to enough dinners to know what was done and not done, but she had to endure the sermon without interruption.

In the background, Ted was eating a chicken leg and grinning at her.

It was too bad of him – Edie was flustered enough already and when he winked at her she had to look away and block him from her mind.

She was already a little feverish at the prospect of being in the same room as Sir Charles again. What was this peculiar fascination he held for her? She had never been drawn to such characters before. The thought that Jenny might be accurate in her surmise that he would notice her and try to seduce her made her feel alternately hot and cold all over.

By the time Mrs Munn's talk was through, Edie felt an uncomfortable band of sweat beneath the elastic of her cap. All she could think of was the way he had looked up at her from the forecourt below, a blend of curiosity and something else, something she had never thought much about because it frightened her.

The trap. The thing that caught so many good women and took them out of the world, where they could have forged a path of their own.

She thought about this all the time she helped to lay the table, placing forks within forks and spoons below spoons. Jenny showed her how to fold the napkins 'the Deverell way' but she was clumsy and could not manage to pleat them properly, so she was sent to set out the glasses instead.

Cars had been pulling up outside the house all evening. Ted Kempe had made several journeys to and from the station as well.

She could hear the muffled voices from the reception room beyond and she tried to make out what people might be saying, but it was too hard. Now and again she heard the fruity, theatrical tones of Lady Deverell, followed always by laughter. This made her knees weaken. Sir Charles's voice was distinctive too, but he didn't seem to amuse quite as much.

Stanhope, the butler, sailed into the room just as the last piece of crystal was set in place.

'Take your positions,' he muttered.

Like frilled centurions, Edie and Jenny stood guard by the table, with four other servants, while Stanhope threw wide the large double doors on the far side of the room to announce dinner.

There were twenty-four at table and Edie found a vicarious interest in looking at the gowns and jewels as they shimmered past, adorning pale aristocratic flesh.

She did not know the woman on Sir Charles Deverell's arm, but she saw him cast the quickest little dart of a glance in Edie's direction before pulling out his companion's chair.

Lady Mary was gorgeous in royal-blue satin overlaid with net, beaded and jewelled at the neckline and on the sleeves. She was transparently a female version of her brother, his dark looks softened and made sleek on her smaller canvas.

The man who limped in behind her must be the other

brother, Sir Thomas. He had a thin moustache that did not look as if it had much more growth in it and his eyes were tired and hooded.

And then – yes, it could only be Lady Deverell, in sweeping floor-length emerald silk that swished about her and was overlaid with a cloud of black tulle. The emeralds at her throat and in her tiara set off the deep red of her hair, while swirls of black beads decorated her bodice and the hem of her skirts. She was like a creature from another world, and yet she was so familiar that Edie's throat tightened and ached.

Lord Deverell, at her side, was a grizzled, faded nobody.

Edie felt a blush of transferred shame, as if all the gossip that must inevitably be attached to their marriage had infected her. But she was nothing to do with it.

The guests were mainly elderly, it seemed, with a sprinkling of younger people, perhaps their children. Everybody was talking about the grouse and salmon seasons, so perhaps they were fellow landowners from the local area.

She could not take her eyes off Lady Deverell, who smiled as brightly as the electric lamps at the theatre, dazzling the candlelight into a dim second place. But her smile was strange, not quite natural. At times it almost looked as if it wavered at the edges of her lips and then it found renewed purpose and flashed again in its full glory. Her eyes wandered, frequently settling on Sir Charles, who seemed to know a lot about their baffling topic of conversation and held the floor with effortless authority. She leant towards him when he cut across or contradicted his father and gave him an extra gleam of her teeth. She was amazingly beautiful.

Lady Deverell looked towards her, sharply, as if she had noticed Edie's unbroken gaze. Edie dropped her eyes and looked instead at Jenny, who signalled that they were to serve the soup which had been brought up from the kitchen.

When she reached the table, Lady Deverell was still looking at her, but not hostilely now. She had a distant, dreamy kind of look upon her face, but it disappeared when somebody asked her about her jewels, whisking her back into the social slipstream.

Edie had been consigned to the end of the table, serving six of the elderly guests, but even at this distance Lady Deverell's radiance reached out to her. Her hand shook and she could barely breathe.

'Be careful, girl,' snapped a dowager in pink and black lace.

A splash of soup had escaped the ladle and spotted the cloth.

'Oh, I am so sorry,' blurted Edie, desperate not to draw attention to herself.

The tiny contretemps had reached the notice of Sir

Charles, however, for Edie became hotly conscious of his eye upon her. If only he would look away.

She avoided his gaze as studiously as she could, attending to her other guests, but when she glanced back up, he still watched her.

Her grip on the ladle slipped and it fell with a clatter back into the tureen.

Lord Deverell frowned and several ladies tutted, their jewels flashing as they turned to grimace at each other.

Edie apologised again, on the verge of tears. This was all a terrible mistake. She would catch the mail train back to London and tell papa she was sorry, she had been wrong and he had been right, could she now take back her old life, please?

'Leave her be.'

The voice was rich and commanding and it belonged to Sir Charles.

'She is new, I think. Isn't that so?'

Edie nodded, wanting to be anywhere but this place, with all these eyes upon her.

'Yes, sir.'

'Well, then. First-night nerves. You know all about them, don't you, *mama*?' The way he said this, with a sneer, to Lady Deverell made Edie gasp, and she was not alone.

'Charles!' Lord Deverell reproved his son.

'Sorry, did I speak out of turn?' He sat back, dabbing his napkin at his lips with an insolent air.

Lady Deverell was flushed but it only made her more beautiful. She levelled a combative stare at Sir Charles and shook her head.

For a moment there was silence while stepmother and stepson locked everybody else in the room out of their mutual tension, then somebody complimented the soup and everybody rushed to agree.

Edie, for the moment, was forgotten, and she melted back into her place with gratitude, waiting for the first course to be finished.

The fever that had affected her on her first sighting of Lady Deverell eventually wore off and Edie was a better mistress of herself when called upon to serve the other courses. She was thankful to be at the end of the table furthest from the family, able to watch them without having to get too near.

Lady Mary sulked about coming back from the London season too early and missing the best closing balls, while Lord Deverell heavy-handedly reminded her that there was a good reason for that, which made her sulk all the more.

Edie exchanged a look with Jenny that asked, 'What reason?' Jenny responded with a tiny shrug.

Conversation was far from lively. Sir Charles occasionally attempted to stir things up with a sly barb or two, but nobody seemed to be in sufficient spirits to react in the way he wanted. Sir Thomas barely spoke at all, glaring down at his plate as if he saw the face of a mortal enemy in it.

Edie was lulled by the low murmurs, the scraping of knives and forks on fine china, the low light and the ambient warmth into a kind of daze. Her legs and feet ached and her head was so fuzzy now. She had been awake since five o'clock in the morning and she had walked as many miles inside the house as she had outside it.

Could they not just finish their meal quickly and let her go to bed?

Through half-shut eyes, she saw the red-gold glow of Lady Deverell and the gleam of Sir Charles's teeth, dangerously bared. Points of light from various gems danced across the walls and ceilings behind them. The wallpaper pattern was a repetitive curl of red and gold, a curiously soothing thing to look at. She fixed her attention on it, lulled, comforted. She leant back against the door jamb, feeling her legs twitch a little and then …

A kick on her shin.

'Keep upright,' hissed Jenny.

She had been on the point of falling asleep where she stood, like a horse. How did anyone live this life without doing so all the time? And this was only her first day.

Somehow she dragged her body through pudding, but it was still another half-hour before the ladies retired to the drawing room.

She swooped forwards to take the dishes downstairs

for the last time. Gathering the last of them up, she made the mistake of looking again at Sir Charles, who was smiling at her as he poured himself a brandy. The smile struck Edie as predatory and she made a hasty escape to the kitchen, feeling like one of the grouse they had spoken of shooting at.

'Told you,' said Jenny at the bottom of the staircase. 'He's got an eye for you already. Watch yourself, girl.'

'I don't want to watch anything,' said Edie, stacking the dishes up by the sink, thanking her lucky stars that she wouldn't be washing them. 'I want to shut my eyes and fall into my bed.'

'Aren't you coming for a game of cards in the kitchen?'

'I simply can't. I'm half asleep already.'

'Fair enough. Sweet dreams, then. I hope they won't be of *him*. I don't want to see you go Susie's way.'

'I won't.'

* * *

Edie's dreams were of nothing, or, if they had substance, it soon melted from her memory. Her first consciousness was of a foreign place, a bed too hard, a pillow too flat, and a peculiar smell of other bodies and their exhalations.

She was the only one abed. The other three girls were dressing already, yawning and tying each other's apron laces.

The rain still beat dully against the little square-paned window and somebody had thought to light a candle, even though the summer dawn had broken half an hour since.

Edie had never risen this early, save on a handful of special occasions, and she bitterly resented having to leave the warmth of her bed to engage in a day of more hard and mystifying work.

The girls seemed disinclined to talk, going about their morning ablutions in pale-faced trances. The memory of Charles and Lady Deverell at last night's dinner hit Edie once more – a big, nauseating blow. Why had she been so stupid as to get herself noticed? All she had had to do was serve some soup, for heaven's sake.

'How was the bed? Could you sleep in it?' asked Jenny, coming up behind Edie as she brushed her hair, having waited patiently for the use of the room's only mirror.

'Oh, it was a little narrow, but comfortable enough,' she said vaguely.

'I was so pleased to have a bed to meself, I never worried about its being narrow,' confided Jenny. 'Had to share with two sisters back at home. Have you got brothers or sisters?'

'None.'

'You won't be missing them, then. Is your ma and pa alive?'

'I live with my father. Lived,' she corrected.

41

'He'll feel your absence, then. Only child gone away from home.'

She pursed her lips sympathetically. Edie, feeling underhanded and low for garnering the girl's simple compassion, merely smiled tightly and put the brush down.

'Could you arrange my hair? I have no skill for it myself.'

'You'll have to get it,' said Jenny with a laugh. 'Heavens, you need to be able to do these things. You'll never rise to lady's maid if you can't fix hair.'

'You're quite right. I wonder, Jenny, would you let me practise on you sometimes?'

'If you like.'

There was a silence while Jenny's fingers worked deftly on Edie's heavy auburn hair.

'You've got such a lovely lot of it,' she said, fixing the cap on top with a quantity of pins. 'It's just like Lady Deverell's – that glorious colour too. I've always longed to be her maid and get my hands on those locks. I can play with yours instead now.'

Edie laughed. 'I've been told I have a look of her sometimes. Do you think so?'

Jenny narrowed her eyes, looking over Edie's shoulder into the mirror.

'The hair, yes. The eyes, no. Hers are blue, yours are brown. And your nose is completely different ... but I think in the shape of the face ... Well, let's say I

42

wouldn't get you mixed up from the front, but I might from behind, if your hair was down.'

'There are many worse people to resemble,' said Edie.

'Yes, look at me, I'm told I favour Little Tich.'

Edie burst out laughing. 'Oh, you don't!' she exclaimed. 'That's a wicked and cruel thing to say.'

Verity, the senior housemaid of the group, stood in the doorway tutting.

'Enough of that,' she said. 'You'll be late for breakfast. Jenny, you aren't her lady's maid, for heaven's sake. If she can't do her own hair, it's high time she learned.'

Downstairs – such a way downstairs – Edie served herself a ladleful of porridge from the big pan and sat down at the long trestle. She did not want to draw attention to herself, but she had questions on her mind and hoped somebody would be able to answer them.

In the event, Ted did the job for her, without her having to say a word.

'Morning, Topsy,' he said, ruffling her hair as he passed. 'Can't stay, I'm afraid – got to take His Lordship to London.'

'He is going away?'

'Yes, some shindig at the club, birthday do, I think. Nice little jaunt to the Smoke for me. Wish you could come.'

'Ted,' reproved Mrs Munn. 'That will do.'

He saluted her and made a brisk exit, grabbing his peaked cap from the nail by the door as he went.

'In view of yesterday's somewhat inauspicious start,' Mrs Munn continued, addressing herself to Edie, 'I'm going to have Jenny keep an eye on you again today. If there's any repetition of the fiasco with the mirror, I'll have to consider letting you go. Is that clear?'

'Perfectly, Mrs Munn,' said Edie, feeling like a recalcitrant schoolgirl. No Latin prose had ever been as challenging as the mysteries of cleaning and serving, though.

* * *

'Ted likes you,' said Jenny, kneeling down beside Edie to sweep the first of a great many fireplaces free of ashes.

'Oh, he's a ladies' man, though, isn't he? I bet he's like that with all the girls.'

'Not all of them,' Jenny insisted. 'A lot of the girls are after him, though. He does wear that uniform well.' She let out a tiny sigh.

'Oh, Jenny, do you …?' She left the question delicately poised.

'It's a silly daydream, that's all it is. Plain little Jenny Wrens don't land fellows like that. I'll live and die in this place, I don't doubt.'

'Oh, don't say that.' But Edie knew Jenny was right. Men were scarce these days and those who remained were keenly sought after.

'I suppose Ted fought in the war?'

'Yes, he was an infantryman. Fought in the trenches, he did. He won't never talk about it though. Says he'd rather forget all about it.'

'And what about … the Deverell sons?' Edie's heart stepped up its pace at the mere mention of the name. Damn Charles Deverell and his insidious ways. 'Did they go to the Front?'

'Yes, both of them. I've told you, haven't I, about poor Sir Thomas and his shrapnel wound. Very unlucky. Mind you, I suppose he's still alive, at least.'

Edie wanted to ask after Charles, but she did not trust herself to speak his name without putting in some nuance of tone that might give her away. Jenny already suspected her of a pash on him. Was she right? No, she could not be right. The man was a perfect stranger, and not a very nice one at that.

Instead, they chatted about inconsequential things while grates were black-leaded and floors swept.

They were working in the morning room, Edie on her knees, making heavy work of polishing the fender, when their joint rendition of 'It's a Long Way to Tipperary' was silenced by the entrance of a family member.

'No, do continue,' Charles said, sinking into a chair and unfolding a newspaper. 'A little music while I read would be rather congenial, as it happens.'

Edie's fingers clenched around the cloth, her arm too stiff to move for a moment or two. She did not dare move, knowing that every inch of her skin from the tips of her ears downwards was burning bright. She willed Jenny to ignore her.

'How's our new girl?' he asked softly. 'Getting into the swing of things?'

Edie made no reply, and Charles did not pursue the conversation. For a deeply uncomfortable half-hour there was no sound but the rustling of newspaper and the scrubbing of iron. She was mortifyingly aware of her bottom sticking out in its tight black skirt, swaying from side to side as she worked. She felt sure that Charles Deverell was watching it. Her skin prickled, an itch at the back of her neck. And something else too – a damp heat between her thighs that she wished would go away.

A masculine cough, the click of a lighter, then the smell of cigarette smoke wafting over her. He wanted her to be aware of him. With rising excitement she wondered, what would happen if Jenny was not in the room?

Would he come over to her, crouch down beside her, tell her he knew that she thought of him, put his hand on her spine and rub it up and down, moving ever lower until he reached her bottom …

This was not a profitable line of speculation. She shut it down and forced herself to concentrate on conferring a high shine upon the poker and the shovel instead.

The only person to come and crouch beside her was Jenny.

'Next room,' she whispered. 'Grate's looking lovely, too, that's a nice job you've done.'

Only because she had displaced all her thoughts about Charles into hard work, Edie realised. The next task might not absorb her so thoroughly.

She picked up her trug and tried to walk primly out of the room without looking at the indolent Lord in his chair of state, but at the last minute she flicked him a sideways glance and saw that he was watching her.

She lifted her chin higher and stared ahead.

'Dinner at eight again? I'll look forward to it,' he drawled as she hurried through the door.

'What was all that? Why are you flirting with him?' hissed Jenny, once they had attained the freedom of the corridor.

'Flirting with him! I'm doing no such thing. I didn't even look at him, didn't even answer his question.'

'To him, that's flirting. The more you run, the harder he chases. The worst thing you can do is ignore him.'

'But that makes no sense. Are you saying that I should, should … make sheep's eyes at him and then he'll lose interest and pursue some other poor girl? Perhaps I should offer myself to him. Is that what I should do?'

Her agitation seemed to quell Jenny's suspicions, but she did not sound entirely convinced when she said, 'I'm sorry. You weren't flirting, I know that. But I'd make sure I was never alone in a room with him if I was you.'

He ruins girls. He could ruin me.

47

Chapter Three

Carrie, the indisposed housemaid, was better and so Edie was not called upon to serve the family at dinner that night.

Instead she sat in the kitchen with the cook, the scullery maids and various low-level male staff, drifting in and out of their conversation while she stitched at a rent she had made in her sleeve.

'You're accident-prone, you, aren't yer?' remarked Mrs Fingall, tiring of some talk about how Lady Mary had reacted to a mail delivery that morning.

'I'm afraid so,' said Edie. 'I'm fearfully clumsy. Have been from a child.'

'Perhaps service ain't for you,' suggested the cook. 'All that precious china up there. Clumsy people ought to keep away from it. Gawd, ain't you never sewed before? You're making a hash of that too. Here, let me.'

She sat beside Edie and took over the operation, her sausage fingers surprisingly deft with the needle.

'Little bird tells me,' she said in a low voice once the youngsters had started joshing each other about sweethearts, 'that one or two fellas round here is sweet on you.'

'Oh, no,' protested Edie, wanting to get up and run away, but trapped by the thread that Mrs Fingall held taut.

'I'm sure you've been warned about our Sir Charlie,' she carried on. 'So I won't repeat what's already been said. But Ted's a lovely lad. A real prize. Do you think you could look kindly on him?'

Put on the spot, Edie could not pluck one single word from the air.

She swallowed and shook her head, then nodded, then shook her head again.

'Oh, I am not here for … for that kind of thing,' she whispered.

'Of course not. And quite right too. Just, you know, if you ever was so inclined … you could do a lot worse.' She winked.

A bell rang and Edie glanced up at the complicated system of pulleys and levers that hung on the far wall.

'Sir Thomas for you, Giles,' Mrs Fingall called out.

The footman leapt up from the table and dashed away.

'I'd get to my bed if I were you, dear,' said Mrs Fingall, cutting the thread with her teeth and tying a final knot. 'They'll be finished at dinner soon and they won't need you for anything more.'

'Yes, I think I will,' said Edie, eager for some solitude.

Alone in the attic, she looked out of the window and thought about how far she was from home, in more senses than the strictly geographic. She had never realised how easy her life was, nor how free she had been compared to most women. And not just the servants either. Lady Mary was discontented, straining against the yoke of her father's expectations for her. Most women lived in prison. She had heard it said but had never understood it as fully as she did now.

She sat on the bed, pulled her knees up to her chin and thought of Sir Charles. It was different for him. He could do as he liked and nobody called him to account. It made her angry, made her want to seek him out and slap his face.

But, of course, that was impossible.

What about Lady Deverell? Was she the most imprisoned of all, forced to play a role for the rest of her life, even though she had fled the stage? If only she could ask her. If only things could be simple.

The thunder of feet on the back stairs drove her to undress quickly and slip into bed, where she feigned sleep before she could be questioned on anything further.

'Sir Charles wants her,' she heard Jenny say.

'Do you think she'll fall for him?'

'They all do, don't they?'

A sigh.

'If only he'd fall back,' said Verity. 'But he never does.'

'Surely Lord Deverell'd kick him out if he got another girl in the family way.'

'Maybe. Remember how it was when they found out about Susie?'

There was a collective shudder.

'You could hear the shouting right across the lawns.'

They fell silent then and Edie waited, curled up on her side, until each body creaked into its bed and the candle was snuffed.

As the girls drifted into sleep, Edie thought back to Mrs Fingall's words at the trestle table. Could she think of looking kindly on Ted?

Ted.

It would not do to be mooning over a chauffeur. He was lovely, of course, but no doubt he was the same with all the girls. He was a natural flirt, that was all.

Besides, there was to be none of this lovey-dovey frippery for Edie Crossland. She had not spent the last seven years wedded to the Women's Suffrage movement to be swept off her feet by a fellow in a peaked cap who dropped his aitches. It was inconceivable.

No, he was a helpful friend, and that was as much as he could be. Love was the silly trap into which so many good women fell. It was not going to catch her.

And why was sleep staying so stubbornly away tonight? An hour ago, as she toiled up the back staircase, she had been fantasising about her old bed with its pile of pillows and patchwork throw. Every limb ached, her feet were blistered and her eyelids were gritty with the day's exertion, and yet her mind would not let her be.

It persisted in going back over the emotions of the last forty-eight hours, so that she swirled in a vortex of fear, exhilaration, curiosity, humiliation, attraction.

The narrow bed was less than comfortable, and the air of the high-up room was thick and humid. She needed to clear her head.

Slippers and dressing gown on, she stole out of the stifling dormitory and down the uncarpeted back stairs, as quietly as she could. At first, she had no notion of where she might wander, but it soon occurred to her that she could find Lady Deverell's room and stand, albeit divided by the door, in the close presence of that fascinating woman.

She had had the opportunity to drink her in at yesterday's dinner, but today had brought disappointingly few glimpses of the red-haired beauty. She had watched her cross the lawn in her riding habit, head low and stride determined. How much better, though, to perhaps see her, through a keyhole, in repose. The mask she wore every day would be stripped away and she would see the woman behind it, unadorned and unshielded.

Edie slunk on silent feet along the confusing maze of corridors she had negotiated earlier in the day, trying to remember which had led where.

A wrong turn took her to the library, and she was at once thrilled and soothed by its familiar bookish smell, naturally drawn to the shelves where she squinted to make out the gold lettering on the spines. But the night was too cloudy and the light from the arched stained glass windows too dim as a consequence.

There would be no reading in here tonight.

She found at length the right staircase and the corresponding corridor and walked along it swiftly, taking no notice of portraits and busts that might otherwise interest her, until she was in the wing that housed Lady Deverell's private rooms.

Did she sleep with Lord Deverell? He had a private bedroom and dressing room at the far end of the same corridor. She knew this was a usual arrangement in the grandest of the old family houses, but it struck her as strange. Did they make appointments for love? Or were the separate rooms a mere formality, an age-old habit they did not possess the modernist urge to break?

Here was her door.

And, oh.

What were these noises coming from behind that door? Surely Lord Deverell was in London? He must have returned straight after the gathering, Ted driving him through the night back to his wife's side. He must be in the grip of passion.

Edie put her hands to her furiously heating cheeks,

guilt-ridden at her snooping now. She should not be here. She should go back to bed immediately.

And yet she found she could not come away from the luxurious moans and sighs that poured through the keyhole.

The act of love. That thing she despised and feared, and yet was fascinated by. She had read Freud and found it terrifying, throwing the book aside in repulsion. No man would make her want to do such a thing.

But what *was* such a thing? She had never seen it, and reading about things was not always the same, loth as she was to admit the treacherous fact.

Lord Deverell, she knew, was a man nearing his sixties, while his new wife was barely forty. Did she desire him, truly? Surely everybody knew it was a transaction – his wealth and status for her fleshly charms and charismatic glamour.

But *love*?

Perhaps it was. And, if so, what did love look like? She bent to the keyhole, all the while in a kind of horrified trance, her body driving her towards actions of which, in the light of day, she would strongly disapprove.

At first, she saw that the room was in dim light, the gasoliers on the wall turned down low. The huge four-poster bed could be seen only from an angle that hid the heads of the occupants, but she could see the lower portion, and two pairs of feet protruding from the covers.

The larger pair lay between the smaller, and the sheets and counterpane rose up from them into an arch – an arch that moved, quite vigorously and in a rhythmic pattern that matched the low grunts emitting from the unseen upper half.

If this was love, it seemed awfully brutal, thought Edie with dismay, and really little more than animalistic. The creak-creak-creak of the bed springs masked some words being spoken, but then a female voice grew louder and higher, and they became distinct.

'Yes, you awful, awful beast of a man, have your way with me.'

Edie grimaced. It sounded so *savage*, almost as if she hated her husband. Perhaps she did.

And then tears came to her eyes as she matched the violent, half-delirious voice with the mellifluous tones she had heard on stage, playing Beatrice in *Much Ado About Nothing*. This was what she had come to – loveless coupling with an old man who had bought her.

'Oh, Ruby Red, you're mine, you are,' vowed a deeper voice, snarled up in pain by the sound of it.

'I've told you, don't call me that!' objected Lady Deverell, and then her words were muffled, as if he had placed a hand across her mouth.

'I'll call you what I damn well like, you bitch.'

Edie drew in a great breath, almost nerved to hammer on the door and drag that dreadful man off his poor wife. But then she heard the most unexpected sound, a high-pitched melting into pleasurable surrender, still coming from behind the obstructing door but none the less clear for it; then falling, sobbing, into a deep sigh.

'That's it,' hissed Lord Deverell, almost inaudibly – but by now Edie's ear was honed and she caught every syllable. 'You love it, don't you? You love what I do to you. Oh, God.'

And now it was his turn to tumble into that dangerous uncontrollable place his wife had just visited.

He made the most terrible, frightening sounds, like a man raging into battle, and Edie saw his feet stretch straight out, every muscle tense, then relax.

The feet flexed and moved, all four together, while the coverlet tent collapsed. The voices lowered to murmurings and languid kissing.

Edie, feeling horribly sick, stood straight, wanting very much to run outside and get some air, regardless of the lashing rain, which had begun again.

She heard Lady Deverell from behind the door say, 'Oh, darling, must you?' and then – oh, heavens! – the Lord's reply, very close to the door.

'I promised Mary. She'll garrotte me if I disappoint her again.'

Was that Lord Deverell? Suddenly she was not at all sure. But it could not be …

Edie almost fell over her feet in her haste to get away.

A very quick examination of the corridor around her yielded no curtained alcoves in which to hide, nor was it possible to get to the staircase in time. The handle was already turning.

Perhaps one of these other rooms would be unoccupied?

But before she could try one, the door was open and in the corridor in front of her, resplendent in paisley silk dressing gown, was …

But she could not let her jaw drop, could not make any kind of exclamation.

Now she had to use all of her own dramatic powers, or everything was lost.

She stiffened and widened her eyes, making them stare out of her face at the man who stood in front of her.

'Good God,' he said. 'What's this?'

She said nothing, maintaining her tense, glassy-eyed posture as she walked slowly towards him.

A streak of lightning almost made her jump, but she mustn't. She must appear oblivious to all around her.

He took a step closer, his head on one side. Edie saw a gleam of recognition brighten his grey-blue eye.

'It's the new girl, isn't it? The parlourmaid?'

Edie stood her ground and stared as if looking straight through him.

'The old sleepwalking gambit, eh?'

He snapped his fingers in her face.

She did not flinch.

'Looks like stronger measures are called for,' he said, and he took hold of her arm and brought his face, dark with wicked intent, so close to hers that she could smell Lady Deverell's perfume on him. He was going to kiss her! No, he could not ...

She pretended to come to her senses, letting her limbs loosen and her breath rush from her in great gasps.

'Oh,' she exclaimed. 'Whatever is this? Where have I come to?'

She tried to shake herself free of him but he was not having it, and he marched, dragging her along with him, to the nearest empty room, into which he unceremoniously pushed her.

'Please,' she remonstrated. 'Please let me go back to bed. I didn't mean to be here, I swear it.'

He took his hand from her and folded his arms, glowering darkly down at her.

'I don't know who you are or what you saw,' he said in a low, menacing tone. 'But, whatever it was, you'll do well to forget it. Do you understand me? Not a word to anyone.'

'I promise, sir, I won't ... I didn't ... anyway. I don't know what you mean, I'm sure.'

'Hmm, I'm sure,' he said, looking at her assessingly, his eyes all over her, making her flush hot and drop her gaze to the ground.

'I'd better get back,' she said, half-turning.

He put his fingers under her chin, gently holding her in position, shaking his head and tutting his disagreement with this proposition.

'You *are* the new parlourmaid, aren't you?'

She nodded, constricted somewhat by his unyielding grip on her face.

'What's your name?'

'Edie. Edie Cr–, uh, Prior.'

'Edie Cruuur-Prior?' he repeated, tauntingly. 'Unusual name.'

'Just the Prior. I changed my name when my mother remarried. I forget, sometimes.'

He regarded her for a silent stretch of time, during which Edie committed his face to memory – its angles and shadows, the prominent nose, the full, sensual lips, the gleaming eyes, the lustrous dark hair, the cruel, handsome whole of it.

He looked utterly heartless to her, and glitteringly magnetic at the same time.

She was more afraid than ever.

'You know who I am, of course?'

'You're Sir Charles, I think, sir.'

'That's right. I'm Charles Deverell, Lord Exley, heir to the estate. How's life in service so far, Edie?'

'Tiring,' she said, tripping over the words in her anxiety. 'I'm tired. I should sleep.'

'Yes, they treat you like working dogs down there, don't they? My hounds have a better life. But I'll give you a little tip, Edie. Be a good girl, and you might find that there are perks to your job.'

His fingers brushed up her cheek, so lightly that the caress in them could almost be attributed to the air.

'Are you a good girl, Edie?' he whispered.

Weakness rinsed through her limbs. She had no reply to offer.

'Tired,' she whispered, her lips quivering.

He seemed to take a step back, though in reality he did not move. The seductive intensity in his eyes broke and he smiled, half-laughing.

'Yes, you're right, it's late and I don't have much more in me, much as I'd like to test the proposition.'

'You and Lady Deverell–'

He held up a finger.

'I've told you. Seal your lips. Well, until I want to unseal them, that is.'

That dazzling grin again, unsettling as a punch to the solar plexus.

'I suggest,' he continued, 'that you take the three wise monkeys as your template while you're working here.'

See no evil, hear no evil, speak no evil.

'I understand, sir.' She looked towards the door and he relented.

'Run along then, Edie Cruur-Prior. Perhaps I should speak to Mrs Munn tomorrow about having a lock put on your dormitory door. But only if I can have a key.'

She turned and fled, running through the corridors and up the staircases, losing her way half a dozen times, until the low-ceilinged corridor that housed the staff dormitories appeared at the head of the uncarpeted back stairs.

All three of her roommates were deep in sleep, making the most of time away from dishpans and dustpans. A flash of lightning lit the room and she noticed how red and coarse Peggy, the young scullery maid's, hands already were, and her only fourteen years old.

Edie inspected her own hands, pale and unblemished. How long would they remain so?

Her stomach was in knots and her head whirling when she lay down and tried to sleep through the thunderous rain. This had been a terrible idea. She had knowledge she did not want now, about Lady Deverell, and she had played directly into the hands of Sir Charles, who might now hound her with seduction attempts.

Which she would, of course, repel.

Of course.

He was attractive and all that, but he was dangerous. Far too dangerous, a giant 'Keep Away' sign in masculine form. She couldn't afford to take risks.

But he chased her into uneasy sleep, as if the warmth she had felt radiating from his dressing-gowned post-coital body had seeped into her pores and remained there, a vestige of his presence tormenting her from a distance.

In her dreams, his fingers brushed her face again, and then they went further, snaking into her hair, luring her closer, until their bodies touched and then their lips. If dream kisses were like real kisses, then how did people ever stop? The richness of the sensation turned her inside out and left her helpless and overwhelmed.

***

A hideous clangour shook her out of Charles Deverell's dream arms and ripped his dream lips from hers. The other girls were already out of their beds, yawningly splashing their faces in the basin or pulling on uniforms.

She took twice as long as they did to get ready and had to rush breakfast. She did not have time to talk at all until she and Jenny were in the corridor with their feather dusters and their tins of wax, ready to set to work on the skirting boards.

'What does Sir Charles generally do all day?' she asked.

Jenny gave her a furious look.

'I want to know so that I can avoid him,' Edie explained.

'Oh, I see. He goes out a lot, motoring in that new monster of his. Plays tennis with Lady Mary. Walks his dogs.' She looked up as if the ceiling might give her more information. 'Not much, when you think about it. What I'd give to live his life.'

'Does he have nothing more to occupy him at all?'

'He has some dealings with the estate and some of Lord Deverell's landed tenants. There's a manufactory outside Kingsreach that he sometimes goes and ... does things ... at. I don't know. It ain't my place to know, is it?'

'I suppose not. And ... Her Ladyship. Has she a great many interests?'

'Lord, why are you asking me? She is always going out to lunch. And she works for a lot of charities, sits on committees, all that kind of thing.'

Boredom has thrown them together. Boredom and disaffection.

And passion. But Edie did not want to think about passion.

She had no choice but to do so, however, when she and Jenny entered the morning room to clean it and found Sir Charles there again, as he had been yesterday. Was he here because he knew she would be?

Edie kept her head down, passing behind his chair in the hope that he might not notice her.

But the hope was vain.

'Our Lady Macbeth,' he said, putting down his newspaper.

Edie, whose hands already shook, was almost over-come with panic. What on earth would Jenny think of this? She made no reply and rubbed harder at a greasy fingermark on one of the window frames.

63

'You'll have to remember your taper next time,' he added. 'Won't you?'

There was a silence. From the corner of her eye, Edie saw Jenny's horrified countenance. Presumably she would have to answer, now he had asked a question.

'I'm not sure what you mean, sir,' she said.

'Hmph. Have it your way.' The newspaper rustled again and no more was said.

***

'What was all that about?' asked Jenny furiously, once they were out of the room.

Edie, enjoying the sensation of being able to breathe again, shook her head.

'I've no idea.'

'Lady Macbeth?'

'I don't know Shakespeare.'

'I bet you do, with all your London theatre-going. What's he on about?'

'I've told you,' said Edie, and she couldn't keep a rising note of antagonism from her voice. 'I don't know.'

Jenny was put out and conversation was scarce for the rest of the morning. At lunch, Jenny sat with all the other girls at the opposite end of the table, whispering and casting glances over at Edie.

Her heart sank. She was friendless here.

Until Ted strode in, put his peaked cap down on the end of the table and snagged one of her slices of bread and butter.

'Hey!'

'Cut yourself another,' he said. 'I've just driven all the way back from town at a steady forty miles per hour. I've earned my daily bread.'

He sat down beside her, warming her with his presence and his cheeky smile.

'You're still here then,' he said.

'Somehow,' she replied with a grimace, then she whispered. 'I'm not sure how long I'll last.'

'When's your day off?'

'Wednesday.'

'Well, I hope you'll last till then. Cos I'd like to take you out.'

'Oh!' Edie blinked rapidly. Was this a proposition? Was he expressing romantic interest in her? She was so inexperienced that she hardly knew if his intentions were amorous or merely friendly.

She decided to assume the latter.

'Well, perhaps a walk out into the country would be nice,' she said. 'Or ... something of that kind.'

'His Lordship's got a shoot on that day. I won't be needed. I'll see what's on at the picture palace, shall I?'

'Well, I suppose so,' she said dubiously.

'Don't knock me out with enthusiasm, girl.'

She saw Mrs Fingall beaming approval as the others muttered and looked daggers. It seemed she couldn't please Jenny and her friends – Ted and Sir Charles were a rock and a hard place, apparently. But which was which?

'Mrs Munn, I think Edie knows her way around now,' said Jenny as the housekeeper came to join the meal. 'May I go back to working alone?'

'Does that suit you, Edie?'

'Yes, ma'am.' Edie sighed. It didn't, not really. She still had so much she wanted to learn from Jenny. But if she wanted to believe stupid things of her, then that couldn't be helped.

'I'm not entirely sure you're ready, but I'll give you a chance.'

* * *

Edie was assigned to the seldom-used upper rooms of the East Wing and she spent the afternoon alone amongst the treasures, having no company but her thoughts. She listened constantly for footsteps on the stairs or in the passage, dreading an unexpected rendezvous with Sir Charles, but apparently he was out.

Looking through the window, she saw Lady Mary with a tennis racquet and wondered against whom she would be playing. Lady Deverell came out a few moments later, similarly equipped, and Edie was transfixed, watching the pair disappear around the corner towards the courts.

Lady Deverell and her stepdaughter. Was their relationship cordial? What if Lady Mary found out about her brother? What if *anyone* found out? Lady Deverell would be ruined, that was for sure.

Perhaps Sir Charles loved her and would stand by her … but that surely couldn't be the case if he was trying his luck with every pretty housemaid that came along.

No, she was his plaything and he might even have her ruin in mind. It was despicable. *He* was despicable. He ought to be stopped – but how?

Carrie was once more indisposed at supper time, so Edie, much against her will, was detailed to serve the family.

She kept her eye on Lady Deverell, waiting for her to steal a look at Sir Charles, but she did no such thing for the duration of the meal, unless addressed.

What a wonderful actress she was. Edie found herself as full of admiration as of distaste. Eventually, however, she realised why Lady Deverell was not attending to her stepson. She was watching *her*.

She had noticed, without seeming to even look in their direction, how Sir Charles touched her under the table when she served the soup and spoke low words into her ear. Although he kept his face expressionless, the messages were inflammatory.

'Will you sleepwalk again tonight?' he murmured.

'No, sir,' she whispered back, trying not to slop soup over the edge of the ladle.

Then, when she refilled his glass, 'Sleepwalk to my rooms. First floor, East Wing.'

At the spooning of the green beans, 'I will expect you.'

She did not dare reply, certain that everyone must see how her cheeks burned and her bosom rose and fell. She kept a very tight grip on all the serving implements and managed not to drop or spill anything, but it was a severe test.

And now, with Lady Deverell watching her every bit as avidly as Sir Charles did, she felt like a hapless pawn, forced into untenable positions wherever she went. This is what it is to be poor, she thought. This is what life is like for so many girls. Poverty robs one of choice.

And if, after yet another day of soul-sapping drudgery, a pretty girl sought out a little pleasure and glamour in the arms of a rich, handsome man, who could blame her? What else awaited her in life but scrubbing and death? Poor Susie Leonard had only done what thousands before her had. Did she regret it? Would Edie?

* * *

She lay awake, her mind a kaleidoscope of confused and conflicting thoughts.

She knew what she had come here for, but now it seemed she had been shown a further purpose.

She got out of bed, once she was sure everybody else was asleep, and tiptoed to the stairs. She stopped several times and thought of turning back, but her need for knowledge and understanding drove her on until she arrived in that fateful East Wing corridor and stood, trembling from head to toe, at the chamber door.

No, she could not knock. What if this was, after all, the wrong door? And, despite how she had planned to proceed, there was no guarantee at all that she would not find herself, very swiftly, in serious danger, all her plans in smithereens.

She took a few deep breaths. This was lunacy. She would find herself on the morning train back to London the very next day, driven by a purse-lipped sad-eyed Ted, her reputation in ruins, her name a byword for scandal.

She stepped back. She would return to her room.

The door opened and she almost screamed, her knees giving way so that she staggered.

Sir Charles looked out at her through the crack, then he held out his hand.

'I've been waiting for you,' he whispered. 'Come on. Don't just stand there.'

'It's not what you think,' she whispered back. 'It's a mistake. I'm not …'

'That kind of girl? Of course. Come in now. Or do I have to come over there and get you?'

She stepped forward and he took hold of her wrist, quickly and firmly, and drew her inside the bedroom.

'Well, Lady Macbeth,' he said, cupping her cheeks in his hands, standing far too close.

'No,' she said, trying to shake her head free and failing. 'Don't touch me.'

'Don't touch you? You've come to my bedroom in the dead of night and you're asking me not to touch you?'

'Please. Not yet.'

'Oh.'

He dropped his hands from her and cocked his head to one side, examining her through narrowed eyes.

'What have we here?' he mused.

Edie felt as if his fingers were still on her skin, still pushing through her hair. She burned in the places he had touched.

'May I sit?'

He waved a hand towards a sofa in the corner.

'I've brandy in the bedside cupboard if you'd like ...'

'No, no.'

He sat down beside her and took her hand in his, despite her attempts to pull it away.

'So, then – what is it you want to say to me?'

She couldn't speak at first, her courage ebbing away, but when he began to stroke her fingers, she found her nerve and blurted it out.

'I don't think you should be doing ... what you're doing ... with Lady Deverell.'

He squeezed her fingers tight and let out an incredulous little laugh.

'I fail to see how it's any of your business ... what was your name again? ... Edie.'

'Actually, I think it is my business. I think it's everyone's business because we all have to live in this house and if Lord Deverell finds out ...'

'He won't.'

'He's your *father*. And she's your father's *wife*.'

Charles was silent for a moment, then he tapped Edie's fingers.

'Do I detect the heady scent of blackmail, Edie? Because I can assure you that you don't want to get on the wrong side of me. You don't want that at all.'

'No. No, you've completely misunderstood me. I'd never blackmail anyone.'

'Good.'

He was so close to her. Their thighs touched, his in silky robes, hers in a coarse linen gown. He smelled off-puttingly masculine. His scent wound itself into her resolve, weakening it and strengthening it at the same time.

She liked having her hand wrapped in his. She liked it so much she wasn't sure she could stand his letting go of it. He was some kind of sorcerer, casting a malign spell on her ... why hadn't she known one could feel like this?

His forehead brushed hers. If she wasn't careful, she would let him kiss her before the time was right. She had already accepted, at the very depths of her, that the kiss was inevitable. But she could at least put it off until she had stated her case.

Pull yourself together, Edie.

'So you refuse to stop ... consorting with your step-mother?' she said sharply.

He burst out laughing.

'Consorting? What kind of housemaid are you? You're the quaintest little thing. It's rather appealing.'

'Please. I'm quite serious.'

'You are, aren't you? I'm fascinated by you. Why is this of such concern to you? And why do you think you can come to my rooms and dictate whom I allow into my bed? I should smack your bottom and send you on your way.'

Edie clenched her fists tight, including the one that lay in his hand.

'You wouldn't understand my reasons,' she said. 'But I see I can't persuade you.'

'Oh, you haven't even tried,' he said in a low voice, bringing his lips perilously close to hers. His breath smelled of mints and the traces of post-prandial brandy. 'Go on. Persuade me.'

She wanted to know what his stubbled cheek would feel like on hers, quite badly.

Not yet.

'I'll make a bargain with you,' she said, clinging on to the remnants of her self-control.

'Oh, will you, by Jove?' His voice was so wickedly low, right in her ear. 'A deal with the devil? A Faustian pact? Out with it, then. Don't ask me to kill any kings for you though, eh, Lady Macbeth.'

'If you'll leave Lady Deverell alone ... I'll ... let you ...'

Dear God, do I mean this? Will I?

'Let me...?' His breath, hot, fanning her neck.

'Kiss ...'

Too late. It was already happening. They were kissing, and she had received no undertaking from him that he would stay out of Lady Deverell's bed.

And now, kissing, a thing she had wondered about often in a vaguely anthropological kind of way. An act seemingly devoid of biological function. The other beasts did not kiss so why did humans? How could the meeting of mouths create a bond or inflame a desire? And what of the secretions inevitably exchanged in the course of such activity? Was it not rather *unhealthy*?

No, no, it was not unhealthy, it was superlatively lovely. Heavens, how lovely. And the desire was kindled so quickly that one stood no chance of repelling it. Within seconds it had seized one, taken one's body and laid it wide open to the ravages of passion.

Edie had never expected the ravages of passion. She

had thought they only existed in the questionable novels the maids enjoyed.

Anyway, it wasn't *passion*, exactly, was it? More a sort of revelry of the senses. Such revelry that her attempt to keep a grip on herself by means of mental commentary soon failed and she was defeated.

His Lordship's lips …

They pressed her onwards, whisking her up inside until she quivered like a helpless creature caught in a net.

When he broke off, she had to gasp for breath.

'Have you ever been kissed before?' he asked.

She noticed that he held the back of her neck with one hand – how had it got there? Worse, her own hands were gripping the lapels of his robe as if to stop him getting away from her.

'Of course,' she lied.

'I'd find it hard to believe you hadn't. But you're trembling so violently – as if you've been attacked. You're afraid, aren't you?'

'No.' Again, it was a lie.

'Don't fib. What are you afraid of?'

'All right. I haven't ever kissed anyone before. You were right. And I'm only kissing you so that you'll keep away from, from Lady Deverell.'

His hand tightened, a little painfully, on the scruff of her neck.

'Really?' He had taken mortal offence. She should

have phrased it differently. 'You're *only* thinking of our dear Ruby Redford? This is an ordeal for you, then?'

'No, it's not an ordeal. As it happens, it's rather pleasant. But I don't care for you, sir, nor do I have any feelings of love or anything of that kind. You're attractive, I'll allow, and that makes this easier, but I'm not offering you my heart. I don't even like you.'

Sir Charles stared, apparently dumbfounded for a change.

Edie had a creeping sensation that she had said too much, been too blunt. She squirmed in his grasp, assessing escape opportunities.

'Who the devil *are* you?' he whispered. 'Housemaids don't go saying this kind of thing to their lordly protectors. Don't you understand, this is an *honour*.'

'Was it an honour for Susie Leonard, too?'

'Jesus.'

He let go of her and sat back as if struck.

'I don't know what your game is, Edie,' he said slowly. 'But I'll find out.'

'I've told you what it is. If you'll leave Lady Deverell alone, I'm willing to grant you certain liberties.'

'Don't you ... aren't you ... girls just don't *do* this kind of thing.'

'This girl does. This girl isn't going to be made a fool of for love. My body is mine to use as I wish, and if it can save ... some heartache for somebody ... then why not?'

'I never heard anything more preposterous in my life.'

'You don't accept my offer? Then I'll go back to the dormitory.'

She stood.

'No, you bloody well won't.' He patted the seat beside him. 'Sit back down now.'

She wavered. She did not want to leave now with her objective unmet. But perhaps it would be best all round, after all, if they could agree to forget this encounter and continue as before. Something told her Charles would not accept this and she would be back in London before the week was out.

She sat down.

'Perhaps we should draw a line under this night,' she suggested warily.

'Perhaps we shouldn't. Perhaps I can't.'

'Can't you?'

'You can't leave a man with so many unanswered questions,' he said. 'It's cruel. And besides … I want you.'

Her throat tightened, a convulsion of fearful excitement overwhelming her senses.

'You can't have me unless you stop what you're doing with her.'

'You don't mean that.'

'I do.'

'You say you don't want me, but when I kissed you …'

He put out his hand and brushed his knuckles against her neck and up under her hair.

'Don't pretend you didn't want it,' he whispered.

She couldn't deny it, and neither could she prevent the way her heart hammered and her blood rushed.

But she could save herself. She could at least do that.

'You can't have your cake and eat it too,' she said, wrenching herself away from his touch and standing. 'Leave Lady Deverell alone and I'm at your disposal. But until then, goodnight.'

She whirled around and ran for the door, suspecting he would give chase.

She was right, but she made it to the corridor while his enraged cry of 'Edie!' still rang in the air. She didn't dare look back but, by the time she had reached the servants' back staircase, nobody was at her heels and she was able to lean back against the wall for a moment and let the giddy swaying of her head settle.

What on earth had she just done? And what would happen now?

He wouldn't say anything, she decided. It wasn't in his interests to have her sacked and besides, as a housemaid she should be beneath his notice.

Slipping back into bed, she could not help but think of how differently things could have been. She could have been in Sir Charles's bed, in his arms ... what would that be like? When kisses went further ... Oh, she could not think of it.

She had offered a man her body.

What was a body after all but flesh and blood and bone? It was nothing. To offer it to somebody was nothing. Wrongdoing came from the heart and the mind, the intention to do harm. To experience physical pleasure with another – this was surely not wrong, for who suffered from it?

She should not be feeling guilt or shame about this – she had sworn that she would not be held down by those old foes of her sex. But she couldn't help it. It was so much easier to argue a position than to embody it. How could she have known that these interloping emotions would ruin the purity of her mission? Before she drifted into sleep her pillow was wet with tears.

Chapter Four

When she woke up, a sensuality lingered upon her, the remnants of her dreams, which were in turn the remnants of her unsatisfied desires.

She bade her roommates good morning, but none of them replied. She was left to pin her own hair and tie her own apron, and was late for breakfast yet again.

If they're so sure I'm going to sleep with Sir Charles, then perhaps I should, she thought fiercely, splashing her face with cold water before running downstairs. At least then I wouldn't be in Coventry for nothing.

'Are you cleaning the morning room?' she asked Jenny dully as they collected their dusters and mops from the cupboard.

'That's yours,' said Jenny smartly. 'I don't expect I'll be wanted in there.'

'Look, there's nothing going on ...'

But she couldn't finish the sentence. There *was* something going on.

'Hope not, for poor Ted's sake,' said Jenny, and she bustled off in the opposite direction to Edie.

'If you're on your own today,' said Mrs Munn, emerging unexpectedly and making Edie jump, 'I'll be along at various times to keep my eye on you. You're much slower than you should be and I'm concerned that the cleanliness of the house will suffer. Jenny says you tend to daydream. Check that, please.'

'Yes, ma'am,' said Edie, only half-listening.

'Still on for the pictures tomorrow?' asked Ted, passing her on the way to the morning room.

'Oh, yes, of course,' she said.

She'd have said yes to anything. Only one thing occupied her mind – would Sir Charles be in the morning room again?

He wasn't, and she could hear the clatter of knives and forks on china from the breakfast room a little further along. Presumably he was in there. If she did this room very, very quickly …

She tried her hardest to sweep the grate and clean the surrounds with all haste, but she got ashes on her face and black lead under her fingernails, while all the metal was smeared and needed an extra rub down.

Muttering curses under her breath, she tried to improve her haphazard job, wondering if she could get away with just a lightning-quick brush of the feather duster across everything else.

But it was too late.

Sir Charles entered the room while she still kneeling on the hearth rug, clouds of soot around her.

'Oh dear,' he said, and, to her horror, he came to stand directly behind her, looming over her. 'You seem to be making things worse rather than better.'

She sat back on her heels.

'Perhaps you could do a better job,' she said.

'Perhaps I could,' he said.

He crouched beside her and her heart seemed to stop beating.

'Look at those hands,' he said. 'They weren't made for this.'

He reached to take one, but sharp footsteps from the next room sent him into retreat before he could do it.

'I beg your pardon, sir,' said Mrs Munn. 'Good Lord, Edie, what are you about?'

Sir Charles hid behind his newspaper while the house-keeper endeavoured to put Edie back on the correct path to cleaning the fireplace.

'I can't do this for you every day,' she tutted. 'Really, were you this inept at your last place? I begin to wonder if they wrote that reference to get rid of you.'

The harsh words brought tears to Edie's eyes.

'Steady on,' said Charles.

'Sir?' Mrs Munn stood and turned to him while Edie did not dare look.

81

'Bit uncalled for,' he said. 'It's only a fireplace.'

'I daresay it is,' she said coldly. 'But it's my ultimate responsibility, so you'll excuse me if I take it seriously.'

'Of course,' drawled Charles, lighting a cigarette. 'Carry on.'

Mrs Munn removed Edie from the scene for an extensive tutorial in grate-polishing. Edie supposed she ought to be thankful; Mrs Munn had repelled the danger from Sir Charles quite effectively for the time being.

'You shouldn't have been alone with him,' she said in a low voice, applying polish to a rag which she passed to Edie.

'I've heard about Susie Leonard, ma'am. It won't happen to me.'

'Really? Well, Susie was a silly girl but a very fine housemaid. Perhaps you are her polar opposite. A poor housemaid with a sensible head on her shoulders. We can't have everything, can we?'

She cracked a rare smile, which Edie could not help returning, feeling rather privileged to be on the receiving end of it.

'I am trying my best,' said Edie.

'I daresay you are, and you can't do more than that. But this is Deverell Hall, Edie, and we have standards that must be maintained.'

'I'll get better, I swear.'

Mrs Munn nodded.

'Now, I'm leaving this to you. I'll come and see how you've managed it in twenty minutes' time. I expect it to be gleaming fit to blind me by then, do you understand me?'

'Yes, ma'am.'

***

Edie was almost done with the Blue Drawing Room when Lady Mary entered in her riding habit.

'I say, it's the new girl, isn't it?'

'Yes, ma'am.'

'I don't usually chat with the maids but I hear you're from London. Is that true?'

'Yes, ma'am.'

Lady Mary threw herself into one of the chairs – one that did not seem designed for having bodies thrown into it.

'Wish to God I was there,' she muttered.

'Ma'am?'

'Oh, it doesn't concern you. I'm desperate for a trip to town but pa's being a crashing bore about it. He has the most abominably old-fashioned ideas about everything. I keep telling him these are the 1920s but I'm sure he mishears me and thinks I've said the 1820s.'

'I'm sorry to hear that, ma'am.'

Lady Mary mimicked the bland phrase then kicked the leg of the chair.

'Do you have a fellow?' she asked.

'Excuse me, ma'am?'

'Oh, you know what I mean. A young man, a swain.'

'No, no, I don't.'

'Then get one. And make it quick, before my brother makes love to you. He will, you know.'

Edie twirled her feather duster round in her fingers, at a loss for words.

'If you'll excuse me, ma'am,' she said.

'Oh, God, he already has.' Mary let out a bark of laughter. 'There'd better not be another little Deverell bastard on the way. Pa's spleen won't stand it.'

'You've no call to make assumptions about me,' said Edie coldly.

Mary drew herself up in her chair and stared.

'Oh, don't I, madam? Well, I stand corrected. But speak to me in that tone again and you needn't expect lover boy Charlie to come to your rescue. Because he never does, you know. He doesn't really care about anyone except himself.'

Edie nodded, sick with nerves now.

'If you'll excuse me,' she muttered for a third time.

'Oh, go on, then. Thought you might be fun, but you're a mouse like the rest of them. Scurry along.'

Edie passed a wary, strung-up day listening for footsteps and peering around corners. When Sir Charles was seen getting into his motor, she was able to gain relief from her suspenseful state for an hour or two, but his return brought the butterflies back to her stomach.

Twice she crossed the path of Lady Deverell, who had nothing to say to her, but watched her intently as she passed. Of Lord Deverell she saw almost nothing, and she dreaded that he might have gone away again, and Charles would pay his stepmother another visit that night.

Enquiries in the servants' kitchen confirmed that this was not the case, however – he had been out preparing for the following day's shoot, that was all. To her even greater relief, Carrie had recovered from her illness and Edie was not called to serve the family at dinner that night.

Instead she sat by the kitchen fire and tried to darn a stocking, though the skill was not one that came easily to her. One of the footmen played the fiddle, and folksy tunes drifted through the servants' quarters while the scullery maids danced.

Ted cut through the frolicking, taking one girl gallantly by the waist and swinging her around until she squealed, before dropping her and coming to sit opposite Edie.

'Raw weather for summer, ain't it?' he said. 'Autumn's come early. This fire's never usually lit at this time of year.'

'At least it's stopped raining,' remarked Edie, biting off a length of thread.

'How did you get on today? Any more disasters with the polish?' Ted grinned and stretched his long legs out in front of him.

'No, at least, I hope not. I had a run-in with Lady Mary, though.'

He leaned forwards, his cheek muscles twitching.

'Oh? What happened?'

'Nothing really. She just seemed to want to needle me. She was put out about some trip to London that had been cancelled. I suppose I was the nearest body to take out her frustrations on.'

'Yeah, that'd be it,' said Ted, settling back in his seat. 'There were a few whispers about her behaviour last time she was up in town. Burning the candle both ends. Out and about with people His Lordship wasn't so keen on.'

'She's a young woman. She's bound to want to enjoy herself.'

'Deverell don't see it that way. He thinks girls should be like his aunts were, sitting around all day flapping handkerchiefs and smelling violet drops. Playing something on the piano if they felt very daring.'

'Gosh, thank heavens for the twentieth century,' said Edie with feeling. 'I hope Lady Mary will benefit from it eventually.'

'Over his dead body,' said Ted contemplatively. 'Those are my thoughts on the matter. That's a shocking job you've done on that stocking. Give it here.'

Edie watched his big hands and long fingers at work with the needle and thread, wondering why, if a man found this kind of thing easy, she did not. Everything ended up tangled and hopeless when she put her hand to it.

'There.' He handed it back, beaming. 'We're still on for tomorrow, aren't we?'

'Tomorrow? Oh! Yes. I'm free from midday, I think.'

'We'll walk up to Kingsreach together then. Wish I could drive you but I can't use the car for my own business. As long as the rain keeps off, it's a nice walk.'

'I know. I walked here from the station.'

'Oh, yes, so you did.' He shook his head, regarding her inquisitively. 'You're a curiosity, you are.'

'No, I'm not.' She blushed and bowed her head, always afraid that her face might give some crucial secret away.

'I'll work you out,' he said, reminding her alarmingly of Sir Charles the night before. She didn't want anybody trying to gauge her motives, let alone two men. Two attractive men.

'I'm not some mystery story, you know.'

'Aren't you? I'm not so sure. Anyway, best go and tinker with me engine. Sweet dreams – dream about tomorrow.'

He ruffled her hair and disappeared, off to the garage.

Edie, tired and bored without the company of the other maids, took herself off to bed early. Tonight she could sleep. Lord Deverell was at home, so there was no need to fear for any more assaults on his wife's virtue by his son.

There was no need to visit Charles.

No need – at least, no practical need.

But her body itched to get out of bed and put on her gown and find him. All she could think of was what he might be doing, what he might be thinking, there in his room with the paisley silk hangings and the aromas of Turkish tobacco and Russian leather and spicy cologne all twisting together and ravishing the air.

There, in his room, his dark hair on the pillow, his eyes on the ceiling, or a book, or looking out of the window or ... thinking of her. Did he think of her?

Or was she no longer of interest, now she had delivered an ultimatum? Was that game over and done with?

She thought she couldn't bear it if so. She squeezed her eyes tight shut and thought of home. Within minutes she was deep in sleep.

* * *

On Wednesdays, she didn't have to clean the morning room. She was permitted the ineffable luxury of a lie-in and she had only light duties to perform until her half-holiday officially began at midday.

She saw the clock hand jerk to the twelve and she made a run for the back stairs, ready to change into her own clothes and meet with Ted.

Too full of the joys of limited freedom to remember

to be cautious, she turned a corner and ran straight into Sir Charles. She had presumed him to be out shooting with the rest and he was wearing shooting attire – tweeds and a peaked cap and all the rest of it – but he had no gun and looked grimly purposeful.

She froze and took a step back but he was too quick for her.

'Got you,' he exclaimed, seizing her by the wrists. 'Well, well, well. You've been avoiding me, Miss Prior.'

'I haven't.'

'I waited for you in the morning room.'

'It's my day off. I didn't have to clean it.'

'Your day off? Wednesdays, eh?'

He relaxed his grip and took her in, from frilly cap to sensible work boots.

'Is this your idea of mufti?'

'I was on my way to get changed. You aren't with the shoot.'

'Well spotted. I came to fetch a spare gun for an unexpected extra guest.' He drew closer, his head on one side. 'So, where are you going to, my pretty little maid?'

Going a-milking, sir, she said.

'I told you. I'm going to change.'

'I don't think you should change. I like you as you are.'

'Please, sir, I have to go. I'm meeting somebody.'

His face, slack with lust, stiffened.

'Who? A man?'

'A friend. Please, let me go.' She tried to wrench herself from his hold.

'A male friend?'

'It is none of your business.'

He seemed to think otherwise, bringing his face right down to hers so that their foreheads bumped together, but a voice from the front door stopped them in their tracks.

'Charles?'

The throaty tones of Lady Deverell were unmistakable.

'I say, Charles, are you there? Did you get the gun? The fellows are all impatient to move on.'

Her footsteps echoed across the tiles and Charles dropped Edie's wrists. She darted straightaway up the back stairs.

At the first landing, she heard Lady Deverell's voice again, a purr now.

'Charlie. Whatever *are* you doing?'

She didn't want to stay to find out.

* * *

Oh, it was horrible, she thought furiously, throwing her uniform on to the bed and buttoning herself into the plain white blouse and blue hobble skirt she had worn on her journey. Sir Charles and Lady Deverell would not leave each other alone and they would be found out and the most terrific furore would ensue. If people spoke in hushed tones of the Susie Leonard affair, what on earth would they make of this? It would be in all the papers.

She put on her straw hat just in case the vague threat of sunshine proved more than idle, threw a light shawl over her shoulders, picked up her handbag and made her way to the garage to meet Ted.

'Only a little bit late,' he said, dapper in a striped blazer and highly polished boots, looking almost foreign out of his uniform.

'Oh, look at us. We are like two regular people,' said Edie.

'Well, I should hope that's what we are.'

'You know what I mean. Uniforms rather take away one's sense of identity, don't they?'

'I don't know. Sounds like you've thought more about that than I have.'

He offered his arm, rather formally, and Edie wondered if she had offended him.

'I didn't mean that I *don't* see you as a regular person,' she said timidly as they set off towards the Kingsreach road. 'Of course I do.'

'That's all right then.'

They turned the corner of the house. On the front steps, Sir Charles stood with Lady Deverell. Edie kept her gaze severely before her, focusing only on the point where the path away from Deverell Hall disappeared into wooded darkness.

Why did he have to see her with Ted? What if she had now made trouble for the chauffeur? She had the oddest fear that Charles was standing behind them, levelling his gun at their backs. Her neck prickled and she started to walk much faster.

'Steady on, girl,' laughed Ted. 'We've three hours yet till the matinee showing.'

'Oh, I know, I'm just a little hungry. Looking forward to taking lunch somewhere. What's it like in Kingsreach? Any nice places?'

'I like the Cross Keys in the market square. They do a decent lunch and a good pint too.'

'Oh, a public house,' said Edie, who had never been to such an establishment.

Ted laughed. 'You make it sound like I'm taking you to Timbuktu. Last time I checked, they did have pubs in London.'

'Of course. I preferred the Lyons Corner House in Coventry Street, though. Did you ever go there? It's frightfully jolly.'

Edie felt a pang of regret at being so far from the buzz and excitement of the London streets and cafés.

'I can't say as I did. Perhaps you can take me there one day.'

She felt heat rise to her cheeks as he squeezed her forearm. Ted seemed to indicate that he had romance in mind. It was most awfully inconvenient. Why couldn't a chap be content with friendship?

'I don't know when I shall be in London again,' she said vaguely.

'Do you miss it?'

'Oh, I've hardly been away long enough. It's odd not to be able to just go out and get whatever one wants, whenever one wants it. Everything is such a long way from here.'

'Left any broken hearts behind you?'

Edie sensed flirtatious danger in the question, which she tried to laugh off.

'Gosh, no. Well … no.'

Ted drew in a breath and tried to draw more from her with his steady gaze.

'All right, there was a young man, a friend of the family, but he was considerably more interested in me than I was in him, I'm afraid.'

'You're running away from him?'

'No, no, I'm not. That's not why I'm here at all. In fact, he helped me to find this position.'

Stop, you've said too much already.

'Man sounds like a fool, sending a girl like you away from him. What's his game then?'

'He doesn't have a game, he just respects my wish not to be … embroiled in … that kind of thing … with him.' Edie picked little darts from her skirt, trying to edge away from the hedgerow.

'What's his name?'

'Pat. Patrick. We're friends, that's all. It's perfectly possible for a man and a woman to be friends without the complication of romance.'

'You believe that, do you?' Ted's expression made her cheeks burn.

'If you don't, then you should turn around and take me back to the house.'

Ted sighed and they walked on for a while in silence that was broken by the distant pop of gunfire.

'Do you like the pictures?' asked Ted, once they were close to the estate's edge.

'I've never been, I'm afraid.'

'You've never been? And you a London girl and all.'

'I'm more a theatre-lover … what's that?'

They turned to look behind them for the source of the approaching racket.

'Sounds like Charlie's motor,' said Ted and, sure enough, the cream-coloured car appeared around a bend, shattering the peace of the green-canopied road.

'I thought he was with the shoot,' said Edie, horribly apprehensive, more so when the vehicle showed signs of slowing down to a halt as it drew nearer.

'Kempe,' said Sir Charles, lolling behind his steering wheel and staring insolently at the holidaying servants. 'You're wanted at the Hall.'

'I can't be, Lord Deverell said –'

'Are you calling me a liar?'

'Of course not, sir, but –'

'Let go of the girl and get back to work then.'

Ted stood for a moment, poised on the brink of argument, then his shoulders dropped and he exhaled noisily.

'Right,' he muttered. 'Edie, can you forgive me? I'm sorry to let you down this time, but I swear I'll make it up to you.'

'It's all right, it can't be helped. I'll walk back with you.'

She shot an unnerved glance at Sir Charles, who shook his head.

'Don't be silly, Edie,' he said. 'You've got the day off. Use it. Where were you going? Kingsreach? I'll give you a lift. Hop in.'

Ted looked horrified, but he couldn't say anything.

'Oh, I don't know about that,' said Edie, caught in a tight spot.

'Nonsense, I won't take no for an answer.'

He opened the passenger door.

Ted whispered something that sounded like 'He's right about that.'

'Are you still here, Kempe? Run along, there's a good man.'

Ted turned and stalked furiously off.

Edie looked after him, undecided whether to run and catch him up or stay here with her devilish tempter.

'You've no business pursuing me like this,' she said in a low voice, in case her words should drift on the wind to Ted's ears.

'You've a short memory, Edie. I believe it was you who had an interesting offer to make in my bedroom the other night.' He paused just long enough for Edie to start wondering if her legs were about to give way. 'Where was he taking you? Some tawdry dive, I suppose?'

'The picture palace. And he mentioned a public house ... I forget its name.'

'Tut tut. I think we can do better than that. Why are you still standing there?'

He patted the seat beside him.

'I can't be seen in Kingsreach with you, for heaven's sake! Imagine the gossip.'

'Who said anything about Kingsreach? Come *on*, Edie.'

'I don't think it's safe ...'

'Worried for your virtue, are you? The same virtue you offered me on a plate not two days ago. Come on, we haven't finished our little discussion on that subject, have we?'

'Oh. Haven't we?'

'No. Look, I'm considering your offer. I just need to give it a little more thought.'

He patted the seat again and this time she climbed in beside him.

Chapter Five

'Good girl.'

His approval needled her and she shut the door sharply, her knees pressed tight together.

'Why aren't you at the shoot?'

'Why do you think? I'm not having you running around Kingsreach with chauffeurs. Cigarette?'

'Oh ... no, thanks.'

He lit one for himself and started the engine again. The car jolted off, almost jerking her out of the seat, but once it settled the ride was surprisingly smooth and fast, cutting a swathe through the damp green lanes. Such a thing did not belong here, Edie thought. A noisy, smelly man-made monster amongst nature's abundance – it did not fit in.

It was important to fit in.

'Where are we going?'

'You'll see.'

'I feel rather as if I'm being kidnapped.'

'You are.'

'Gosh.'

She swallowed and looked at Charles's hands in their driving gloves, so sure and confident on the wheel. Perhaps she ought to learn to drive. It did seem rather marvellous, to be whisking along like this with the wind trying to get at her hair under her straw hat. It was just as well she'd tied the ribbon so firmly.

'You don't have a chauffeur of your own?'

'I neither need nor want one. I like to decide my own course. That way, if I want to make a diversion, I can.' He made a sharp right turn into a narrower, bumpier lane.

Edie screamed, not having expected this manoeuvre, finding herself thrown against him. He kept one hand on the wheel and put the other about her waist, holding her close.

'Exciting, isn't it?' he drawled.

He drove on a half mile or so, Edie trying to prise his fingers from her waist all the while, before leaving the road where the verge was broken, presenting an ideal little parking space beneath a grove of trees.

'Oh, why have we stopped?' cried Edie, feeling a great affinity with damsels in distress down the ages.

'I wanted to take in the view.'

Since that view was of unbroken fields of corn, Edie rather doubted this.

'If you think you can use force to seduce me –' Edie

kicked his ankle hard. He dug his fingers into her waist before removing them to rub at the injury.

'You little beast,' he hissed, eyes flashing with something not entirely of anger. 'You needn't suppose you can get away with that.'

Edie shuffled to the far edge of her seat, her fingers trembling on the door handle.

'I'm entitled to defend myself,' she said. 'You should have let go of me.'

He reached across so quickly that she hardly saw him take her hands and wrench them away from the door.

'Sit still,' he said, 'and stop behaving like a melodrama heroine. I'm not a rapist. I only meant to talk to you. I suppose that's allowed, is it?'

'If you're telling the truth.'

'Hm, well, telling the truth hasn't always been my strong point but in this case I'll endeavour to do my best. But you must do the same. I have questions I want answering and I won't accept any subterfuge from you.'

He dropped her hands and watched while she folded them in her lap.

She was still shaking and she needed a moment to let the shivers subside before speaking. She stared ahead at the empty road and tried to forget that she was completely alone in the middle of nowhere with a dangerously seductive man.

'You know that word, don't you?' he continued softly. 'Subterfuge.'

She nodded.

'You have an unusually broad vocabulary for a parlourmaid.'

'I went to school, like everyone else.'

'Like everyone else,' he echoed thoughtfully. 'You aren't like everyone else, though, Edie. You're a very different kettle of fish from the little sweethearts one usually encounters wielding the feather duster.'

'Am I?'

'You know you are. Tell me about yourself.'

'There's very little to say. I'm an only child. I grew up in Bloomsbury, if you know it.'

'Yes, I know it. The British Museum and so forth. Quite an affluent quarter, isn't it?'

'In parts. Not all of it.'

'You grew up in some basement hovel then, did you?' He pulled off one of his driving gloves and held it by one finger, inspecting it idly.

'We weren't the poorest but we weren't the richest either,' said Edie briskly. She was trying very hard not to tell any outright lies, but it involved the full engagement of all her wits and she was already starting to tire.

'What does your father do?'

'He, ah, he's …'

'Don't lie, Edie,' warned Charles, fixing an intent gaze on her in which she felt imprisoned.

'He is a teacher,' she said, in a kind of desperately

100

apologetic tone, knowing that this information could be the start of her undoing.

'A teacher? With a daughter in service?'

'He taught me very well,' she said. 'He is a strong believer in social justice and, as such, he thinks one should experience life on all levels and amongst all classes.'

This much was true.

Charles stared for a moment then laughed, throwing his head back on the car seat.

'You're scrubbing grates on your knees at six o'clock in the morning to make yourself a better person?' he exclaimed. 'You don't even need to do it – you could teach yourself, surely? Teach poor children – there are plenty of 'em in London, I hear. Why service? It doesn't add up, Edie. But perhaps your arithmetical skills are less well-developed than your social curiosity. Explain. I need to understand you.'

'Well, you see,' said Edie carefully, coming up with a faintly plausible explanation second by second, 'teaching poor children in London would of course expose me to the lives of the least fortunate. That much is clear. But how does one come to mix with the very highest stratum in our society – the aristocracy? How does one do that without being titled oneself?'

'Oh, that's a very fair point,' said Charles, nodding. 'Of course, dukes and dairymaids mix much more freely now than they ever did, and perhaps that tendency will only increase. One need only look at our fair Ladyship to see an example of the kind.'

Edie made fists in her lap, bunching them tight in the serge of her skirt.

'She is a woman who has made the most of herself, through talent and personality,' said Edie, her voice a little hoarse. 'For that, I believe she is to be admired.'

'She's a gold-digger and a whore,' said Charles.

Edie's hands flew out of her lap and she aimed a slap that found its mark and cracked ferociously through the muggy air.

In a split second she was pinioned at the wrists with Charles's nose right against hers while he bore down on her, breathing heavily.

'You *will* tell me,' he said with barely controlled venom, 'why you are so intent on defending this woman. You know her, don't you? Are you some relation of hers, crawling out of the woodwork for a slice of the family pie? *My* family pie?'

'We have never met before, never,' said Edie. 'Let me up. I'm sorry. I shouldn't have hit you. I hate to hear women called whores. It makes me angry and then I can't control myself.'

He sat up and released one of her wrists, but brought the other to his face, laying her palm flat on the hot red mark she had made.

'What would you call her then?' he asked. 'A woman

who has given herself to a man she doesn't love, for money?'

'Unlucky,' said Edie. 'Unhappy.'

Charles's face contorted with scorn. 'Unlucky? Unlucky to marry my father? Unlucky to live in one of the finest houses in England.'

'And unlucky to get herself mixed up with you.'

He drew back from her at that, calculating his next move. Edie thought he looked like a serpent poised to strike. But he did not strike.

'Your offer still stands?' he asked, almost offhandedly, as if enquiring after her comfort.

She wasn't sure it still did. She thought she ought to withdraw it. Clearly she had had no idea what depths she might be flinging herself into with this man.

'Because I've decided I'd like to take you up on it,' he said softly, putting two fingers beneath her chin so that she couldn't look away.

'Have you? You'll stay away from Lady Deverell?'

Every pore of her skin burned. How did he know the perfect way to touch her?

He has practice. Lots of it.

He nodded a brief assent.

'No, say it. Swear it.'

'What a puzzle you are. Yes, all right, I swear it.'

You've done it now, Edie Crossland. You've signed yourself, body and soul, over to this man. But must the

*body and the soul be indivisibly related? Can I get away
with just giving him my body? I must work to keep my
soul intact, whatever else he takes from me.*

Having adopted this dualistic philosophy, Edie felt
safe to proceed.

'Very well,' she said with awkward bravery. 'You may
take me as your mistress. But I have conditions.'

He laughed. 'Of course you have. I'll hear them, but
first ...'

His hand slid around the back of her neck and he
held her there for the duration of the kiss he planted,
tenderly at first, upon her lips. It felt like the summer
air around them, a zephyr, a whisper of a thing, but it
soon grew. Edie found sensations in it she had never
expected. It stirred up a storm in her head and her belly
and then even lower, even to her knees, which turned
to water while the kiss showed her more and more of
her unspoken desires. How could she feel so protected
and yet so endangered? She saw herself on the brink of
throwing herself open to this man, of giving him anything
and everything he might want. Yet she must retain some
measure of control, or he would ride roughshod over
her; and that was not the plan.

All the same, she could live in that embrace, live with
those lips upon hers and his hands, at her nape and waist.
At first, she did not think of doing anything with her
own hands, but as their sighs deepened and the whirl of

delight spun more wildly, she clutched at him, seeking his hair, his face, his shoulders.

Then he did two things that alarmed her into breaking the kiss. First, he pushed the tip of his tongue between her lips as if he meant to feed it to her. Secondly, he grazed his knuckles against the side of her breast, tending towards her stiffened nipple. A sense of how terribly unseemly this all was, taking place in a motor car of all places, sent a cold shiver of shame and regret through her and she pushed him off.

'Oh, Edie,' he moaned, leaning his head against the green leather and giving her a look of inflammatory sorrow. He stroked her cheek and she came fractionally closer to him again, their faces almost touching. 'I think you must like me, just a little.'

'I don't intend to like you,' she whispered. 'If I care for you, it will make things far too difficult.'

'I'll make you care for me,' he said. 'I'll make you fall in love with me.'

'You won't.'

'I will.'

She could not prevent herself allowing him another kiss, but this time he did not go too far. Indeed, he did not go far enough, for she thought that, after all, she wanted him to touch her in places that had never before been disturbed. Her curiosity had been aroused – amongst other things.

'We are in broad daylight in a public place,' she said, as much to convince herself as caution him. 'If anyone should chance by ...'

'I want to take you under a haystack,' he drawled. His face was pressed to hers, cheek to cheek, lips to ear. 'I want to do all the most unspeakable things imaginable to you.'

'About those conditions,' said Edie.

'Oh, damn those conditions. Tell me later. Sit up and do something about your hair. I'm taking you out to lunch.'

* * *

A few towns along the river, out of the range of local gossip, Charles took her to a place with tables at the very banks of the water, where the waiters served one with pink lemonade in very tall glasses, and fresh fish caught that morning.

'Fish knives,' said Charles, picking his up and surveying its glint in the afternoon sun. 'Pa won't have them, thinks they're terribly infra dig, but I find them quite useful, don't you?'

'We've always used them,' she said, sipping at her lemonade.

'I daresay you have,' he said, and his Cheshire-cat grin made her kick herself for giving away another example of her middle-class background.

She stared down at the latticed ironwork of the table, unsure how to make polite conversation with a man who fully intended to take her virginity before much more time had passed.

'I want to hear your conditions,' he said.

Some ducks sailed by, quacking happily. It seemed entirely the wrong place and time for such a conversation, but Edie tried to gather her thoughts.

'You know the first one. About leaving Lady Deverell alone.'

'Yes, yes. She was just a diversion anyway. I'd rather have you. Much rather. What else?'

'You're not to get me ... I don't want a baby.'

At this moment the fish arrived, trout with scalloped potatoes and a salad.

Edie watched Charles's face as he acknowledged the food and asked for condiments. He looked perfectly unruffled, as if they had been talking about the weather.

'That's easily taken care of,' he said, once the waiter had retired. 'You needn't worry about it.'

'Susie Leonard –'

'Susie Leonard wanted a baby. She wanted my baby. She thought I'd marry her if she had one.'

'You should have told her you had no intention of doing so. What will her life be now? What about your child's life?'

'The child is well provided for,' he said abruptly, attacking the fish's soft flesh. 'Susie will never go without food or lodging.'

Edie exhaled gratefully. 'That was another of my conditions,' she said.

'Well, I've met it. I'll take you to visit her if you like. You can judge for yourself.'

'So you see the child?'

'I pop down there when I can.'

'Is it a boy or a girl?'

'A girl. Charlotte. Not my choice, but she insisted.'

'She named her after you.'

'So it seems. Look, I know it reflects badly on me. It all happened very soon after I came back from the war. I was blindsided, I wanted to forget ... she helped me ...'

'You're asking for my sympathy? You seduced an innocent girl.'

'She wasn't a virgin.' Charles tore at some bread from the basket, seeming to enjoy Edie's consternation. 'Somebody else had had her cherry, and do you know who it was?'

'Of course not.'

'Your friend the chauffeur.'

'Ted? Oh no.' Edie couldn't believe this. Ted was a good man, a gentleman in his way. Surely he would not have ... 'You're saying this because you want me to stay away from him.'

'Yes, I do want you to stay away from him. In fact, that might be a little condition of mine, while we're playing this game.'

'How do you know it was Ted?'

'She told me. I'd say the child had a look of him, but she really doesn't. She's the living image of my sister at that age. All the same, I could very easily have denied paternity and walked away. I didn't. I think you should like me for it.'

'I suppose you could have been worse.'

The fish was too fresh and the accompaniments seemed slimy. Edie had no appetite for the food, imagining her stomach round and balloon-like, like Susie's must have been. Imagine if he did get her pregnant. What on earth would she do then?

'Well,' she said decisively. 'Susie Leonard might have wanted your baby but I categorically and absolutely do not. So please see to it.'

'If you were a real parlourmaid you'd jump at the chance to get your own cottage and a steady income instead of living that life. You're here for a holiday of sorts, I think. Or perhaps you're running away from something? Oh, yes, that's it, isn't it? You're escaping. Unlucky Edie, to run straight into my arms. Poor unfortunate damsel.'

He was enjoying his speculations, nibbling at the last crust of bread after mopping up the remaining sauce.

'Nothing of the sort,' she said. She was aware of sweat gathering at the back of her neck. The day was too hot and the table lacked a parasol. 'I think I should like some shade. Could we go and sit over there, underneath that tree?'

'Of course. Have you finished?' He looked doubtfully at her plate. 'I always thought you maids ate like horses. You're going to need to do better than that, my girl, once I've got you in my clutches. I want you in peak condition.'

'Oh, stop it,' she muttered, hotter still at the thought of what he had in mind for her.

He called for ices to be brought to the little bench beneath the weeping willow and sat down beside Edie, taking her hand in his as they gazed at the water. Just watching it flow onwards had a refreshing effect, and the ices fought off the worst of the discomfort, cooling Edie down to a bearable level.

'Any more conditions?' he asked lightly.

A swan glided past. How incongruous this was.

'I don't think so,' she said. 'Just … if you could try and be … nice … about it.'

He seemed to melt at that, his face almost sad.

'What you must think of me,' he said. 'I am a terrible man. I know it. I can't help it. But I won't be terrible to you, Edie Prior. I couldn't be terrible to you.'

It would be all lies, of course, and she should not feel reassured, but she did. He might be a rake and a wastrel and all sorts of other awful things, but at his core she felt he was a man of his word.

'I hope so,' she said.

'And now, here are my conditions for you,' he said, brightening. 'You will eat three square meals a day. You will not work so hard that you fall asleep the minute you come off duty. You will avoid Ted Whatsisname. And you will enjoy yourself when you're with me. Do you think you can do that?'

'I don't know,' she said truthfully. How could she avoid Ted? And what if sex turned out to be dreadful?

'Promise me you'll try.'

'I promise.'

'Right. Good. Have you finished that ice? Come on then. I'm taking you out on the river.'

Edie always remembered that afternoon as if it were accompanied by music, perhaps Delius's *Summer Night on the River*, which she had heard conducted by Thomas Beecham. Its idyllic, impressionistic quality suited that lazy, warm afternoon, floating with this man, soon to be her lover. Her thoughts, all bunched up and tense, dissolved under the sun's power and she became a creature of sensation. Her clothes clung to her and she felt heavy and hot between her legs and wonderfully light-headed. When the skiff found a bend of the river that was deserted, Charles would let the boat drift while they kissed, endlessly and with a languor that protected them from extremes of passion. Besides, they would capsize the boat.

Love and sex might be wonderful after all. If it felt this way, she could scarcely blame the maids for losing their heads and hearts.

But how would she keep from losing hers?

Chapter Six

'I'd better drop you off here,' said Charles, slowing down as the car approached the entrance to Deverell Hall. He drove a little way past the gatehouse, although the estate manager must surely still be at the shoot, before stopping around the first bend of the driveway.

Edie wondered how one ended an afternoon like this. Should she just get out of the car and go? Or …?

Charles stubbed his cigarette out in the dashboard ashtray and reached for her.

'Desperate to get away from me, eh?'

'No, just … you know. Nervous.'

She looked up the road as if expecting company.

'It's all right. Everyone's busy. But you're sensible to think about it. We have to make sure nobody suspects, or you'll be out on your ear.'

'Perhaps, after all, it's too risky.'

'It's risky, but worth the risk. I think it is, anyway. As for you, that's between your strange desire to protect

Ruby Redford and your own conscience.'

There's more to it than that.

'I don't see when we'll get the chance.'

'Oh, we will. I can't say when. But I'll let you know when the time comes.'

'Will you?'

'Yes. Wait for me. You will wait for me, won't you?'

His fingers were on her cheek, and he looked so serious, or as close as he came to it, that her heart contracted.

'You sound as if you're going off to war,' she said.

He shut his eyes at that, then, when he opened them, leant in to kiss her.

'Go, before I have to take you here in this car,' he said, with a rasp.

Edie opened the car door abruptly and began to march along the path, not waving at Charles when he drove slowly by, his eye upon her.

Once he was out of sight, she collapsed on to the verge, buried her face in her knees and burst into tears.

She had never meant for this to happen, but the taste of him still on her lips, the memory of his arms around her had changed her. Everything was different now. She felt as if the tenderest thing could wound her to the core.

Damn that man, but perhaps he really could make her love him?

'You're just scared and confused, a stranger in a strange

land,' she told herself sternly. 'You're bound to feel a little adrift. Chin up, girl. Keep your wits about you.'

The little pep talk gave her fresh impetus to continue the long walk back to the house.

If only servants were able to enter without having to pass through the kitchen. The last thing she felt like doing was walking past all their inquisitive eyes. What if they knew somehow? Or even if they did not, it would be easy enough to guess. Charles would have been missed at the shoot, even if he had made it back in time for the dinner. And Ted! He would know what a girl looks like after she's been kissed.

Her thoughts troubled her all the way around the side of the house, but they were interrupted by the rather strange sight of Giles emerging from the rhododendron shrubbery with his jacket buttons half-undone and his hair falling over his brow.

He stopped short when he saw Edie and looked behind him in a panic-stricken kind of way.

'Cat,' he explained breathlessly. 'Ran off with a good steak in its mouth. Gave chase. Gone, though. No chance.'

He shook his head vigorously.

'Oh, dear.'

Giles held up his hand, excusing himself mutely before running off in the opposite direction.

Edie squared herself, ready for any line of questioning that might be fired at her on her return. As it happened, she needn't have bothered.

The moment she set foot in the building, cook cried, 'Thank God you're here, Mrs Munn needs a word.'

She hurried to the office, grateful for the absence of Ted, and was told that a staffing crisis had arisen due to two more maids falling foul of the contagion that had laid Carrie low. It was her evening off, Mrs Munn understood that well, but would she consider rendering assistance?

'It's all hands on deck, I'm afraid,' said Mrs Munn with a sigh.

'Oh, of course. I don't have any other plans. I'll go and get into my uniform, shall I?'

'Thank you. I'm very much obliged, Edie.'

***

The shoot dinner was large and involved a great deal of lifting and fetching and carrying and pouring. Jenny and the others seemed to have suspended hostilities, all of them sympathetic to her having to work on her evening off.

'Rotten luck,' whispered Jenny. 'Where did you go? We saw Ted come back.'

'Just walked into town and went to the film by myself,' lied Edie, uncomfortable at the necessary deception.

Jenny seemed to accept this, which suggested that Ted had not mentioned being sent ignominiously back to the house by Charles. She wondered if he had returned only to be told that Charles was lying about him being needed. That would land her in hot water, she thought. Ted was no fool.

It was a challenge to work in the same room as Charles, but she avoided his eye and kept to the far end of the table, serving jolly and rather drink-reddened old gentlemen their beef Wellington and their port. If he looked at her, she tried not to notice.

'Where did you go, Charles?' she heard Lady Deverell's ringing tones enquire. She felt herself weaken all over immediately, her heart fluttering at the potential danger. 'You were very much missed.'

'I told you, I wasn't sure I was up to it,' he said. 'You know how I am around gunshots these days. I'm sorry to bring it up, but it was you who raised the subject.'

There was a general murmur, sympathetic in tone, and somebody changed the conversation to talk of a forthcoming hunt ball.

It was a relief to Edie when she was allowed to leave the room and return to the kitchen. Being so close to Charles was a special kind of torture and she was head-achey with the tension of it as she sat down at the long trestle and helped herself from trays full of leftovers.

She had barely bitten into a smoked salmon pinwheel when Ted sat down beside her, making her stuff the food into her mouth more quickly than she had intended.

'Nice afternoon?' he asked, a little sourly.

'Nicer if you'd been there,' she said, after swallowing the food rather uncomfortably.

'Really?'

'I wish you hadn't had to come back.'

'I didn't.'

'You didn't? You didn't come back?'

'No. I didn't *have* to come back. His Lordship didn't need me.'

Edie looked at him with what she hoped mimicked incomprehension.

'So why were you sent back?'

'I thought you might know the answer to that.'

She shook her head.

He popped a miniature choux bun in his mouth. It seemed to lift his mood.

'Ah, well, all's not lost,' he said. 'It's a nice evening, after all that rain. Come out for a walk with me in the gardens.'

'Are we ... is it permitted?'

She thought of the footman, who had chased the cat through the rhododendrons. Presumably it was not forbidden then. All the same, she very much wanted to avoid being alone with Ted in a situation that might be observable from the main house. If she broke Charles Deverell's conditions, what then?

'Of course, you noodle,' he said cheerfully. 'If we stick to the parts nearest the kitchen. Come on, eat up.'

118

'I'm ravenous,' she said.

'What did you do for lunch?'

'Had to buy myself a pork pie. Ate it next to the river.' Half-true.

'The river, eh?'

'Yes. It's lovely there, isn't it?'

'Hmm.'

They both ate, stolidly and silently, for a few more minutes before Edie felt her appetite was sated.

On the way out to the garden door, Edie told Mrs Fingall that she was sorry to hear about the lost steak.

Fingall looked utterly confounded.

'D'you what, dear? Lost steak?'

'Yes – the cat, you know.'

She shook her head. 'I don't know about any steak, but you've lost me.'

'Oh. No matter.'

Outside on the gravel that paved the herb garden, Ted was curious.

'What was all that about?'

'I saw Giles earlier, coming out of a shrubbery, looking quite dishevelled. He told me he'd been chasing a cat that stole a steak. I suppose perhaps he didn't tell Mrs Fingall, though surely she'd have missed it?'

'Oh,' said Ted. 'Giles.' The way he said it, as if a long-held suspicion had been wearisomely confirmed, made Edie glance at him with kindled interest.

'What about him?'

'It ain't for me to say. And I don't want to go upsetting you with rumours.'

'What rumours?'

'Like I said, none of my business.'

Edie stopped and bent to take in a blissful lungful of basil.

'This is a house of rumours,' she said. 'I've hardly been here five minutes and already I know of several.'

'There's rumours about you,' said Ted. He put a hand on her elbow. She couldn't move.

'What nonsense,' she said, straightening up, spine stiff. 'Rumours are what people discuss when there's nothing to talk about. Idleness and boredom, that's all.'

'Not much scope to be idle and bored in the servants' hall, Edie.'

'No, but when one's whole life revolves around bowing and scraping to a handful of people, those people have to carry the weight of all the wild imaginations of the servant girls combined.'

'How you do talk. You want to write a book, you do.'

'Perhaps I shall.'

'Don't you want to know what they are? The rumours, I mean.'

'I'm not remotely interested.'

Edie tossed her head and began to walk swiftly up the path, towards the vegetable beds.

Ted dogged her footsteps.

'Don't be like that,' he said. 'Don't go all high and mighty on me.'

She turned, trying to hold herself at indignant full height.

'Then don't bother me with vile gossip,' she said. 'I won't hear it. I daresay it's all come from Jenny and I know what she says, and she's quite, quite mistaken.'

'All right, all right. I'm sorry. Come and sit in the summerhouse. It'll calm you down.'

The summerhouse was pleasant, a little damp-smelling after the recent wet weather, but surrounded by velvety roses, foxgloves and sweet williams, all the more lush and brilliant from the rain.

'You've gone absolutely bright red,' said Ted softly with a rueful little smile. 'You didn't need to get in such a passion, you know. I'm your friend – I don't deserve to be shouted at.'

'I didn't mean to shout. I just hate all this silly tittle-tattle. All I want is to work hard and fit in, and nobody will let me.'

'They're jealous of you.'

'I can't think why.'

'Because just look at you! You're a stunner, aren't you?'

'Oh, don't be …'

'And – don't take this the wrong way – but everyone says as how Sir Charles can't take his eyes off you.'

Edie buried her face in her hands.

'Stop it,' she begged. 'I don't want to think of it.'

'Hey.' Ted curled his fingers around hers and prised them away from her skin. 'Look. What did he do to you?'

'Don't ...'

'Today. He came after you, I know that. It was nothing to do with me being wanted at the house. So ...'

'He didn't do anything. He drove off and I didn't see him again.'

'He didn't try it on? Oh, pull the other one, Edie, it's got bells on.'

'If you're determined to call me a liar ...'

Edie stood, brushing off her skirts, her hands shaking with anger and anxiety.

'No, for God's sake, Edie, I don't mean to –'

But it was a golden opportunity to stalk away and out of this uncomfortable conversation, and she knew she had to seize it. However much she wanted to stay and talk to Ted. However much she wanted to blurt the whole ridiculous situation out to somebody.

But there was not a soul she could tell, apart from the God she only half-believed in. She settled for that, recounting the events in her head as she lay looking up at the sloping ceiling in the dormitory.

But then she had to break off as she remembered the touch of Charles's lips, the feel of his hands at her breast. God would not want to know about that, surely.

When would it be? When would she go to him and give herself? How would it be, to be naked in front of him? What would he say? What would he do?

She tormented and tantalised herself with these thoughts until they unwound into sleep, where they re-emerged in dreams, shockingly erotic or terrifying.

* * *

Three days passed, the house full of visitors staying over from the shooting party. There was no opportunity for furtive meetings or even a swift whispered exchange. Charles drove the guests all over the county, or played tennis or croquet with them, or took them fishing on the lake.

Edie waxed floors and polished mantels and watched through the windows.

Ted apologised for his remarks and they reached a cautious rapprochement, though she did her utmost to avoid being alone with him. He was busy, for the most part, ferrying house guests about, and they met only at the supper and breakfast tables.

Edie drudged and slept and dreamed and kept herself as invisible as she could but on the third day she had to serve at a grand banquet with dancing and watch Charles Deverell squiring a beautiful young woman in jet beads around the floor. He was a good dancer but a better flirt. The woman, whoever she was, was clearly very taken with him.

But when the dance ended, he uttered some words of excuse or apology and left her looking after him as he walked out.

Where was he going? She couldn't, of course, follow him – she was circulating amongst the guests with a silver tray of champagne cocktails – but to her dismay she noticed Lady Deverell leave in the same direction minutes later.

Her stomach leaden, she tried to accept that Charles was going to break his word and everything was over. At least she would keep her virginity. But that did not seem much of a consolation at all – more like a disappointment.

There were the beginnings of tears in her eyes and thoughts of catching the morning train to London on her mind when a voice in her ear behind her said, 'Is one of those for me?'

Charles.

She jerked forward so suddenly that the glasses fell from the tray, crashing in crystalline splintery puddles on to the floor. A fuss of tutting and exclamation erupted from the nearest guests.

'Sorry, sorry, all my fault,' said Charles to all and sundry. 'I crept up behind her. It was silly of me.'

'I'll fetch a dustpan and brush,' said Edie, all but running from the scene, away down to the kitchen.

Mrs Munn was not best pleased.

'Careless,' she clucked, as Edie, on her hands and knees, swept the fragments up. 'And clumsy. The best Waterford crystal. It'll all have to be replaced.'

'I'll take care of it,' said Charles, who lounged nearby looking devilish and mouth-watering in his white tie and tails. 'Don't worry. It was my fault.'

Mrs Munn did not seem remotely mollified by this; if anything, it made her even crosser.

'*You* can get back to the kitchen, young woman,' she said to Edie. 'You've done quite enough damage for one evening.'

'Oh, let her stay,' remonstrated Charles, and Edie felt a prickle of discomfort. He shouldn't be drawing attention like this. Lady Deverell cut through the brilliantly sequinned crowd and stood beside Charles.

'What's the matter?'

'Just a minor breakage,' said Charles. 'I'm to blame, but this poor girl seems to be catching it.'

'You're to blame?'

'I crept up behind her, jogged her elbow. It was an accident.'

'You're such a beast,' said Lady Deverell, and there was real venom in her words.

'I've never pretended otherwise.'

'Come on, Edie, downstairs, now.'

Mrs Munn shepherded her away. She was not

ungrateful to be away from such intense scrutiny but all the same she couldn't help wondering what Charles had been about to say when he made his startling appearance. Was tonight going to be the night?

Not any more.

* * *

At breakfast the next morning, Mrs Munn had a face to sour the milk.

The atmosphere at the table was subdued, with much yawning after the previous late night. The last guests had not retired until three, and somebody had had to clear up after them.

'Everyone's leaving after breakfast,' said Jenny, stirring her porridge with a listless hand. 'Thank God.'

'No more big events for a few weeks,' said the butler briskly. 'Well done, everyone. You did Deverell Hall proud.'

A few eyes turned, swiftly and surreptitiously, to Edie, as if to say *What about her?* But nobody said anything.

After breakfast, Mrs Munn rose and said, 'Edie, I'd like to see you in my office, please.'

Panic twisted inside her, shortening her breath.

She followed Mrs Munn out of the kitchen, hearing susurrations at her back. Rumours, gossip. Was she going to be sacked?

126

She sat opposite, waiting for the death knell to sound.

'I don't know how to put this,' opened Mrs Munn.

Yes, definitely the sack, then, though she couldn't imagine Mrs Munn finding the words that hard to speak.

'I'm terribly sorry about the crystal,' she blurted in mitigation.

'Never mind the crystal, that's not what I want to talk to you about.'

'Isn't it?'

'No. I've had a rather unusual request, from Lady Deverell.'

Edie bristled, feeling goose pimples rise on her skin.

'Lady Deverell?' she whispered.

'She seems to have taken a fancy to you. She wants you to be her lady's maid.'

'She …?'

'Yes, it's highly irregular. I've explained that you have no experience in that role and can barely manage parlour-maid duties but …'

She made a strange whistling sound, which was presumably meant to indicate the mysterious whims of the grand and great.

'Does she not already have a maid?'

'Indeed she does! And a very good one. Poor Sylvie, what is she to do?'

Edie was lost for words. She felt she ought to turn the job down but, for one thing, she was not sure she could if Lady Deverell wanted her and, for another, it was a marvellous and unexpected gift, a huge step towards achieving what she had come here for.

Unlucky Sylvie, yes – but if she knew the real state of things, perhaps she might be able to look upon her demotion with a little less rancour.

'What should I do, Mrs Munn?'

'Do? What a question. You have no choice in the matter. If Lady Deverell wants you, then she must have you. Go and remove your belongings from the dormitory. You will have a room of your own, upstairs from Her Ladyship's.'

'A room of my own?'

'Yes, and of course you have seen that Sylvie's uniform is of better quality material that what you are wearing now. It need not be so hard-wearing. You will take your meals in here with me and you will not mix with the other servants except on special occasions.'

'Did Lady Deverell … say anything? I mean, did she say why?'

'I haven't the slightest idea. Now do go and pack your things. I suppose I have an advertisement to draft.'

***

Edie took each step on the long climb to the servants' quarters slowly, to counteract the mad gallop of her mind.

Why on earth had Lady Deverell asked for her? Did she know something? What could she know?

Exhilaration was tempered by fear. She had no idea how to be a lady's maid. She would have to do her hair – how could she possibly manage? She would fail and then she would be thrown out. But before that happened, perhaps she and Lady Deverell would forge a friendship, a relationship. How wonderful that would be.

She packed her few possessions back into the bag she had brought, then carried it down to Mrs Munn's office.

'Order of the boot?' asked Giles, with polite sympathy, as she passed him on the stairs.

'No, quite the opposite – promotion,' she told him.

'Promotion? Really? You've only been here five minutes.'

'I don't understand myself, I'm afraid.'

'Who're you taking over from?'

'Sylvie.'

He whistled and then stood with his mouth open for so long that Edie felt the need to escape.

'Don't ask me,' she said, hurrying down again. 'Ask Her Ladyship.'

* * *

Mrs Munn, her face grimly set, led her to Lady Deverell's rooms in the East Wing, then up a level to the floor overhead, where the rooms were smaller and mostly unoccupied.

'This is your room,' she said, opening the door.

Inside, Sylvie sat on the bed, sobbing loudly. An open valise half-filled with belongings thrown higgledy-piggledy lay on the floor.

'Oh.' Edie turned to Mrs Munn in distress. 'Surely there must be some time for Sylvie to …'

'Lady Deverell wants you from today. The room's yours now. Sylvie must sleep in your old bed for tonight. If she wants your job as well, she can have it. Otherwise, she must find her own alternative.'

'It is cruel,' raged Sylvie, looking up at them. 'Lady Deverell is cruel. I have been an example of a good lady's maid. But she is not a real lady and now it is clear. Oh, now it is so clear.'

'I won't listen to this, Sylvie,' admonished Mrs Munn. 'Finish your packing and come to my office in your own clothes, please.'

'She will steal my uniform? It will not fit her. She is too tall.'

'I will provide Miss Prior with her uniform. Bring yours with you when you come down.'

Edie stepped into the room, taking her life in her hands.

'I'm sorry,' she said.

'I'll leave you to sort yourselves out,' said Mrs Munn, retiring.

'You are sorry? That is no good to me. Take your sorry, keep it. It will not feed me or my family in Rouen.'

'I didn't seek this position. You are undoubtedly better suited to it than I am. If it were up to me, I'd ask Lady Deverell to keep you.'

Edie wasn't sure she meant this, but it seemed to soften the Frenchwoman a little. She dabbed her eyes, sniffed and threw a cosmetics bag into the suitcase.

'I don't want to work for her anyway. *Putain*.'

She threw a jar of face cream on top of the other things.

'Don't you like her?'

'She is silly, spoiled, vain, vulgar, stupid.' With each epithet, Sylvie added another item to her case, hurling them so hard Edie thought they might break.

She stood well back and made for the large square window. What a light and pleasant room this was. She lifted the sash to allow some of the warm, over-ripe August air in.

She thought it best to say nothing more. Sylvie clearly needed to give vent to her sorrow and rage, and she had no intention of standing in her way.

Instead she looked out at the departing cars and carriages crowding the drive, while Sylvie threw things and ranted in French.

Having slammed the valise shut, the ousted maid remembered Edie's presence and turned to her.

'I will be gone from here soon,' she said. 'I have decided to go to London. But I will give you one warning. Keep

131

your eyes and your ears shut. Things are going on in this house that you don't want to know about. I am happy to be away from it all. Happy, I tell you! I pass it to you, willingly.'

Edie supposed that she meant the affair between Lady Deverell and Charles, but she mustn't give herself away, so she merely shook her head and wished Sylvie the best of luck for her future.

Sylvie gave her a look of disgust and flounced out, valise in hand.

Edie sat down on the bed – more comfortable than the one she had failed to become accustomed to upstairs – and tried to accept that she was now Lady Deverell's personal maid. She wondered what Charles would make of the appointment. Would this ease or hinder their plans? It would make any liaison difficult to conceal from Her Ladyship, she supposed.

The thought of Charles induced a flutter and she lay down on the bed, suddenly weak. She was still there when there was a knock on the door and a stone-faced Jenny appeared, some garments over her arm.

'Your new uniform,' she said, throwing them on the bed. 'Got yourself comfy, I see.'

'It's a stroke of luck. I wasn't expecting it.'

Edie sat up and fingered the lacy edges of her apron. 'I'll bet. You seem to have one of those faces that fit. Well, I wish you joy of it.'

She stalked off.

It didn't matter if she was unpopular in the servants' hall, Edie reminded herself. She would hardly have to spend any time down there any more.

She tried on the new uniform and found that it fitted her much better than the last, arranging itself around her bust and hips so that her silhouette curved gracefully in and out in all the right places. The little cap was trickier to pin to her hair than the plain cotton affair she had worn before. It was delicate, trimmed with Brussels lace, and she was hardly aware she had it on. Only the mirror revealed the truth.

She was still looking at the figure she cut as a lady's maid when the door to the chamber opened again – no knocking this time – and Lady Deverell stood behind her, still in her dressing gown with her mane of red hair about her shoulders.

Never having seen her so, Edie was struck almost dumb.

'Oh,' she said, whirling around. 'I'm sorry.' Though what she was apologising for, she couldn't really say.

'Sylvie's gone, then, has she?'

'Only just.'

'Thought she'd kick up more of a fuss, to be honest.'

Edie agreed she had every right to, but kept her opinion to herself. She should curtsey! Why hadn't she curtsied?

Her quick awkward bob made Lady Deverell laugh.

'Mrs Munn said you were inexperienced. She's always right, of course. Good old Munn. That just made me want you more.'

'If you don't mind, ma'am, I'm not really sure why you wanted to engage me.'

'Oh, darling, it doesn't do to question these things. I'm your gift horse.' She bared all her teeth, big and gleaming. 'Don't look me in the mouth, whatever you do.'

'I'm very grateful, of course, but …'

'But?'

'I'm afraid you might find me a little inexpert after Sylvie. With hair, in particular.'

'Darling, I know how to dress hair. I'm better at it than half the lady's maids in England. No.' She sat down in the wicker chair beside the bed. 'I don't need a coiffeuse.'

Edie laid one palm flat on the dressing-table surface. She felt the need of its support. Lady Deverell had a most peculiar look in her eye.

'When I first saw you, last week at the charity dinner, something about you drew my eye straight away. It wasn't your clumsiness, either, though plenty of people noticed that. I felt as if I knew you, as if we'd met before. I've been racking my brains all week and I simply must ask you. Have we?'

'No, ma'am, never. I have … seen you before. But you wouldn't have noticed me. I was in the audience.'

'Oh, you've seen me on stage?' Lady Deverell stared. 'You've been to London?'

'I'm from London, ma'am.'

'Really? Not a bumpkin like the other parlourmaids? How extraordinary. What possessed you to come here?'

'I wanted a change of air.'

Lady Deverell clearly found this as unbelievable as her stepson had. She let the words linger in both of their ears, a smile slowly curving to the fullest extent.

'How fascinatingly opaque. Well, you've certainly found that here. The back of beyond. Ditchwater is relatively exciting.'

'I've been too busy to think of anything, ma'am.'

'Of course. A servant's life is much the same in Mayfair as in Kingsreach. So we are not acquainted?'

Edie shook her head, not trusting her voice.

'I'm not the only person to notice you, of course,' Lady Deverell continued, still with her wide, beguiling smile.

Edie knew she was supposed to supply some filler for the ensuing pause.

'Aren't you, ma'am?' she said helplessly, feeling that she knew what might be coming next.

'Oh, come now. We all know when a man's interested in us, don't we? You've grown up in London, as I did. I could spot a prospective suitor from the age of eight.'

'A man, ma'am? I was asked to the picture palace by His Lordship's chauffeur, if that's what you –'

135

'That's not what I mean, and you know it.' The smile was thinning out now, cracking at the corners.

'I hardly know ...'

Edie looked desperately at the window. There was no other escape route.

'Are you a sly one, Edie Prior? Are you a little liar? Or are you truly a naïve little fool, as you try to make out?'

Edie shook her head, her body in revolt, her palm slippery against the shiny dresser now.

'If I've noticed him looking, I'm sure you have. Sir Charles. My beloved stepson.'

'I don't ...'

'Keep clear.'

'I've heard the rumours.'

'They're all true.' She paused. 'Just out of interest, what rumours have you heard?'

'A girl had his baby. Former parlourmaid, I believe.'

'Oh, that one. Yes, that's definitely true. And you don't want to follow in her idiotic footsteps, I presume? He didn't marry her, did he? And he won't marry you.'

'I never thought for a moment –'

'Good. Gold-diggers don't prosper here at Deverell Hall.' She paused and chuckled.

Edie hardly knew where to look. She could hardly laugh along with her.

'Except me, of course,' said Lady Deverell. 'But there's only one Ruby Redford. Truly original, truly unique.

That's what the drama critic at the *Standard* said, and I'm pretty sure the Deverell men would agree with him.'

She looked towards the door at that and lowered her voice.

'If you're to be my lady's maid, Edie, there are certain things you should know. But if I tell you, you must be clear that they must never, ever be repeated. Not to anybody – none of the servants, not even your closest friend.'

'I'm not a tattler, ma'am, never have been.'

'You'll find out eventually, so I might as well tell you now. When His Lordship's away, as he is once a fortnight or so, I sometimes receive a visitor.'

Edie could scarcely believe Lady Deverell was about to confess her affair with Charles, and she felt sure the flush of her countenance gave away her prior knowledge, but she simply swallowed and waited for more.

'It'll shock you, I'm sure, but it would shock you more if you found out another way – I have a little dalliance going on with Charles. It's nothing serious. And it's none of your business. So if you see him in my chambers, you'll know to turn a blind eye, won't you, dear?'

'Y-yes, ma'am.'

'Good girl. Oh, dear, you really are shocked, aren't you? Don't be. There's only five years between us, and I doubt there's a married noblewoman in England who hasn't taken a lover at some time or other. I'm sure Hugh

137

has some tart on the go in St James's. His club seems to have an awful lot of functions lately.'

'Did Sylvie know?'

'Oh, dear me, yes.'

'Aren't you afraid she'll ...?'

'She knows better than that. Who'd believe her? It would look like sheer malice, a nose out of joint. And she would never work again. I know it makes me sound awful, but I've lived my life surrounded by male attention. I miss it, Edie. You can't imagine what it's like ... I hope you won't judge me too harshly. Not that I care if you do. Anyway, Charles seems to have taken a shine to you and I don't care for rivals. I like to keep them where I can watch them. What a way to earn a promotion, eh? But I'm sure you'll be super. Now, if you don't mind, I'd really like a bath. Could you be a dear and run one for me?'

Edie followed her downstairs to her suite and did as she was bade. The bathroom was relatively new, all its fixtures and fittings of shiny copper pipe. Hot water steamed from the tap quickly. Did she have to do anything about towels? Soap? Laying out a bathrobe?

She found most of what she needed in various hampers and cabinets.

This is what I wanted. To be close to her. How much closer than this? Running her bath, attending to her intimate needs?

Why did it feel so hollow, and so frightening?

'I think it's ready, ma'am,' she said, poking her head around the folding door once she had turned off the taps.

'You think it is? I'll have to see. Could you lay out my clothes for the day? Something suitable for driving, I think. I'm considering a visit to the Chudleighs at the Grange.'

She left Edie with this mystifying instruction. What was suitable for driving and visiting? She stepped into the vast walk-in wardrobe and breathed in the luxury that surrounded her. Silks and furs, satins and velvets, yards of bugle beading and sequinned hems. She put her face against them, gathered handfuls of them, feasted her eyes on the rainbow of colours. But none of them seemed suited to driving.

A little further back she found daywear, along with tweeds and riding habits and all manner of more serviceable garments. She decided on a matching skirt and jacket in navy and white with a pearl-buttoned blouse.

But what to wear underneath? Drawers full of underwear had to be consulted, and this was an embarrassment to Edie, who had never had charge of another woman's smalls before. It seemed so indecent to rifle through the piles of knickers and stockings. She chose silk, to keep Her Ladyship cool, in a dull gold colour. As she laid it out, she wondered if she would be called upon to attach the suspenders and tighten the bodice. Why on earth couldn't she dress herself, as Edie had to? After all, she must have spent decades wrestling with costumes. It was not as if she was a helpless little human ornament, like some of the fine ladies one heard of.

She still held the knickers in her hands when the door opened again.

Edie turned to see Sir Charles, freshly washed and dressed and smelling rather strongly of an expensive cologne, on the threshold.

'Oh, so it's true,' he said.

'Go,' whispered Edie in a panic, flapping the knickers at him. She could hear Lady Deverell's bathwater sloshing about, but this still seemed absurdly risky.

Charles did not care about risk, though. She should have known that by now.

'She wants to keep her eye on you. Be careful.'

'Listen, perhaps we shouldn't ...'

'Oh, no, you don't.' He came closer.

She tried to step away, but he caught her by the wrist and pulled her to his chest.

'You don't get out of it that easily,' he whispered into her ear. 'This makes things a little awkward, yes. But it can still be done, believe me. Tonight, Edie. Tonight's the night.'

'How can it be?'

But he sauntered away without another word, leaving Edie fit to faint.

Her hands still shook when she brought Lady Deverell's warm towels into the bathroom.

'Oh, don't be shy,' said Lady Deverell, placing a fortunate misconstruction on Edie's nervousness. 'You've seen a naked woman before, I suppose?'

'Of course,' said Edie, willing herself to stop dithering over that dreadful man.

All the same, now Lady Deverell mentioned it, it did seem rather odd to be in the same room as her naked body, even if was mostly concealed beneath the milky, soapy surface of the bathwater.

She was magnificent through and through, thought Edie with a flicker of pride, glancing at her swan neck and elegant collarbone. Below it, her breasts were full and high, sloping down to the water, beneath which they disappeared long before her eye reached the nipples.

Not that she wanted to see them. The thought made her hot with embarrassment, especially when she considered that Charles had seen every scrap of that fragrant skin. The back of her neck began to crawl and a wave of nausea almost made her stagger so that she had to put a hand on the side of the bath for support.

'I say, you look quite green. Are you all right?'

Lady Deverell sat up straight, water ploughing and plunging around her. *Nipples. Don't look.*

But she couldn't tear her eyes away and the sight of them made her obscurely angry, choking her words of reply.

141

'I'm a little ...'

'I daresay you haven't had breakfast, have you?'

'No.'

'Well, that's no good, is it? I'll have something sent up for you when I go down. Go and sit down in the bedroom. I can dry myself.'

Edie was in the little bedside chair, her forehead on her knees, when Lady Deverell walked back in, wrapped and turbaned in towels.

The events of the morning had defeated Edie and now her head and heart were a horrible stew. She was not at all sure she could pursue her plan any more. It seemed to have reached its crisis, much more quickly than she expected and too soon to show her hand. If she did it now, she would be laughed out of Deverell Hall, or worse.

But, if she stopped and thought, coolly and collectedly, she could see that she had the best chance of all now. She could find a way into Lady Deverell's affections. At the very least, she could maintain a modicum of her attention. And wasn't that, after all, the only thing she asked? Why spoil it with mistimed revelations?

She sat quietly and swallowed her panic and let her confidence reassert itself at its own pace.

Just don't think about Charles. Just don't think about it and it'll go away.

'You still look ghastly,' said Lady Deverell cheerfully, inspecting the clothes Edie had set out for her. 'Oh, that old thing. I haven't worn it in months.' She picked up the skirt and sneered at it, but she did not demand it be exchanged for another.

'I think it would suit you,' said Edie, risking a look up.

'Well, perhaps you're right. No, don't get up. I can manage. Just this once.'

Edie put her forehead back on her knees while Lady Deverell attended to her own costuming.

'Goodness, I hope it isn't morning sickness,' she said, a little sharply.

'Absolutely not!' cried Edie.

'All right, calm yourself. You've heard what can happen to maids in this house. It's not completely beyond the bounds of possibility, is it? I wondered if my stepson had made a very early impression on you, that's all.'

Edie couldn't answer this without lying, so she remained silent.

'He *is* terribly attractive, after all,' Lady Deverell continued, her eyes on Edie as she fastened her stockings. 'Don't you think?'

'If you like that sort of thing,' said Edie.

'Oh, I think we all do, don't we, dear? Dashing man, full of charm, dripping with compliments. And an absolute genius between the sheets –'

'Oh, don't!' Edie couldn't help herself.

Lady Deverell stood tall, a glamorous amazon in dull-gold underwear.

143

'I'm so sorry. I mustn't drive you into his arms, must I? That's not the idea at all. Never mind. Admire from afar, if you must, but it can't ever go any further. He's heartless, Edie, that's what he is. Completely heartless.'

And are you not?

The tip of Edie's tongue quivered with it.

'Poor Hugh,' said Lady Deverell, speaking for the first time of her husband. 'If he knew he was surrounded by vipers.' She sighed. 'I've tried to be a better person, but it isn't who I am. We are none of us perfect, are we, Edie?'

'No, ma'am.'

'But the least perfect of all is Charles Deverell. Well, now, this skirt looks rather marvellous, I must say. You have a keen eye, Edie. I'd forgotten how it flattered my figure. Do you think you might help me pin up my hair?'

She tried, but her skills in this area were so miserably lacking that Lady Deverell excused her the task.

She was ordered back to her seat while Lady Deverell went down to breakfast.

'Don't bother about taking it in Mrs Munn's room,' she said. 'I'll have a poached egg sent up. Then there's some mending to be done – Sylvie will have put it in the work-basket in her room. Oh, I beg your pardon – your room.'

She was as good as her word and a poached egg on toast with weak tea arrived on a tray a quarter of an hour later. The maid who brought it set it down on the dresser with a clatter and no word.

Edie ate and drank and felt a little better, though the persistent twisted feeling at the pit of her stomach did not recede. That was the Charles feeling and it could not go until he did. She knew it, and so did her body.

* * *

Lady Deverell did not come back to the room that morning and Edie was left alone to wrestle with needle and thread and try not to botch the job of mending more than a four-year-old might. She wasn't entirely convinced of her success, and the possibility that Charles might sneak into the room at any moment made her fingers clumsier than ever.

In the event, he did not. When the maid came in to make the bed – Jenny, as luck would have it – she was alone with her thimble and her hunched shoulders.

'Morning, Jenny,' she said, longing for a friendly face, a smile, a word of comfort.

But it was not to be forthcoming from the parlour-maid, who sniffed.

'Better for some than others,' she said, plumping the pillows with a violent hand.

'I didn't ask for this. I know I am not suitable.'

'Ain't for me to pass comment.'

Edie could squeeze no advance on this from the tight-lipped Jenny, so she gave up and silently went to help her with the bed, only to be rebuffed.

'Not your job,' she snapped. 'Leave it.'

So Edie left it.

***

Lady Deverell came back up after lunch for her gloves and hat.

'I'm off on my visit now,' she said. 'I shan't be back until after tea. I'll need my dinner things laid out.'

'What should I do?'

'Do? Why, don't ask me. Do what you please. Take a walk, read a book. It's all the same to me.'

A walk, then, it was, in the stifling fever-heat of the early afternoon. Bugs settled in her hair and clammy warmth sheened her skin. It could hardly be called pleasant. The ground had still not hardened from the rains, and it seemed more storms were on the way. The heaviness of the air would have been unsettling enough in its own right, but it was almost unbearable combined with the fear and confusion in Edie's mind.

From behind a bush, she observed Charles and Mary playing croquet on the back lawn – or at least, a very enervated, lazy version of it, each move interspersed with cigarettes and gin and tonics.

Languid as he was, there was an energy to his movements that signified optimism and high spirits. Was he thinking of tonight? But how could it happen, if she slept in that cubby above Lady Deverell's room? How? Or would she be in Charles's bed? But surely that was dangerous too.

There was no use thinking of it.

If Charles was lively, Mary was the opposite, her hair drooping along with her rather bohemian flowing gown. At least it looked cool in this weather, but her pretty face was permanently twisted into a scowl and she seemed to be regaling Charles with some list of slights or frustrations, taking it out on the croquet ball, which she whacked much harder than necessary.

They seemed quite close, as brother and sister, Edie thought. But what about the other brother? She couldn't even recall his name for a moment. Tom, that was it.

She tore her eyes away from Charles, in his linen shirt and light trousers, and deliberately took the path that led away from that lawn.

The grounds were beautifully landscaped and each wind or twist seemed to reveal some new and lovely surprise. Fountains, pavilions, statues, cunningly concealed little rose gardens – all evoked startled pleasure, removing Edie from her troubling world and taking her to a wonderland.

Reaching the shores of the lake, she noticed a set of crumbling stone steps that led to some kind of grotto just at the level of the water.

She was halfway down before she heard strange noises, unrelated to the rushing water that seemed to pour in a continuous stream from the lake to the subterranean chamber. Mingling with its splashes were heavy breaths, grunts, moans – unmistakably human and male.

She retreated quickly back up the steps and waited by a tree to see who, if anyone, might emerge from the cavern. It couldn't be Charles – he was with Mary. And His Lordship had been in the library with his estate manager when she left the house. As for the servants – when did they find time? Was it even a human? The sound had been so rough and bestial – could it be the coupling of a pair of animals? Or spirits?

She shivered. *Don't be ridiculous.*

But this place was so quiet, so still, so like an unearthly garden transplanted to the Thames valley. Perhaps she had left reality and stumbled on an alternate universe.

A head of messy light-brown hair became visible above the old stone wall, as its owner mounted the steps. The face that came next into view was familiar – Giles, the footman. He had his arm around somebody, helping them up, it seemed.

Oh!

Edie had to press her fingers into her chin, covering her mouth.

It was Sir Thomas. Every bit as dishevelled as Giles, limping across the grass in his arms.

They were lovers. She knew, of course, that such love existed, but she had thought it something that happened only in London, in a certain type of sophisticated milieu, amongst men who had formed crushes on each other at Oxbridge.

The thought of a strapping, down-to-earth young working man like Giles being homosexual was almost impossibly exotic to Edie's mind. Surely it never happened that way?

Was that what it was? Almost despite itself, Edie's mind tried to find alternative explanations for what she had heard and seen. Perhaps Giles was trying to help Sir Thomas heal his wounded leg by engaging him in some form of physical training and she had heard the exertions produced thereof.

Or ... or ...

They were kissing. Kissing right there on the shore of the lake, and then Sir Thomas laid his head on Giles's shoulder and they talked, their voices drifting up to Edie even if the words were indistinct.

She took advantage of their distraction and stole away, all the time thinking over their situation. Surely they would never be able to tell anyone of their love. How sad and wasteful it seemed, that their lives would be lived out in secret.

But then, that seemed to be the Deverell way. Secrets, so many of them, in every corner. And tonight, Sir Charles would add to his sum.

Chapter Seven

A flash lit up Edie's little room, drawing her to the window. The rain was already pouring down in sheets from misshapen purplish clouds. The air crackled, but the humidity did not seem to have broken yet. If only it would.

Lady Deverell had told her, during her undressing, that Charles had gone to meet friends in town and would not be back until morning. If it was true – and he certainly hadn't been at dinner – then what was he thinking of? Had he forgotten her?

He must have thought better of it, she decided, but she felt something a little more than relief. Something, in fact, rather like disappointment.

All the same, she had gone about her preparations for bed as if she expected a lover. She had put on scent and, unusually practical, had laid a dark-coloured towel on the undersheet, having heard that there may be some loss of blood on such occasions.

Such occasions.

As if the breaching of her hymen were a form of coming-out dance.

But perhaps it would not happen and she would save herself for some misty future man who would love her and want to marry her and all that. But then she would have to bear children, and she wasn't at all sure that was part of the Edie Crossland life plan.

Had Charles got the things? The French things? She couldn't remember exactly what they were called.

She watched the rain course down the glass and thought of the pensive look on Lady Deverell's face when she had bade her goodnight.

'Run along to your little bed, little maid,' she'd said. 'His Lordship will be here soon enough. He had that look on his face at dinner. The look I dread.'

'Your Ladyship?' Edie had enquired mildly.

'The bedroom look,' she said with a sigh. 'Goodnight now.'

The bedroom look. It was the look Charles Deverell wore almost permanently; at least, every time he looked at her. The thought of it made her stomach flutter.

Thunder rumbled and she caught sight of a dark figure, running across the lawns towards the house. Somebody caught in the rain, a servant returning late from an afternoon off, perhaps.

Or ... no! Was it, though?

She squinted but she couldn't make out any characteristics through the streaming windowpane. She leapt back from the window, just in case, and flung herself into bed. It was too hot to pull the covers over so she lay on the towel, wondering if she ought to put it back in the airing cupboard after all.

How was she meant to sleep in this heat, with this uncertainty, with the presence of Charles so predominant in her mind? She couldn't sleep if he came and she couldn't sleep if he did not. It was unfair of him to have this effect on her. It was hateful of him. He was hateful.

Her doorknob turned and she sat bolt upright, panic setting in. She took hold of the candlestick at her bedside and ran behind the slowly opening door, weapon in hand, heart competing with the thunder outside.

The intruder crossed swiftly to the bed and put a hand on the mattress to establish that she was not there.

A man. Charles.

She exhaled, and the sound of her breath caused him to turn around and see her.

'What on earth are you doing with that candlestick, you little fool?'

'I wasn't sure it was you.'

'Of course it was me – who else would it be? Oh, Kempe, I suppose. You'd better not have given him anything you shouldn't.'

'You're soaking wet.'

'I've swum oceans to be in your arms.'

'Oh, shut up! Don't tease.'

'Just …' He came closer and took the candlestick from her. 'Come here.'

His hair was plastered to his scalp and his face shone with damp. His clothes looked soaked through, the jacket heavy and waterlogged, the shirt transparent.

He threw the candlestick on the bed, shrugged off the saturated jacket and hung it on a bedpost.

'I've got a towel,' she whispered, snatching it up and offering it to him.

'First things first,' he said, taking it off her and dropping it to the floor.

He hooked an arm with inescapable swiftness around her waist and pulled her into him. Immediately her nightdress was wet through, but it was a warm wetness and it seeped into her bloodstream somehow, speeded by the press of his lips against hers.

She did not mind the raindrops now. They added another layer of sensuality to the kiss, an intangible veil, melting into steam. She wound her fingers in his dripping hair and knew beyond doubt that she would give herself to him tonight.

Once she was thoroughly wet through and weak with the blissfulness of him against her, he sat her down on the bed, picked up the towel and dried his hair vigorously.

153

'Took the motor into Maidenhead,' he explained. 'Had to put the wicked stepmother off the scent. How was she? Doesn't suspect, does she?'

'Of course she does. That's why I've got this job.'

'Well, yes, I know that. You'll need to practise your poker face, my dear, when you're around her. Damn it, I can't get dry. Left the car halfway up the drive, didn't want to wake anyone.'

'It's an awful lot of trouble to go to.' Edie was both flattered and afraid.

He put the towel down and sat beside her, taking her hand. His shirt was still drenched and clinging to him.

'You're worth it,' he said, impressive in his solemnity.

'You don't know that,' she said with a nervous little laugh.

'I will know it, before you're much older. And I think I'll prove myself right.'

He cupped her face and kissed her again, slowly and tenderly. This was already an addiction, Edie realised. She had not meant to enjoy it this much. If she was not careful she would find herself in deep trouble.

'You know what I'm going to do to you?' he said softly, smoothing down her loosened hair.

'I don't, precisely. I mean, I know the mechanics ...'

He hushed her. 'No, my love, that's not what I mean. You know what I'm going to make you?'

'Make me?' she stammered, dismayed beyond measure at how insistently her body was crying out for his touch.

154

'Mine,' he said. 'I'll make you mine.'

She shook her head, trying to inch away from him, but he was not having it and kept a tight hold of her.

'No, I won't be yours. I'll still be myself, Edie ... Prior. I won't belong to you, or anybody.'

He leant his forehead against hers, their noses touching.

'You're a stubborn little witch, but I'll make you love me.'

'You won't.'

'Oh, you don't know it yet, you poor little innocent, but what we're about to do changes you. A woman can't give herself to a man without falling in love with him. It's inevitable.'

'I don't believe it.'

'You'll see. They all do. You will.'

'I won't. I'm not some silly goose of a girl. You can't think that ... doing this thing ... to me will change me. I am determined that it shall not.'

'You won't be told,' he said, shaking his head. 'But I won't rest until I have your heart ... right ... here.'

He held out a hand and curled the fingers into a fist.

'No rest for the wicked, then,' said Edie, finding that she relished this sparring.

'That's me, is it? The wicked?'

'I'm afraid so.'

'Hm, well, you may have a point. Heavens, I must get these wet things off before I succumb to pneumonia. It's not a sick bed I want to be lying in tonight.'

He stood and began removing his waistcoat, then his wet shirt.

Edie, fascinated by her first sighting of an unclothed male torso, watched from the bed. He was lean and spare inside his clothes, but with some muscular strength. There was a little dark hair on his chest, which the rain had reached, flattening it to sleekness.

He took off his shoes and his drenched socks and finally his trousers until, in only his underwear, he lay down on the bed and drew the covers up to his waist.

Lying propped on his side, he said, 'Well, come on, then. Get that nightie off and come here. No, stand up and face me. I want to see you.'

Edie felt suddenly as if she were on one side of an insurmountable peak. He really expected her to undress while he watched her?

'I'd prefer to just get into the bed,' she said.

'Oh, would you? Little Miss Coy, are you? It's a bit late for that, my love. Don't be prim and proper. Show yourself to me. I promise I won't laugh.'

She screwed her eyes tight shut and then he *did* laugh.

'You said you wouldn't!'

'I'm sorry, I'm sorry, it's your face! Come on. Open your eyes.'

Keeping her gaze fixed on the floor, she pulled the lawn cotton nightdress over her head and dropped it on the chair nearby.

She was naked, all of her on display to him. She tried to cross her arms in a position that would hide the worst of it.

'No,' he said reprovingly. 'Don't cover up. Move your arms and look at me.'

She had to force herself, her hands moving slowly to her sides, but she managed it somehow. When she raised her eyes to his, she was struck forcibly with a bolt of terrifying excitement. God, the way he looked at her, as if he would eat her ...

He crooked a finger.

'You're beautiful,' he said. 'Now come to bed.'

She was grateful for the opportunity to hide herself under the covers, but he stopped her, hanging on to them and refusing to let her have any.

'No,' he said. 'I want to look at you. Lie still and let me ...'

Leaning over her, he placed one hand at her collarbone and began to trace its line, from one side of her neck to the other. His feathery touch brought her out in goose pimples and made her scalp tingle.

'Don't be ashamed of your body,' he said. 'Don't be afraid of it. You girls are always so afraid of your bodies ... as if they're your enemies ...'

'They are,' whispered Edie. Hers was a renegade, a rebel that had broken away from all good sense and discretion and seemed hell-bent on joining forces with Charles.

His fingers skated and swirled around her shoulders and upper arms and then, without warning, they were at her breasts, circling the perimeter of one until a bold thumb pressed on her nipple, making her gasp.

'Mm,' he said. 'Is that nice? Do you like the way I touch you?'

She did not want to reply. Surely it was obvious – why make her say it?

He stopped, his fingers hovering less than an inch above her.

Oh, don't stop, please …

'Yes,' she admitted, snapping it out.

'Just as well,' he said, resuming his ministrations. 'Because my fingers are magnetically drawn to you and I doubt I'll be able to prise them off.'

'We must be opposite poles,' whispered Edie, feeling herself falling into the unknown, head over heels.

'Perhaps,' he agreed, both hands now at work on her, stroking and squeezing, while his head dipped low, fanning hot breath on her nipples. 'Which of us is south and which north? Oh, I think I know. You are cold and heartless north. I am passionate south.'

The tip of his tongue flicked at her right nipple and she squirmed violently.

'Oh,' she exclaimed, trying to think and finding it dreadfully hard under these circumstances. 'The south pole is not warm. It is bitter.'

'Must we discuss world climate now?'

His mouth closed fully over her nipple and he sucked at it. A silken thread of pure pleasure wound down to the spot between her legs that seemed to be so warm now. Almost too warm, and she was aware of that furtive trickle that sometimes accompanied her most secret thoughts.

His head below her chin, attached to her breast, was a curious sight. She watched him, trying to keep track of where his hands were roaming. One played with her other breast while the other moved lower, over her stomach. His knuckles grazed the curve and swell of her waist and hips, tracing her outline.

She wondered what she should do, if anything. Was it acceptable simply to lie here and bask in the glory of these new stimulants – or should she reciprocate in some way? What was the done thing?

'Should I ... would you like ... shall I touch you?'

He raised his head and she was confronted with the rude sight of her nipple, raised and red and shining. She swiftly averted her eyes and looked at Charles, who wore an expression of comic pensiveness.

'Dear Edie, you bear no responsibility for tonight's pleasures. I know what I am about, and so all you need do is place your trust in me. Follow my lead and don't worry about anything but enjoying yourself. Will you do that for me?'

'I'll try.'

'I hope you'll succeed.'

'I don't want to be a disappointment to you.'

'Oh, Edie, Edie.' He buried his face briefly in her breasts, then looked back at her. 'There's no question of that. No question at all. You could only disappoint me by ordering me out of the room. I trust that isn't going to happen?'

'No. I honour my contracts.'

'Contracts?' He screwed his face up in frank bemusement. 'Where do these notions come from? You are unfathomable. But I will fathom you. Oh yes, I will plumb your depths.' He interspersed these last words with kisses, then Edie gasped as his hand pushed at her inner thigh, causing her to spread her legs.

'Now, be a good girl and give yourself up to me,' he whispered.

A good girl would not be doing this.

A good girl would not be allowing a man to gently part the lips of her sex and rub the inner folds with pressuring fingertips. Would a good girl feel this surge of divine pleasure at the touch of a man on her exposed swollen bud?

'You want me,' said Charles, presenting it as a fact in his low, assured voice. 'Even if those lips won't speak it, these will.' He tapped at the cleft and moved slowly down her body until he knelt between her thighs, staring

160

between them until Edie thought she might die of shame. She shut her eyes and turned her face away, trying to blot out the image of her most intimate parts being inspected with such naked rapacity.

Without breaking the lazy rhythm of his fingers, Charles leant over and kissed her stomach, several times, each kiss landing lower than the last.

Edie began to twitch, nervous of where the mouth might venture next. She was mortifyingly aware of how her juices flowed and how they must be covering his fingers. She was really no better than she should be, after all. And now he knew it. Oh, this had been a mistake. The way he made her feel placed her in his power in a way she had not expected.

The sensations conferred by his strumming fingers built, slowly but unstoppably, until she wanted to twist away and wrench them off her. When he kissed the soft skin just beneath her lower lips, she moaned before she could stop herself.

'Mm,' he said, his voice a warm buzz against her thigh. 'You want me.'

Still with her head turned sideways and her eyes tight shut, she felt him move back over her, maintaining the inexorable work of his fingers, using his other arm to prop himself an inch or so above her. She felt his heat above her, the tickle of his chest hair on her nipples. She wanted to feel his skin on hers. It was better than all the finest fabrics she had ever worn, better than feathers, better than fur.

'Open your eyes. Look at me.'

She couldn't. How could she look at the man who was touching her so scandalously, and to her obvious, treacherous joy?

'You can't hide from me. Everything of you is mine. Open them ...'

His fingers slowed and then stopped, as if preparing to end the waves of wild ravishment that had possessed her.

She looked at him indignantly. 'Why? Why can't I keep my eyes shut?'

'Lots of reasons,' he said. 'I'll give you two. One, I don't want you pretending that you're somewhere else, with someone else, doing something else. I want you here, with me, one hundred per cent, taking responsibility for the fact that you want and need and love the things I'm doing to you.'

Edie felt mutinous, wanting to throw him off, slap his face, anything to alleviate her mortal shame at how strongly he made her respond.

This made him even more horribly smirky and satisfied than ever, though, so she composed her features before he spoke again.

'Don't you?' he said, challenging her almost beyond endurance.

Why did he have to be such a beast?

'Edie? Answer me.'

'It's all right,' she sulked.

He laughed out loud.

'Oh, this is *fun*,' he said. 'I think I'll get more out of you than that before I've finished. Anyway, I said I'd give you two reasons for keeping your eyes open. That was one. The other is that I want to see your expression when I make you ...'

His voice dropped and his fingers resumed their devilish work between her lower lips.

She struggled for breath, and for mastery of her facial features, her native obstinacy making her want to retain a blank expression to spite him. But neither of these things were governable, and she surrendered first to hectic gasping, then to the twitching of her cheeks and eyes. Finally, the huge surge of sensation washed every other consideration away.

Something beyond her experience was coming to claim her, something Charles Deverell called forth. She rolled her eyes back but he reproached her for it.

'No, not the ceiling, *me*. Yes, you're nearly there, aren't you? Oh, so nearly there.'

His manipulations of her were no longer lazy. His fingers were firm in both pressure and purpose, and they had found a secret part of her that went deeper than flesh. The unsettling pleasure emanated from a core far inside and radiated outwards until it spilled from her in so many different ways.

However hard she might try to hide her response, there was no chance of it now. Her body gave her away a hundred times, in the tension of her muscles, in the arching of her spine, in the high breathy wail of her voice, in the widening of her eyes and, most damningly of all, in the way she pushed that intimate part of her against his wicked fingers, as if begging for more.

She had been taken over by a force more powerful than she could ever have prepared for. It was at once shameful, terrible, frightening and utterly rapturous.

Charles did not laugh at her, exactly, but she had the feeling that he was cackling triumphantly in some inner place. On the surface, though, he was gentle and solicitous, smiling at her throughout her outpouring.

'Oh, yes, my girl, that's it,' he murmured, pressing his hand against her parted lips, still rubbing. 'That's what I do to you. You look so scared, love. You come so sweetly, just the way I thought you would.'

She felt the itch of tears at the corners of her eyes. She shut them, determined that she would not be bullied into opening them again until she knew she was safe, and turned her face from him.

'What's this?'

Although she was spent, he kept his hand where it was, reminding her of how she was possessed by him now. He had made a mark on her and she could never wipe it clean.

'Edie?' He spoke more sternly now.

She swallowed and held her peace. He did not own her. He could not make her do anything. The impulse to cry passed and she let her muscles relax.

'It doesn't mean anything,' she said at last. 'It is a mere function of the body.'

'How terribly romantic you are.'

'Stop teasing. It isn't fair.'

He was silent for a while, then he reached down to stroke her hair.

She flinched.

'Don't be ashamed, Edie,' he said. 'What we are doing isn't wrong. It's natural. It's a pleasure, to be embraced.'

'It isn't that,' she said, finally brave enough to open her eyes and look at him. She wanted her gaze to be hostile, but the sight of him knocked her off course. Was he right about the inevitability of falling in love with him? Oh God, what trouble she was in, if so. 'It isn't shame, or not entirely.'

'What is it then?'

'Anger. I'm angry with myself, and with you. I'm angry that I've let myself be … moved … by you. And I'm angry that all these sweet words you're saying have been said before, to who knows how many poor girls, all of whom believed it, more fool them.' She paused, even more angry that her breath was becoming ragged, another prelude to tears.

'You won't believe me when I say this, but you aren't those other girls, and never will be. And I don't want any more girls like that. It was all a long time ago, anyway. My reputation as a rake was made largely pre-war. I'm not that man any more.'

'You'll say anything as long as it gets you what you want.'

'Not to you.'

'Liar.'

'Oh, I'm the liar, am I? I don't think so. I know who you are.'

She sat up, her heart beating wildly.

'What … do you mean?' The words almost would not come out through slackening lips.

'Damn it, I wasn't going to say anything.'

'Too late. You've done it. Tell me what you mean.'

He took hold of her hands and leant in close to her, his breath warm on her face when he spoke.

'You're her daughter, aren't you? Or some member of her family. But my money's on her daughter.'

'Why do you think that?' But it was a whisper, hardly convincing.

'It's pretty obvious, Edie. This whole situation – your desperation to protect her from ruin at my wicked hands. You wouldn't be doing this without a very compelling motive. But why do you want to protect her when she has clearly been no mother at all to you? She doesn't know you.'

'Not yet. Not yet she doesn't,' whispered Edie. 'It wasn't her fault. She had to forget me. She wasn't given a choice.'

Charles held her face in his hands, his thumbs brushing away the tears that now fell.

'Oh, what a tangled web ...' he said quietly.

She seized his forearms and held them tight.

'You won't tell? Will you? I know you hate her but please ...'

'Well, you've certainly given me a stunning piece of ammunition. No, don't look at me like that. I won't say anything. Not yet, at least. I can't promise I never will, Edie. For heaven's sake, be reasonable. This woman is a living piece of deceit and my father is the poor fool she's duped into supporting her for the rest of her life. At some point, I will have to tell him.'

'Charles, please, I'll give you whatever you want ...'

'Don't.'

His tone was harsh and his fingers tightened around her face, pushing against her cheekbones.

'Don't,' he said, more levelly, 'turn me into some monster who uses this to force you into something you don't want. I'm many things, most of them bad, but I'm not that. I won't take you just so *she* gets away with her duplicity.'

'So you're ... this is ended?'

'No, Edie, it isn't ended. I'll take you, but only because

you want to be taken. And you do. The blood of that lying whore might run in your veins but you will be honest with me.'

'I'll be honest with you. I hate you. I hate what you are making me and I wish I'd never laid eyes on you.'

He dropped his hold on her and looked at her steadily, drawing a deep breath.

'Well, that's rather unequivocal, isn't it?' he said. 'I see how things stand.'

He rose from the bed and began gathering up his wet clothes.

Edie reached out, hesitantly, then dropped her arm.

'You won't ... go to her?' she said, faint at the thought.

'If I'm unwelcome here ...' he said, but his attempt at a sneer didn't quite come off. He was hurt, she realised. She had hurt him. But he deserved it! Oh, it was too difficult.

'You're so cruel,' she said.

He held his clothes against his chest and stared at her.

'I only want to be kind,' he said. 'Kind to you. But you're afraid of what you feel for me and I can't fight that tonight, not after all that's been said.'

'Charles ...'

'No. I won't go near your precious mother, don't worry. I don't want a part of any contract. I want you. I want you to come to me. And I think you will. Goodnight, Edie.'

She stared at the space he left in the room for a very long time, unable to move or think.

When she lay down, she put the towel to her face and breathed in the smell of his wet hair and his cologne and his cigarettes. Damn him. Damn him to hell.

* * *

The day she found out about her mother had been truly awful.

Her father had been giving a party for the launch of a friend's book and all the usual bohemians and aesthetes were in attendance, including papa's publisher, a man whom she had known since childhood but who had never ceased to make her feel uncomfortable in his presence. Barrington Long had that effect on all women, she divined, and most were experienced enough to laugh him off or brush him away like a fly. Edie longed to achieve that level of poise and confidence, but she did not have it yet.

She concentrated on playing the hospitable hostess, mingling with all the different guests, discussing books with the writers and politics with the firebrands. They all doted on their 'little Edie', who had sat on cushions listening to radical ideas and new philosophies since she was scarcely old enough to toddle.

Still, as was his wont, Barrington Long had found a chance to monopolise her, creeping up behind while she stood on the balcony taking some air from the smoggy Bloomsbury sky.

'Ah, Edith,' he said, his hot breath at her shoulder. 'You have outdone yourself tonight.'

'Oh, it's down to Mrs Fry really,' she said carelessly. 'I only chose the menu.'

'You chose it divinely, my dear.'

'Thanks. Perhaps I might go in and ...'

'Not on my account, dear Edith? I so wanted to speak to you.'

'Really? What about?'

'About what a big grown-up girl you are now.'

Edie felt sick and tightened her hold on the wrought-iron balcony.

'I'm an adult woman, if that's what you mean.'

'Yes, I suppose it is. And a damn fine one, too. Filling out in all the right places.'

'Do stop. I don't like to hear this.'

She felt him shake when he laughed behind her.

'I sometimes wonder if you really are your mother's daughter,' he said.

'What? Did you know her?'

Edie turned around now and frowned at him.

'I should say so. We all did. Intimately.'

'What on earth do you mean?'

'I'm sorry, my dear, take no notice of me. I'm a little bit the worse for wear.'

'No, I insist you tell me what you mean. Are you saying that you were her lover as well?'

'No, I wasn't. Wishful thinking. She's a damn fine woman and we all envied your pa no end.'

'*Is* a damn fine woman? Don't you mean *was*?'

'Fuck.'

Edie had heard the word before – it was rather fashionable, indeed, in the circles her father moved in – but she slapped Long round the face all the same, then ran into the drawing room in search of her father.

'Tell me the truth about my mother,' she demanded, after disengaging him from a cluster of guests. 'The truth. All of it.'

'Oh, Edie …'

'Is she still alive?'

'I'd hoped it wouldn't come to this …'

Yes. She was still alive. And, what was more, she was famous, and married to an aristocrat. She couldn't make her father tell her much more about the circumstances of her birth, but she gathered that Ruby Redford had given the baby over to him, explaining that she was better off that way. Theatrical life was not for a baby, and Ruby had a career to consider and a scandal to avoid. 'These things happen.'

Enraged by her father's years of silence on the matter, Edie had packed her bags and stomped off to stay with her friends the McCullens, in their chaotic but friendly tenement in Holborn.

It was there that the plan had been hatched. They had been so optimistic, so entranced with their cleverness, so sure it would effect a wonderful reconciliation between mother and daughter, as well as striking a blow for the workers, though they were vaguer on how that element would come into play.

But lying in her bed that night, thinking about Charles on the floor below, Edie did not feel clever at all.

She only felt even more out of her depth than ever.

* * *

Distant thunder still rolled around the house when Edie woke from fitful sleep the next morning. Dreams both erotic and disturbing broke into elusive fragments. She needed a glass of water urgently.

Sipping at it, she revisited the night's events and tried to predict how they would affect the day. Was it all lost with Charles? The thought was an unwelcome wrench, a churn of the stomach. But why should it be? If he would leave both her and Lady Deverell alone, then surely she had the result she wanted?

She dressed hurriedly, yawning, and went to take her station in Lady Deverell's chambers.

'Good morning, my lady,' she said, nervous at addressing the sleepy face on its silken pillow. She had the most absurd presentiment that Lady Deverell *knew* – knew everything, about Charles, about her, about their relationship. Keeping a cool head was going to be difficult today.

'Mm, is it morning already?'

Lady Deverell turned her face away and pulled the covers higher.

'If you'd like to sleep later –'

'No, no, don't go. My bath. I'll be ready directly.'

It was only then that Edie realised Lord Deverell was not in the bed with her. Perhaps her dread of his 'bedroom face' had been misplaced?

But, once Lady Deverell was bathed and dressed, she confirmed that Lord Deverell had indeed come to her room.

'I thought I might find him here,' confided Edie, trying her level best to drag a comb through her mistress's luxuriant locks.

'Oh, he never stays. He snores, you see. I send him packing. The sheets will need to be changed, if you don't mind seeing to it.'

'Oh – of course.'

'I know it should be a housemaid's job but it feels too … intimate, somehow. I prefer to have my lady's maid do it. That way, only two of us know the truth of the matter, rather than the whole house.'

'Well, three, really,' said Edie unthinkingly, but this seemed to displease Lady Deverell, who pursed her lips.

And when Charles visits, nobody can gossip about how

the sheets needed washing, even though Lord Deverell was away. Edie thought Lady Deverell's preciousness was more about practising deception with ease than about fine scruples. Did she blame her? Should she?

She found it easier to blame Charles.

The thought of him made her wrench the comb a little too forcefully, so that it snagged in her mistress's hair.

'Ouch! Watch it!'

The door opened and, before she could turn around, Edie saw Charles in the dressing-table mirror. He wasn't dressed and looked rumpled and louche, his dressing gown untied at the waist, his dark hair standing straight up. There were shadows under his eyes and somehow they made him look even more desirable.

Edie's fingers shook as they closed around the comb.

'I thought you were out,' said Lady Deverell, a satisfied cat-with-the-cream smile on her face.

'Town was a bore. Came back early. Good God, girl, what are you doing?'

He took the comb from Edie, brushing against her hand in the process. She stepped back sharply, a shock flashing through her.

'Don't you know how to brush this incredible hair?'

'Charlie, you mustn't. You shouldn't even be in here, you bad boy. What if Hugh comes in?'

But Lady Deverell's reproaches were idle enough and she bent her head back, deriving pleasure from his skill with the comb. He put it aside and began to use the hair-brush instead, teasing the auburn mane into submission.

'You see, Edie,' he said, lifting his hooded eyes towards her in the mirror. 'Gently does it. No need for force.'

She was transfixed, unable to speak, finding the simple action of his brushing Her Ladyship's hair unbearably erotic. She wanted him to brush *her* hair, to touch her skin, to lay her down, to finish what he started last night.

His hand reached forward to gather Lady Deverell's hair into his fist, but before he could, she sniffed abruptly and frowned. She seized his hand and put his fingers to her nose, then she slapped his wrist so hard that Edie flinched.

'Alley cat,' she snarled. 'Get out of here.'

Edie saw her cheeks flood with crimson, horribly aware that what Lady Deverell had scented on her lover's fingers was *her*.

'She said much the same thing,' drawled Charles, moving away at his own unhurried pace, with a glance over his shoulder at Edie. 'Seems my luck's out.'

Thankfully, Lady Deverell was beyond paying any attention to Edie's blushing confusion. She threw the brush after Charles, hitting the door as he shut it, then bunched her fists and banged them on the dressing-table.

'The bastard,' she said in a choking voice. 'The utter swine. I don't know why I ...' She buried her face in her arms and remained like that for a long time while Edie sat on the windowsill, waiting for strength to return to her limbs.

Was this a message to her? A sign that he relinquished his hold on Lady Deverell, for her sake? Or was it simple clumsy coincidence that he had not bothered to wash his hands and been found out?

Lady Deverell raised her head and directed teary eyes at the mirror, looking towards Edie's perch.

'You know what the really pathetic thing is?' she said. 'The thing that makes me hate myself and hate him more than anything? I'll forgive him. I'll spend a few days picturing him with whichever tart he's had his way with and … then I'll want him so badly I'll swallow my pride and go back to him.' She shut her eyes and seemed to be trying to keep some outburst of emotion at bay for a moment. Without opening them again, she said, 'Don't fall in love, Edie. Don't ever fall in love.'

She could think of a number of responses to this, but none of them would improve Lady Deverell's mood, so she held her tongue.

After a few moments, Lady Deverell appeared to make an effort to shake her head clear of her jealous rage and sorrow and smiled, rather thinly, at Edie.

'Do come away from the window. I don't bite. I'm sorry. It's just that sometimes I feel so lonely here …'

Edie rushed over to her and seized the brush, ready to complete her task.

'Oh, don't be lonely. You have me. You'll always have me,' she said, cursing her impulsiveness a moment later when Lady Deverell cast her a curious glance.

'Always? Do you really think so?'

'Well … perhaps.' Trying to deflect attention from her awkward outburst, she took up a section of hair and pulled the brush through it over and over with compulsive rapidity.

'I say, you don't have a pash, do you? On me? You wouldn't be the first …'

'Oh, gosh, nothing of the sort. Really, I spoke without thinking. Please, don't mind me.'

'There was an exquisite little creature who played Hermia to my Helena once. She was always finding excuses to embrace and touch and kiss. Eventually she confessed that she loved me to distraction. It was terribly awkward. Lovely girl, but … You aren't that way inclined?'

'No.'

'And you don't have a sweetheart?'

'No.'

'Why ever not? Pretty thing like you should have a sweetheart.'

'I thought I wasn't to fall in love, my lady.'

Lady Deverell laughed. 'Yes, that's right. I can't have it both ways, can I? But I suppose some men aren't bastards. If only one could meet them.'

Papa isn't a bastard. You met him.

177

'Well,' said Edie with an attempt at briskness, 'I suppose if one must spend one's life looking after a person, it had better be a person like you. Husbands cannot wear such glorious gowns and I suppose they want laundry done and potatoes peeled and so forth. I think my life here far superior to that.'

'You're a sensible girl, when you want to be,' said Lady Deverell approvingly. 'Oh, dash it, I can't face breakfast if he's going to be down there. Would you go and ask for an egg to be brought up, and coffee?'

'Of course, my lady. But your hair?'

'We'll see to it later.'

***

Edie half-expected Charles to leap out at her from every corner as she made her way to the kitchens; but he was nowhere to be found. Instead, she was intercepted on the back staircase by Ted Kempe, in full uniform.

'Hello, stranger,' he said, tipping his cap and standing back against the wall to let her pass. 'How's things up there above stairs?'

'Lovely, thank you,' she said, eyeing her escape route. 'How are you?'

'Still pretty cut up about the other day, as it goes. Charlie Deverell was up to something, and I think it might have started with E.'

'Oh, don't, I have nothing to do with him.'

'See that you don't, love. He's poison. Listen, what about a rematch?'

'I'm sorry?'

'Your next afternoon off. See if we can get as far as the picture palace this time?'

'Oh, I don't know... Her Ladyship hasn't said anything about afternoons off ... I suppose I still get one.'

'Course you do. Or there's a dance up in Kingsreach next week for the bank holiday – a few of us are going, if you fancy it.'

'I'll see.'

'I hope you can. Save a space for me on your dance card, won't you?'

He winked and made haste up the stairs, leaving Edie to her task.

* * *

When she returned to Lady Deverell's chambers with the breakfast, she broached the subject of her afternoon off.

'You get every afternoon off as it is,' said Lady Deverell, cracking the top of her egg with her teaspoon. 'Good heavens, girl. What more do you want?'

'But would I be free to leave the house?'

'If I told you I wasn't going to need you, yes.'

'And if I said I had business in town on one particular afternoon – could you undertake not to need me then?'

'I really couldn't say. What business might you have in town anyway?'

'Oh ... nothing. It was merely a hypothetical question.'

'Merely a hypothetical question? Where did you learn these expressions, Edie?'

'From my father.' She paused, waiting for Lady Deverell to ask about him. She did not. 'Besides,' she said, 'I've been invited to a dance. Would it be out of the question to attend?'

'Who invited you?'

'Kempe, the chauffeur.'

Lady Deverell laughed, a spoonful of egg halfway to her mouth.

'Oh, he's the housemaids' favourite, isn't he? Lovely, strapping young man – I can see why. And you have an eye for him, do you?'

'He asked me, so it seems only polite ...'

'Only polite? You'd go to a dance with him because it would be bad manners not to? Oh dear, Edie. You aren't a creature of passion, are you?'

You don't know what I am.

'What do you think?' she urged. 'Could I go?'

'When is it?'

'I'm not sure. Some time over the bank holiday weekend.'

Lady Deverell took a long time to chew and swallow her piece of egg white.

'I'm not sure it's convenient,' she said. 'We have a party staying here over that weekend. There will be lots of changes of clothes, driving out into the country, tennis and so on. I might need you rather a lot.'

'I suppose it's in the evening.'

'I suppose it is. Well, I can't promise anything. We'll have to see.'

'It isn't important,' said Edie, who was in two minds about whether going with Ted was a good idea anyway. 'I'm not much of a dancer.'

'Oh, that's a shame,' exclaimed Lady Deverell. 'Dancing is such a pleasure. If you like, I can teach you a few steps.'

'Oh, really, it's not necessary.'

'Nonsense, I'd enjoy it. We'll get Mary to play for us and take a few turns around the ballroom later. What fun. It will cheer me up. Don't be shy – you'll be helping me, honestly.'

* * *

Edie's reservations had not quite melted away by the time Lady Deverell had persuaded Mary to take her place at the piano in one of the quieter back drawing rooms.

'You must know the foxtrot,' she enthused. 'Such a fashionable dance, very popular in London. You really do not know it?'

Edie had watched, but never participated. She shook her head apologetically.

'Mary, let's try a slow one, shall we? Really, Edie, it's not unlike a waltz but in four-four instead of three-four. Surely you know how to waltz?'

Edie showed, while Mary played with an impressive level of competence, exactly how inexperienced a dancer she was. Lady Deverell seemed to greatly enjoy having such a blank slate for a pupil, for she laughed almost the whole way through the dance, throwing her head back and seeming to have entirely forgotten her annoyance with her perfidious stepson.

Edie could not help joining in the giggles, even though she tutted at herself every time she tripped over Lady Deverell's dainty foot or turned so awkwardly that she almost brought the pair of them over.

'Did you ever see such a dancer?' cried Lady Deverell to her stepdaughter. 'Really, she reminds me of a young faun, on her legs for the first time, staggering all over the floor.'

Mary smiled tightly.

'Really, I have no objections whatsoever, for this is the closest papa will let me come to a ball until Christmas, no doubt.'

'Oh, Mary. I do feel for you. It is very hard of him. We shall have a marvellous ball when all our guests arrive.'

'Old relics from papa's days in the regiment, I suppose. Not a man under fifty to be seen. Apart from one's brothers.'

'I suppose you will not want to dance the tango, then?' Lady Deverell smiled broadly at her stepdaughter.

'Come, Mary, come and dance one with me. You do it so beautifully. Edie, I don't suppose you play …?'

'Actually, I do. A very little.'

She went to the piano, from which Mary had risen, apparently eager to take any chance of a turn around the floor, even with her stepmother.

'I will take the male part,' said Lady Deverell, 'and Mary the female. Watch us, Edie, and then you can try your own hand at it. Or foot, I suppose.'

Edie barely watched the dancers, too absorbed in trying not to stumble over her playing, but when she looked up it was to see two beautiful women, dancing fluidly and seamlessly around each other, burning up the space between them almost as if they were real lovers.

She played several false notes in her hurry to banish the thought from her mind, but she knew that this image would come back to haunt her when she went to bed. If it could find space in her mind that was not occupied by thoughts of Charles, that was.

'God,' exclaimed Mary once the music ceased and she laid bent back over the arm of Lady Deverell. 'You had all society at your feet and you came *here*.'

Lady Deverell stood straight and patted down her skirts, turning away from Mary's breathless scrutiny.

'We none of us know what we have while we have it,' she said. 'You want what I had. I wanted what you have. Do you think the world will ever allow us both?'

'The world hates women,' said Mary. 'So it's unlikely. Wouldn't you say, Edie?'

Edie stood up from the piano, looking between the born Lady and the one who had been made so.

'That is a gloomy outlook,' she said. 'We have the vote now. At least, Lady Deverell does. You and I are too young, of course. But I'm sure that will be remedied very soon. We have all seen how instrumental women were in keeping the country going during the war.'

'You may have done,' sniffed Mary. 'I saw very little of it, being packed off to school in Switzerland for the duration.'

'I suppose His Lordship thought to protect you.'

'And yet how cheerily he waved his sons off to the Front.'

'Come now,' interrupted Lady Deverell, clapping her hands. 'We are dancing, not moping in the grumps. Come to me, Edie, and show me how much of what you saw was taken in.'

'Very little, I fear,' she said.

She had barely spoken the words when Mary, back at the keyboard, clattered into an intense rhythm and Edie found herself seized in a close hold.

Much fumbling and tripping ensued, only coming to a halt when a male voice spoke over the gasps and giggles and mild swear words.

'You need someone to show you how it's *really* done.'

Mary slammed down the piano lid.

'Oh, go away, Charlie. You always spoil the fun. This is a Ladies' Excuse Me – no gentlemen required.'

'Yes, but how is anyone supposed to learn the tango like that? Let me be the man – since I am.'

Charles stepped in from where he had been leaning on the door jamb, a look of sardonic fascination on his face.

'Oh, I don't think ...' said Edie, while Lady Deverell simply left the room, calling Edie after her.

She looked back at him, then at Mary, who was making a droll face at her brother, as if fascinated by the sudden *froideur* and wanting an explanation for it. Edie hoped to God he would not provide one, as she scurried away.

What could he tell her anyway? Surely she would not approve of his activities with her stepmother – a stepmother with whom she seemed to be on a reasonably friendly, if jealous, footing.

***

'He wants to plague me,' muttered Lady Deverell. 'He will not succeed. I will have no dealings with him unless strictly unavoidable.'

From around the next corner, the master of the house appeared, so unexpectedly that, for a moment, he and his wife regarded each other with the native bristle of cats encountering each other on some dearly desired territory.

'Ah, Ruby,' he said eventually. 'I have been looking for you. You weren't at breakfast.'

'I didn't sleep well,' she said. 'A slight headache, no more.'

'Splendid. I mean, that you aren't ill, not that you slept badly, of course, ha ha.'

Edie feared Lady Deverell's hostility must be obvious to her husband, she made such a scant effort to veil it.

'What did you want?'

'Ah, yes, thought you might like to take a trip to town. Big do coming up this weekend, what? New frocks might be called for. What do you say?'

'Oh.' Lady Deverell brightened somewhat, granting her Lord a coquettish smile. 'That would be lovely. It seems such an age since I was up in town. We must dine at the Ritz again.'

'Absolutely. Such fond memories of the place. Well, then. Have your maid pack you an overnight bag and I'll have Kempe bring the car to the front in an hour or so. Does that suit?'

'Perfectly. I say, Hugh, might we bring Mary? The poor girl's positively in the dumps.'

'After the bally show we had this season ...' Lord Deverell frowned.

'It's one night. She'll be with us. And she needs new gowns too.'

'Well, I suppose so, if it's your wish, old thing.'

'It is. Go and tell her – she's in the Blue Drawing Room.'

With a smile of ineffable sweetness, Lady Deverell glided on her way, Edie trotting at her heels.

'Am I to come too?' she asked.

'Oh, no, I don't think so. It's just for one night and you aren't exactly expert in matters of toilette yet, are you? I shall have one of the girls at Belgrave Square dress me.'

'I am trying to learn, my lady.'

'I know. Don't take offence, for heaven's sake. I'm merely stating a fact.'

While Edie packed a valise under her mistress's direction, she tried not to think too hard about the fact that she would be alone in the house with Charles. No, not alone – that was absurd. The entire staff, plus his brother, would still be resident. If she wished, she could spend the day and night in the housekeeper's office.

If she wished ...

'Do you miss London, my lady?' she asked, folding a silk slip.

'Every bloody day,' said Lady Deverell, and Edie flinched at the unexpected language. 'I didn't expect to.

Thought I'd had my fill of it and wouldn't look back. But it's in my blood, Edie, in my soul. Oh, I suppose you were hoping you might get a chance to see your father?'

'No, no, it's all right, honestly.'

'Next time I'll take you with me. In the meantime, practise dressing hair. On the kitchen girls, if need be.'

'I think I might, my lady.'

'Good.'

* * *

Sir Thomas was on the steps with Lord Deverell and Lady Mary, waiting for Kempe to bring the car around. Edie wondered if he had joined the party too, but it seemed he had not. Instead he was anxious to hand his father a list of items he needed from town.

'Can't promise all this, my boy,' said Lord Deverell, eyeing the list from beneath heavy brows.

'Perhaps Edkins will be able to get them?'

'I'll see.'

The crunch of gravel signalled the arrival of the car, and Giles the footman took Lady Deverell's valise from Edie's hand and went to stow it in the boot.

By the time the vehicle had disappeared with its pleasure party amongst the enclosing green at the far end of the drive, Edie, Sir Thomas and Giles had been joined by another – Charles.

'Giles, I, er, need your assistance with something,' said Sir Thomas hastily, disappearing inside with the handsome footman.

I think I know what, thought Edie, looking after them.

'We're rid of them,' said Charles, speaking over her shoulder.

He was standing too close to her. She tried to step out of his orbit, but he took her elbow.

'Come for a walk. Soon all the flowers will be dead. Let's gather rosebuds while we may, eh?'

'"To the Virgins, to make much of time",' murmured Edie, allowing him to draw her down the steps and around the corner of the house.

'Precisely so,' he said. 'Who educated you?'

'My father.'

'An educated man and Ruby Redford. Seems an odd match.'

'Perhaps that's why they didn't stay together.'

'Perhaps. You don't know? Your father hasn't told you?'

'He never speaks of it. I didn't know she was my mother until ... somebody else told me.'

Charles stopped and looked down at her, his face a picture of consternation.

'Your father knows you're here, I take it?'

'No.'

He raised his eyebrows and exhaled a long whistle.

'You're a cool customer, Edie Not-Prior. So you're all alone in this?'

'Not quite. I have friends with whom I discussed and developed the idea. It was a bad idea. I see it now. I think that, when she comes back, I will tell her who I am and –'

'Whoa, whoa, whoa,' said Charles, holding her by both elbows now, shaking his head. 'Don't be hasty.'

'It's not your business.'

'It is my business. I don't want you thrown out of here. I want to keep you here.'

'Why? After everything I've said?'

'Because you're a maddening little witch and I can't stop thinking about you. Come on. Somewhere we can't be overlooked. By the lake, perhaps.'

But Edie thought that the combination of Charles and sun and water was not to be trusted, after the way it had affected her in Maidenhead. She chose instead a little summerhouse in one of the less tended parts of the garden, overlooked today by the men in green baize aprons with their wheelbarrows.

'So, then,' said Charles, lighting a cigarette as soon as they were seated on moth-eaten cushions softening an old stone bench. 'Let's get this straight. You're Ruby Redford's daughter. Your father never told you about her. You found out yourself and came up with this hare-brained scheme to work for her. Didn't you think of writing her a letter?'

190

'Of course I did. I was afraid she would never reply. And, in her position, one doesn't know who might happen upon her correspondence. I didn't want to be responsible for jeopardising her marriage.'

'Don't you feel bitterness, resentment, hatred? Or do you reserve such feelings solely for me?'

'Hush.' She flushed deeply, wishing she could make up her mind whether to hate this man or ... not. 'It is hard to explain how I feel. I do feel cheated of something most people have – a mother's love. I do feel disappointed in her and angry with her for abandoning me. But if, after all's said and done, I still have a chance of having a mother – that is what means the most to me. That is the course I feel I must pursue. You do not understand.'

She saw Charles, his face impassive, eyes narrowed, expel a column of cigarette smoke.

'No, I think I do,' he said. 'We all want what we feel we missed. If I could go back and have my youth again ... but it would mean changing history. World history.'

'The war?'

He nodded and took another drag of his cigarette.

'But we aren't talking about me. What if she rejects your advance, Edie? What if she breaks your heart?'

'My heart is strong enough.'

'Is it? Are you as tough as you like to think?'

'I have thought about this. I am prepared to lose. I

191

have a life to which I can return – a good life, where I am loved and valued.'

'Then you are luckier than most.'

'I suppose so.'

'All the same, you might need a friend.'

He put out his cigarette on the floor.

'A friend, yes.'

'Don't hate me, Edie,' he said quietly, holding out a hand to her. 'Let me be your friend.'

'If I have a friend, I need to trust them.'

'Didn't you see what I did for you this morning? I severed my tie with your mother. I did that for you.'

'You said you would tell your father.'

'I won't say anything. Not unless you want me to.'

'You have conditions.'

'No conditions.'

'What, none?'

'You are important to me. I care about you. I'm not making deals with you any more. I'm not trying to trap you or get you into my clutches.'

Edie looked away, out into the gardens where holly-hocks and lupins waved cheerfully in the breeze, a little foreteller of the coming autumn.

Could he possibly mean what he was saying? Or was it all part of his game? A new tactic – Mr Nice. Mr I-might-possibly-want-to-have-an-affair-with-you. He could have tried this tack with a dozen maidservants.

Something deep within her made her want to believe him so much that she couldn't bear to question him aloud.

'If you mean it,' she whispered.

'I mean it.'

'What I said last night – about hating you. I didn't mean that.' She folded her hands in her lap, tense as a tiny animal in the shadow of a predator, expectant of its spring.

'I know.'

'Oh, you don't know.' She turned to him, indignant. 'You always pretend you do, but you don't.'

'If you really hated me, you wouldn't have ...' He smiled broadly.

She caught a breath and looked away, shame crimsoning the very tips of her ears. No, he was right about that. Damn him.

'I want to hate you,' she faltered. 'But I can never quite muster it. I'm sure, if I got to know you better, I could do it.'

'Well, there you are, then. Get to know me better and you can hate me properly. Or ...'

'I won't fall in love with you.'

'That's all right then.'

He was closer to her now, close enough for their faces to meet and touch. He turned his head and spoke softly into her ear.

'Prove it. Let me try to make you fall in love with me and see how long you resist. There is nobody here to see us. We have the house and garden at our disposal for a full twenty-four hours.'

'There is your brother. And Mrs Munn. And all the servants.'

'Never mind the servants. And my brother has his own little scandal to attend to.'

'Oh, you know about that!'

Charles's eyes widened.

'*You* do?'

'Sort of stumbled upon them, by the lake. Oh, they didn't see me, don't worry.'

Charles smiled sadly. 'Poor Tom,' he said. 'But you see; he will be in no hurry to blow any whistles on me.'

'I suppose not.'

'Can you whistle?'

Edie giggled at the tangential turn the conversation had taken.

'No, or at least I have never tried.'

'Never? Try it now. Go on.'

'No!'

But she rounded her lips and blew through them, laughing again when only air escaped.

'Lick them first. Make them moist.'

Edie felt horribly shy.

'Or I shall do it for you.'

She passed her tongue hurriedly over her lips then repeated the experiment.

194

'Blow more gently.'

A third attempt succeeded in producing a low bird-like note.

'You see, you can do it. And now you will always possess the ability.'

'Why on earth do you care if I can whistle?'

'I don't. But watching your delicious pouting lips like that is quite enchanting. It makes me want to ...'

He put a finger to them, letting it glide along her wetted lower lip before pushing it ever so slightly further, meeting the tip of her tongue. Before she knew what she was doing, she sucked upon it.

'That's where my tongue should be,' he whispered, and she had no way of fighting the purposeful kiss he bestowed upon her after that.

The kiss spoke to her. You want this, said his tongue, his teeth, his lips. You cannot pretend otherwise. You want this always, morning, noon and night. Don't blame me for giving it to you.

The fight was over. She wanted him and he knew it.

'Come to my room,' he murmured into her ear.

'I shouldn't ...'

'What's the worst thing that could happen?'

'Lots of things.'

'You might fall for me.'

Exactly.

But she was weary of thinking, of resisting, of reasoning,

of trying to work out the best and least dangerous move. She wanted only to shut it all out and give herself up to a pleasure that now seemed inevitable.

And at least she would *know*, then. She would not be one of those women, single for life, always wondering what the secrets of their married sisters might be. She would have the best of both worlds – the experience of pleasure and the freedom to choose her own path in life.

But might such experience be a Pandora's box, raising unwanted evils to the surface of her life? It was a risk, like everything she did in this place.

It was a risk she would take, along with Charles's hand as he stood to lead her back to the house.

They entered through a little-used door in the West Wing. The beds were all made now and the maids busy in other parts of the house, so they were able to hurry through the corridors and up the staircases unobserved.

Energetic grunts issued from one part of the passageway. Charles turned to her and grimaced. 'Thomas is much more vocal in bed than in life,' he said. He took her hand again and tickled her palm. 'I wonder if you will be.'

The idle speculation brought home the enormity of her actions. She was about to enter his room a virgin and leave it a woman of experience. She wondered if it would show on her face, in her demeanour. Did it change a person?

They arrived at his room and, despite the wide open

windows airing the place, the aroma of Charles hung in the air, larger than him, pervading the atmosphere like a great seductive Deverell cloud.

He shut the door with his foot and held her against him, looking seriously down at her.

'No silly tantrums this time, hmm?' he said. 'You must promise me that you want this, and it isn't some game or deal.'

'You didn't seem to mind it being a game or a deal before.'

'No, but I've thought a lot about you since then. Didn't get a wink last night, in fact. And I've decided that we do this as independent adults who want each other, or not at all.'

'*You've* decided?'

'Haven't you?'

She tried to look away but his searching gaze compelled her to respond.

'Yes,' she muttered. 'All right.'

'So are you going to kiss me?'

She banged her knee mutinously against his, but she did not reject his suggestion, and stood on tiptoes to reach his lips. The minute they touched, he had his hand at the back of her head, keeping her fused with him until she was kissed into a state of knee-trembling sensuality.

'I like that little black-and-white outfit of yours,' he said, breaking off. 'But it has to go.' He reached behind and untied her apron; then his fingers plucked at the dress buttons above. It was so stiffly starched that its removal was a bit of a struggle, but she turned around obediently enough to let him finish.

Her bare shoulders were treated to the featheriest of kisses up to her neck and she shivered, looking at the bed through half-closed eyes. His hands strayed from her upper arms and reached around to rub against her breasts in their light summer camisole. She shut her eyes tight when he discovered her nipples, undisguisably hard and swollen.

'Mmm, how's that?' he whispered, and her answer came by way of her bottom, which she pushed back against him, flexing her hips in a shameless come-hither. Although, she thought half-coherently, he already *was* hither. Could she beg him to come *more* hither?

He kept up this electrifying pressure, stroking her nipples while he kissed the tender skin of her neck ever more ardently, patiently waiting for her desires to soak through her until she was heavy and dripping with them.

When he slid one hand inside the elastic of her drawers, she moaned but made no attempt to squirm away.

'Just like before,' he said, his tongue poking around the soft flesh behind her ear. 'Just as wet and ready for it.'

His palm flat against her tendrilled down, he curled his fingers and slipped them between her nether lips. She abetted him in this, tilting her pelvis forward to bring her eager clit to his attention. He was not slow to act upon her message and he caressed it with firm slow strokes, his other hand still cupping and rubbing her nipples, his mouth now suctioned to hers.

If it weren't for the tight pressure of his arm against her stomach, she thought she would stagger and lose her footing, so unreliable was the strength of her legs now. Nothing existed or mattered but his touch upon her, and her body flowering into wantonness beneath it. If this was ruin, she understood now how some women rushed headlong towards it. To wait for a husband who might never come … oh, why would one, when this could be had so easily, so sweetly?

She remembered the feeling from last night and knew when the first stirrings of that release flickered in her belly.

She whimpered and gyrated her hips, parting her legs wider to urge him on.

But instead, he took his fingers away, laughed and slapped her bottom.

'Get on to the bed,' he said.

'Oh!' she exclaimed, disappointed beyond measure.

'Don't pout at me. You've already had one set of jollies. I want to keep you on the edge now, make sure you're properly hungry for it.'

'You're a …'

'I know, I know. Go on then.'

She sat herself beside a bedpost at the bottom of the

bed and watched from heavily lowered brows as Charles undressed.

'Keeping her on edge', indeed. But she was, she couldn't deny. Her clitoris felt like a lead weight between her legs, as if every drop of blood in her body had concentrated there. There was a tingliness, a weakness almost reminiscent of influenza. That thought made her smirk – *oh, Edie, you are such a romantic.*

'What's funny?' She couldn't so much as twitch an eyelid without Charles noticing, it seemed.

She shook her head and swallowed, watching him unlink his cuffs, his hawk-eyes upon her.

'No, tell me.' He came closer, looming a little in only his shirt and suspendered argyle-pattern socks.

'Just that my head's a little light,' she said. 'It reminded me of the 'flu.'

'I don't think the 'flu's any laughing matter,' he said, raising an eyebrow before removing the shirt entirely.

'I know, just … I'm nervous.'

He crouched before her and took her hands.

'It's natural,' he said. 'But think how many girls have to give themselves the first time to hopeless bunglers. That's not the position you're in. I'll make it good for you, I promise.'

She smiled weakly, then laughed in merry earnest when he stood back up.

'What now?'

'You look so funny in those socks and nothing else.'

'Damn,' he said, reaching down to unclip the suspenders. 'You'd think a rake of my long standing would have learned by now – take the socks off first.'

Edie covered her mouth to prevent any more giggles escaping. The socks made a soothing distraction from the other salient feature of Charles's naked body – the one that was destined to find its way inside her.

Her amusement was soon displaced when Charles, now fully naked, stretched out on his back beside her and said, 'Come here.'

She hesitated, still sitting on the edge of the bed, her neck twisted to look at him – his face, of course. She kept her eyes severely off the *other thing*.

'You're afraid, aren't you?' he said, one arm cradling the back of his head, so insouciant he could have lit up a cigarette.

'No.'

'Come on then. Lie down beside me. Or on top of me. Or sit astride me. I don't mind. Take your choice. Oh, but you can take off your undies first.'

With her back to him, she stood and removed her camisole, drawers and stockings until she too was naked. It felt rather liberating, actually. Not as deadeningly embarrassing as the night before – perhaps that had broken her reserve. She was showing him nothing he had not already seen.

201

All the same, she was a little reluctant to turn around and show him her full-frontal view and she dived quickly on to the bed on her front and lay there for a moment or two of acclimatisation.

'Are you hiding from me? You've got nothing to hide, Edie. Are you still nervous?'

She nodded.

He stroked the nape of her neck, exposed by the tight bun into which, by a process of trial and error, she had scraped and pinned her hair that morning.

'You knew what a naked man looked like, didn't you?'

'Of course.' She raised her face, giving him the full benefit of her scorn. 'I've been to the British Museum. I've seen plenty of statues and artworks.'

'What kind of statues and artworks have you been looking at, to see a man in this condition?' he asked teasingly. 'Give me your hand.'

He managed to chivvy her onto her side, facing him, took her wrist and placed her hand on top of that alarming part of him.

'It's not like the statues, is it?'

'No. It's bigger and it doesn't … hang … in that way they do …'

'No. And do you know the reason for that?'

'Something to do with … no,' she amended, slightly horrified by the feel of the appendage beneath her palm.

'You,' he said, kissing the tip of her nose. 'You are the

reason for it. Wrap your fingers around it ... like that. What do you think of it?'

'I hardly know what to say. It is ... I expected something less ... inflexible. I am also a little taken aback by its size ... width, I suppose.' She shot him a grimace of true fear.

'You don't think I can fit? Ah, but you'll see.'

She clenched the muscles around her own small, tight opening. It seemed impossible but, on the other hand, she had often marvelled at how women managed to get an entire baby through there, so perhaps he was right.

'I have heard it can be painful. The first time,' she ventured.

'Yes. There may be a little blood. Just a little, as a rule. I don't suppose you ride?'

She shook her head.

'Ah, that sometimes does the job for one. Never mind. You can tug on it, if you like. See what happens.'

She yanked her closed hand upwards, so suddenly that he hissed.

'Gently,' he managed to say. 'Squeeze as tight as you like but don't pull too hard. Up and down a little. You see what happens?'

Edie observed the looseness of the skin at the top of the shaft and how it sometimes revealed, on her downward stroke, a little more of the smooth red tip beneath. She also noticed a pale, near translucent, bead of fluid there. Babies. What babies were made of.

'You got the French things?' she said in a gabble of speed, recalling the dangers of the act – dangers her mother knew all too well. Those were footsteps in which she had no intention of following.

'Letters? I told you I did, didn't I? They're in the top drawer. But we don't need them quite yet. Keep ... yes ... doing that ... mmm.'

His face was interesting to watch now; he was deeply flushed and his eyes seemed to flicker under almost-shut lids.

'All right, enough of that,' he said suddenly, clamping his hand on top of hers to still its rhythmic motion. 'Are you still on edge?'

Her mind raced straight back down between her legs. Yes, she was.

'Edie? Are you?'

'I ... don't know.'

'Well, I'm damned sure I am. And if you aren't, I'd better tighten the strings again, hmm? On your back and open your legs for me.'

Edie bristled slightly at his overbearing manner and thought of fighting him, but then, he was the one who knew what he was doing. Perhaps she should just make this as easy as possible for both of them. So she lay down and watched his face, transfixed by the play of light and shadow, the gathering of his brow, the darkening of his eyes as he bore down on her, reinserting his fingers between her soaked lips.

'All right, you're wet enough,' he said, patting her lightly between her thighs. 'I'm going to put this damn thing on, now. Are you all right?'

There was a little dip of concern in his voice and Edie tried to compose her brow, smoothing out the furrows.

'Perfectly. Why shouldn't I be?'

He chuckled as he rummaged in the bedside drawer.

'Stiff upper lip, eh?' he said. His voice was light, but as he turned back, an odd-looking lung of rubber in his hand, there was a strange manic gleam in his eye. 'Stiff upper lip,' he repeated, his tone harder this time. 'That's us, isn't it, Edie?'

'Now it's my turn to ask if you're all right,' she said, propping herself on her elbow, watching him sheath his erection in the tubular covering. 'You sound angry.'

'I'm sorry,' he said. 'I'm not. Not with you. Forget I said it.'

He smiled, a little tightly at first, then he straddled her hips and his face transformed to an expression of heartfelt desire.

'Put your arms around my neck,' he commanded softly. 'Kiss me.'

She reached up, enjoying the novel sensation of her nipples pressed into his chest, wondering how it was that such a simple thing as skin-to-skin contact could feel so addictively good. Their lips crushed together, cheek met cheek and nose rubbed nose. Throughout the kiss, though,

Edie was aware of the insistent pressure of Charles's erection on her lower abdomen and she knew that the moment was coming when she would have to let him in.

Sooner than ever, now, when he lowered her back down, still connected at the lips, until he lay on top of her. His legs were between hers and he rolled his pelvis against her pubis, demanding admission.

'Let me in,' he whispered into her ear.

A rising panic seized her, weakening her legs, but he nudged them wider apart and braced himself above her, kissing her all over in a frenzy – face, neck, breasts, shoulders. The kisses were not quite enough to distract her from the blunt intrusion between her lower lips, bathing itself in her juices. It still felt so *wide*. And so hard.

She was unable to avoid tensing herself as the tip of his shaft made its progress downwards to that impossibly tight place.

'Don't be frightened,' he said. 'It will only hurt for a moment, and I can promise you, you'll have felt much worse if you've ever stubbed your toe.'

She giggled, a little hysterically. 'You make it sound so attractive.'

'I'm not joking.'

He sounded so stern that she pressed her lips together and lifted her bottom a little, as if to show him that she was made of grittier stuff than he gave her credit for and she would go through with it regardless.

'I'm trying to make this as nice for you as I can,' he continued, a little mollified. 'Stop giggling like a school-girl. It's a woman I want here tonight.'

And I want a man, she thought, instantly sobered. And I've got one.

'I'm sorry,' she said. 'I don't know what the form is.'

'Of course you don't. And it's all right to be a little bit scared, love. It's quite natural. Now hush. Try to stay relaxed.'

Her hands were still clasped, locked almost, around his neck and she felt them tremble when the rounded tip of his cock began to push into her.

'It can't,' she gasped, but he kissed her silent and kept up the pressure.

He put one hand beneath her bottom and held it firmly, keeping the cheeks apart to open her further. Somehow, he was sliding in, just a tiny bit at first, but she was spreading without discomfort. It felt so odd, all the same, and not a bit natural.

Goodbye, virginity.

She squinted at the clock on the mantel, feeling somehow that she should record the exact time in her mind. The crossing of the Rubicon.

'Hold tight now,' he said in a strained voice.

She wrapped her arms around his back and clung for dear life while he made a fierce jolt forwards.

She couldn't help letting out a scream – not so much

from the pain, which was momentarily sharp but soon over, but from the expectation of it and the sheer brute force of the movement.

'I'm sorry, I'm sorry,' he whispered, dropping kisses all over her face as if each one were an apology. 'The worst is over, I promise.'

'I've done it now,' she said, the words keeping rhythm with the dull waves of pain radiating outwards from the initial shock. 'It's done. Can't be undone.'

'Sh, it's all right, it'll be better than this from now on. You might not think it now, but you'll come to love this.'

She searched his eyes frankly.

'I'm fine,' she said. 'I won't deny it hurts a little, but I rather like having you inside me. I can't describe the way it makes me feel, but … you needn't worry, you know.'

She wanted to reach up and gather the tenderness in his face, to hold it to her heart. He looked so loving and so relieved. It made her emotions seesaw until she hardly knew what they were or who she was.

'What if,' he said slowly, sliding his hand between their stomachs and down over her mons, 'I were to touch you here …' Now he had his finger on her clitoris and she thought how strange and different it felt now that he was inside her, just below. 'Would that make it better?'

The throb of pleasure his gesture provoked rose up and merged with the ache of pain inside. If he kept that up, it might even defeat it.

'I think … it would,' she whispered.

'All right. Now keep holding on. I'm going to move inside you. I'll take it very slowly, don't worry.'

Edie screwed her eyes shut and tried to concentrate on the spark of pleasure above that gnawing ragged pain. As he worked inside her, with painstakingly slow and small movements, she told herself it would all be all right, it would all be fine, it was what people did, it was what everyone did.

At first he spoke to her, in low reassuring little bursts. Was she all right? Did it start to feel nice at all? Did she know how tight she was, how perfect she was?

It did not feel nice until he stopped moving for a little while and concentrated on rubbing at her bud, so intently that she was able to surrender to the growing pleasure and give herself up to him. Unexpectedly, the knowledge and sensation of his being inside her added a great deal to her climax; taking her to a higher peak than she had experienced before.

When, before she had even had time to float down from her place in the stars, he began to thrust harder and more roughly, she did not feel the pain she thought she would, but was able to keep her legs wide and accept his plunging strokes, even welcome them.

The sting was good, it was what she had needed, that blank unidentified craving that had plagued her since she was young. Tear away all the learning and the reserve and

209

the manners and the anxieties and she was just a little female animal, opening herself to her mate, as her ancestors in the caves had done without half the agonising.

He had nothing to say now, his teeth gritted and his brow taut with effort. He looked quite wild, and quite magnificent, a noble brute pursuing his evolutionary purpose. He was not silver-tongued Charles Deverell any more. He was primitive man.

Oh, she must do this again. Often. She must feel this weight pinning her down and accept these bruising kisses and feel the savage force of what held them together and would not let them come apart.

A moment came when his determination became something else – what was it? Was it fear? Shock? Awe? It looked like all three, and sounded like triumph when he rode to his own conclusion.

She wanted to hold him, soothe him, crush him against her and stroke his matted hair. How different he was in his moment of rapture – how unpolished and without artifice, his mask of suavity dropped in an instant.

She was touched beyond expression. When he laid his face upon her bosom, she kissed his hair and shed a few tears into it. Was he right after all? Was he right about having to fall in love with him?

Now that it was too late, she understood what she had exposed herself to. He had peeled away her defences and here she was, laid bare. Whatever he asked her to do now, she would do. She was a fool. But she would not let him see it. She must never let him see it.

'Darling, precious girl,' he murmured. 'Now you are mine, all mine.'

He shifted position so that he could see her face, which she turned away.

'Oh, don't be cold, love,' he said, with such dismay that she turned guiltily back. 'Have I hurt you too much?'

He stroked her cheek and found the incriminating tears.

'Edie,' he whispered. 'Talk to me.'

'I'm not hurt,' she said. 'At least …' She propped herself up and squinted down at her thighs. Smears of sticky bright blood were upon them, and further stains disfigured the sheet. 'I am, a little, but …'

She lay back down, her speech degenerating to a croak.

'Pretty stupid of Mother Nature,' said Charles, his old tone almost entirely recovered now, 'to make the first time such a botch job. Doesn't she want the girls to do it again? One would think she tried to sabotage herself.'

'Between her and God making childbearing so foul, they've made a mess of things, haven't they?'

Charles chuckled and kissed her.

'At least you don't have to worry about the second one,' he said, fumbling to remove the French letter and tie a knot in its end. 'But they did one good thing. They gave you this.' He pressed hot fingers to her clitoris. 'No earthly use for anything but pleasure. I don't think they can have been entirely against the idea, do you?'

'You're a wicked man,' she said with a yawn.

'But you love me.'

'Shut up. I don't.'

'Ah, you do. Whether you know it yet or not.' He lay back down and spooned her in his arms.

Oh, how delicious it felt, almost as good as having him inside her. Now she even relished the sweet aftershock of the pain between her legs. Everything about him made her weak with longing, from the size of the hands that held her to the vibrations of his deep voice in his chest, tickling her spine when he spoke. God, if he knew what he had done to her ...

'What was your first time like?' she asked, needing to understand more about him. She hoped the question did not give her away, tried to make it sound vaguely curious rather than hungry for more knowledge of him.

'You really want to know? I barely remember it.'

'You must do. First times are always memorable.'

'You're right. I don't want to tell you because, like most things, it doesn't reflect very creditably on me. Suffice to say, I was a bad boy, but she was a happy girl. And when I say girl, I actually mean woman of twenty-nine.'

'Charles! You can't fob me off with that. Tell me.'

'Well, I won't mention her by name, because she's rather prominent in good society, but I was a schoolboy of sixteen, visiting a friend in the summer hols, and she was his aunt.'

'She seduced you.'

'You might choose to see it that way, but I was more than ready to be seduced. It happened after a game of tennis. We were playing doubles, Freddie and I versus his sister and his aunt. It was a hot day – Freddie and sister gave in and went to get changed. But she and I stayed on for more until I lobbed the ball right out of the court and into the shrubbery. I did it on purpose. We'd had this kind of flirtatious rivalry going on all week – anything I could do, she had to do better, and so it went on. She knew I was attracted to her and she played on it, and I knew she did.

'There in the shrubbery, pretending to look for the ball, I made my move. She acted shocked but she was thrilled. It did not take much to get her to reciprocate. She invited me to her room that night and I took her up on it.'

'Poor Freddie.'

'He knew nothing about it, and still doesn't. Poor Freddie's sister, rather. She was a little bit sweet on me, I think.'

'What an idiot then.'

'What are you saying?'

'Nobody should be sweet on you. You squander other people's love.'

'I have done,' he said soberly. 'I've taken it for granted too often. But I'm thinking of changing my ways.'

She craned her neck, looking back at him, expecting to see a mocking smile or some other sign that he was not serious, but she could detect none.

'Are you?'

He kissed her, catching her nose before she turned her face away.

'I hope so. I've had enough of it now. I'm not getting any younger. Bed-hopping in big houses was fun for a while and quite a wonderful antidote to the three years I spent behind barbed wire in Belgium, but perhaps it's time to give it up.'

She caught her breath. 'The war,' she said but he interrupted, putting a finger over her lips.

'Hush, let's not,' he said, then he released her, sat up and lit a cigarette. 'Want one?' he offered, waving the packet at her, but she shook her head.

The giant spectre of recent history had raised its head and neither of them could quite shake it off.

Edie cast around her mind for a change of subject.

'Who seduced whom?' she asked. 'You or ... Lady Deverell?'

She had thought of saying 'my mother' but the words had sounded so freakish on her lips that she retracted them.

'Oh, must we?'

'So many forbidden topics.'

'Look, it doesn't reflect well on me, all right? I did it for my own reasons, which were selfish and vapid and spiteful. Though I still think she's a disastrous wife for my father and he should get rid of her. But I don't want to be telling you what a bastard I am. Not now. Not after we've …'

He put out his cigarette half-smoked and caressed her cheek, looking half-heartbroken.

In his post-coital rumple, baggy-eyed and off duty, he looked more lovable than Edie had ever seen him – a man of sad regrets and dreams and hopes. This was a man she could like, she realised. Oh, why was he doing this to her? Why did he have to make her like him, as well as all the rest?

'I want to make it all better,' he whispered. 'For you.'

'For me?' Her heart thundered. 'I'm just … you've had what you wanted from me, haven't you? I'm just the maid.'

'No,' he said, sounding dreadfully hurt. 'You've misunderstood me. You think I just wanted a quick fumble and then I'd let you go? Christ, Edie, did it mean so little to you? Have I had no effect on you at all?'

'I don't know *what* you want,' she said, suddenly on the verge of tears. 'I don't know what you *can* want.'

'I want you,' he said passionately, drawing her to him so that their foreheads touched. 'That's all. Just you. I want

215

to get into you, to that core of defensive repulsion I keep seeing, and break through it. I want to make you love me.'

'But what if I did, Charles? What could ever come of it?'

He kissed her.

'I don't know,' he admitted. 'Something. But I do know that I'm not letting you go. I can't let you go.'

'What if I want you to?' she asked, every instinct she possessed screaming against the idea.

'Do you?'

'I'm not sure,' she faltered. 'I just don't see how ...'

'Don't try to be reasonable about it. It's passion. It's beyond reason. We can only let it take us where it will.'

'Oh, I don't believe in all that.'

He drew apart from her as if stung, squeezing his eyes shut and pinching gently at her cheeks.

'I will make you believe in it,' he said in a low, intent voice, bringing his face back to hers, then his lips.

She felt the force of his determination in the kiss he gave her then, felt the uselessness of resisting him. The ache between her legs was insistent, a constant reminder of how he had her now, he had her virginity for all time.

'You're quite right,' he whispered, having laid her back down in his arms, 'to try and keep a sensible head on your shoulders. But the more you deny the way I make you feel, the more I'm going to pursue you. I just thought you should be forewarned.'

'I feel like I've accidentally sold my soul to the devil.'

'So you should.'

'We ought to get up. Won't people notice that we're both missing?'

'People? There's only Tom here.'

'For heaven's sake, Charles, the staff are people too!'

'Oh, the staff, yes, yes. One forgets.'

'*I* am a person. And that poor girl you impregnated and then abandoned is a person.'

'I think we've discussed that, haven't we? And established that I did *not* abandon her.' His voice was cold now and he had picked up the unfinished cigarette and relit it.

'You claim to support her and the child, but you made that claim during the course of an attempt to seduce me.' She tried to maintain a brittle, bright tone, but inside she screamed at herself to stop trying to spoil everything between them. 'It could be empty words. Everybody says one shouldn't trust you.'

He puffed, silently and moodily, at the cigarette until it was finished, then stubbed it out swiftly and got out of bed.

Edie reached half-heartedly after him, but he had stalked into the dressing room and emerged a few minutes later with a basin of water and a flannel.

'Stay,' he said gruffly, motioning her to lie back.

He put the flannel in the water, squeezed it out, then

217

applied it to Edie's blood-smeared thighs, wiping off the marks with gentle care. Once they were gone, he rubbed between them, cleaning her lower lips and pubic hair. It smarted a little when the water dripped on her vagina, but she had no wish to stop him and she stared at the ceiling, feeling by turns grateful, angry at herself, resentful and guilty. But a greater emotion bound all those others together, all about him and how she wanted – badly wanted, despite herself – to be kind to him in return.

'There,' he said, his face unreadable. 'No trace of it. It might never have happened.'

What an idea.

'I'm afraid I can't promise to do the same for the sheet,' he said, frowning. 'There'll be talk at the laundry. Luckily the linen is sent out and done in Kingsreach, but the maids'll notice.'

'They'll know it was me,' said Edie. 'They'll know.'

'How can they know?'

'It's obvious.'

'I'll take it off and put it in the fire, if you want. Or get rid of it some other way. I'll say I burned a hole in it with my cigarette. It wouldn't be the first time.'

'Would you?'

'Of course I would. Anyway, get up and get dressed. I'm taking you to meet someone.'

'Oh?'

But he had returned already to the dressing room and

came out only to gather his clothes from the floor and start putting them on.

'Much as I'd rather stay in bed with you for the rest of the day,' he said, pulling on his trousers.

Edie watched with regret as he covered the body that had so recently been on top of her, making love to her. He seemed once more quite distant, disconnected.

'Would you?' she said, longing now for the return of his earlier gentleness.

'Of course. All day, all night, all week, if possible. Get up then. You'd better go up and get changed into your own clothes. I don't want to take a uniformed maid out with me. That'd start the tongues wagging all right.'

She put one leg over the side of the bed.

'Charles,' she said, and her hesitancy made him look sidelong at her while he buttoned his collar.

'You're terribly pale, my love,' he said, pausing to give her his full attention. 'You have stopped bleeding, haven't you?'

'Yes, I expect so.'

'Good,' he said, but he waited for her to speak again.

'I just … it wasn't too painful, you know … in fact … well, I did … like it. Just thought I should say.'

January became June, and his face glowed with a smile she could almost call soppy. He crouched at the bedside, his tie hanging around his shoulders, and took hold of her fingers.

'If you liked that, then wait until tonight,' he said.

She clenched between her thighs, ruefully aware of the twinge of pain as she did so. Did he really mean to try it again so soon?

He caught her apprehension and laughed, kissing her brow.

'You're an innocent,' he said. 'I'm not going to hurt you. There are plenty of other things we can do.'

'Are there?'

'Plenty. Come on. Get your things on and get back to your room. I'll meet you halfway up the drive in the motor in an hour.'

He pulled her to her feet, patted her bottom and continued dealing with his tie.

She scrambled into her uniform as quickly as she could, despite feeling as if she had been kicked between her legs by a horse, and made for the door.

He caught her en route and made her stop for a long, deep kiss.

'I liked it too,' he whispered, opening the door for her and checking that the passage was clear. 'I'll see you in an hour. Don't be late.'

Yes, she felt different as she walked along the corridor. But that was just the residual pain. One could hardly forget about it when one had such a constant reminder. When it faded, would she be back to her old self again? Or would she always feel the absence of what she'd had before, what she'd given to him?

She pushed open her door, her whirring thoughts fixed on where she might be going, and who might notice or gossip about their joint absence, so firmly that she didn't realise at first that she was not alone in the room.

It wasn't until she pulled off her mob cap and looked in the mirror at her disordered hair that she saw another woman, also uniformed, behind her.

She spun around.

'How dare you? This is my private room.'

'You don't need it no more, I think. You have another bed to sleep in.'

Sylvie bared her teeth in a catlike little smile.

'Wait till I tell Her Ladyship,' she gloated.

Chapter Eight

Edie could not quite shake off the idea that she might be hallucinating.

'But you ... you went to London,' she said.

'In the end, I decide to stay,' said Sylvie coolly, taking an unoffered seat at the dressing-table. 'Because a little bird tells me – a little Jenny wren – that my position may be available again sooner than I think.'

'Jenny? What on earth could she tell you? She barely knows me.'

'She does not need to know you. She knows Sir Charles well enough. When he has an eye on a maid, she soon disgraces herself. It is a fact of life at Deverell Hall.'

'There was one maid,' said Edie. 'One. He looks after the child, financially.'

Sylvie laughed. 'And all the girls before the war as well. You are the last in a long, long line. Not a very distinguished one, I'm afraid.'

'I'm not in any line,' retorted Edie, her blood up, ready to defend herself. 'I'm not some sighing little idiot, thinking I can bag myself a lord. You're quite, quite wrong about me.'

'Oh?' Sylvie's composure was maddening. 'But I'm not wrong about you coming here straight from his bed, am I?'

Edie could not lie so blatantly.

'It's none of your blasted business what I do and with whom,' she said.

'So he has had you,' said Sylvie. 'It's quite obvious anyway – I can smell him on you. And your face – that pathetic rapture, that glow. You make me sick.'

Edie's legs were trembling again; she had to sit down on the bed. She winced as her tender nether parts made contact with the mattress.

'Now you have given him what he wants,' Sylvie continued, her voice low with malice, 'I say it will last perhaps a month. Until he is bored of you, or you fall pregnant.'

'That won't happen,' said Edie, helplessly adrift.

'No, you're right, because it will end before then. It will end tomorrow, when Lady Deverell packs you off home without a character.'

'I don't think she'll do that,' said Edie, suddenly struck by a pathway out of this odious predicament.

'No?' Sylvie laughed.

'No. Because then there would be nothing to stop me telling Lord Deverell about her affair with Charles.'

Sylvie screwed up her face scornfully. 'As if he would believe you.'

'Perhaps he wouldn't. But do you know that for certain?'

'Listen, I hate that woman with all my heart, but I did not say a word to Lord Deverell because I know I will be blamed and disbelieved and I will lose my character for ever. No good house will take on, what do you call it, a tattle-tale. Discretion is the better part of service, *non*?'

'I'll do it, if you breathe a word of this. I promise you.'

'Then you will never work again.'

Edie smiled, a twitchy nervous thing.

I don't have to, she told herself, meaning it. Not that she dreamed of really telling Lord Deverell a word of it. But somehow she had to get this devil off her back.

'I don't care,' she said, as calmly as she could. 'I don't care about working again.'

Sylvie looked thunderstruck.

'You are joking,' she said uncertainly. 'We all have to make a living in this world.'

'I don't need this job,' said Edie.

'No, because I suppose you can make better money on your back,' snarled Sylvie, back in full venom again.

'But listen. I'll make a bargain with you, if you want.'

224

'A bargain?' Sylvie was working hard to temper her rage, but her eyes glittered with fury.

'I will be the worst lady's maid that ever was. I'm not far off it anyway. I will suggest to Her Ladyship that she take you back.'

'What? And you will go back downstairs, to the parlourmaids?'

'If that is her wish.'

'You are lying.'

'No, no, I promise you, I am not lying. I am a clumsy oaf when it comes to dressing hair. I can't sew. I fumble with buttons. She will tire of the novelty soon, Sylvie, I am sure of it. And what's more –' she lowered her voice '– this is between us, yes? She has quarrelled with Charles. They are no longer friends.'

'Truly?'

'Yes. Look, can you give me a week? I'll do everything I can to make her sack me. A week is all I ask. Please.'

'Well … I suppose so. It will be less unpleasant than the other way.'

'Yes, yes, we can achieve this without any unpleasant-ness at all. You will be back in your old place and I will have no qualms at all about going back downstairs. And neither Lord nor Lady Deverell need know any more about what goes on behind their backs. Will you shake hands with me and seal the compact?'

Edie rose unsteadily and held out her hand.

Sylvie, dubious at first, took it.

'One week,' she said. 'No more.'

'No more,' agreed Edie.

'Take a bath,' suggested Sylvie before leaving the room. 'You stink of that man.'

Edie could not call down for bath water, though – especially at this time of the morning – so she gave herself a thorough sponge wash instead, before dressing in her own clothes and trying hard not to feel so wobbly and weak.

* * *

'There's a problem,' she said, climbing gingerly into Charles's car.

He raised his eyebrows, gloved hands on the wheel, and waited for her to elaborate.

'Did you know Sylvie hadn't left? She's been lurking in the kitchens, biding her time, waiting for us to have an affair. And now we are ...'

'She knows?'

Edie nodded, her lips pinched.

'Ghastly little creature that she is,' muttered Charles. 'Like a burr, clinging where she's not wanted.'

'She threatened to tell Lady Deverell.'

'Of course she did. Don't worry. I'll see to her.'

'No, Charles. Leave her be.'

His look was puzzled, then he craned his neck to peer

226

over his shoulder as if he feared Sylvie might be hanging on to the rear bumper.

'You want her to tell your ... my ... *her* ... about us?'

'No, but I made her an offer. I said I'd try to get myself sacked for incompetence, so she could have her place back.'

'You said what? Edie, you don't owe that stupid bitch anything.'

'I feel I do, actually. It wasn't fair that she lost her place because Lady Deverell was jealous and suspicious of us. It was never part of my plan that I should displace other people. Better people. People who didn't deserve it.'

He breathed deeply. 'You're a lot better than I am,' he said. 'I don't take prisoners.' He repeated the words in a whisper, making Edie shiver for a reason she couldn't quite comprehend.

'It'll be fine,' she told him. 'I'll go back below stairs.'

'I won't be able to get at you so easily down there,' he objected. 'I want you close.'

'There'll be chances. Or perhaps ...'

Perhaps I'll tell my mother everything and then leave. Go back to London, start everything new and fresh. Get away from you and this horrible pull on me you have.

'Perhaps what? Perhaps you'll let me set you up in some nice little cottage in Kingsreach? Say you will, go on.'

'No, that's not an option, not even for a moment, Charles.'

'You're breaking my heart.'

'You haven't got one to break.'

They sat in silence for a moment before Charles made a determined yank at the gears.

'Right then. Full steam ahead for the young Deverell,' he said. 'I hope you've brought her some sweets. She won't like you otherwise.'

'Your daughter?'

'Charlotte, yes. She knows what she wants. Chip off the old block.'

They drove to the outskirts of Kingsreach, to a slightly ramshackle riverside environ made up of low brick cottages and higgledy-piggledy enclosures of land. Chickens everywhere, and goats and dogs. And children, lots of children in torn pinafores and raggedy shirts, climbing the trees in search of spoiled fruit.

Edie had never seen habitations like these, probably as poor as the London slums but not as dirty, and the children less stunted and haggard than those she had seen in the city streets.

'It doesn't look much,' he said apologetically, parking his car well away from the cottages, but still finding it overrun with curious children as they walked up the lane. 'But she owns it outright – cottage and land – so if she ever wants to sell up and move away, she can. I've heard a rumour the council are planning to build model dwellings down here, so they might make her an offer.'

They were still some hundred yards from their destination when a tiny girl in plaid pinafore and a lace bonnet toddled up, arms held up, chattering unintelligibly.

'Yes, yes, papa is here to see you,' said Charles, lifting the child into his arms.

Edie was not prepared for the effect this little reunion had on her. She felt a kind of agony, as if a dream held in suspension had finally been shot through. Despite herself, despite everything, she had held a vestige of foolish hope that in fact he had not fathered a child with a servant girl and had been unfairly accused. But there was no doubt this girl was his, from the shape of her face and the blue of her eyes.

'Where's mama?' he asked, throwing her gently up and down while she squealed and laughed. 'Is she at home, hmm? This is Edie. She's my friend. I'm afraid she didn't bring you any sweets. What a naughty lady she is.'

He set Charlotte down and reached into his pocket.

'But I didn't let you down, look.' He held out a paper bag which the child snatched up. She picked out a handful of barley sugars and stuffed them all into her mouth at once.

A young woman emerged from the low door of the end cottage, flapping a duster in her hand.

'Charl, where are you, darling?' she called, then she caught sight of her visitors and her face stiffened. 'Twice in a month? I'm honoured, ain't I?'

'Monthly visits were your stipulation,' said Charles, pausing at the wicket gate. 'May we come in?'

'You'd better introduce me to your lady friend first. We must observe the formalities, eh?'

She gave Edie a stony look and put her duster in her apron pocket, blushing as if ashamed to be caught so.

'Certainly. Edie Prior, this is Susan Leonard. Susan Leonard, Edie Prior.'

'Mother of his child,' said Susie, nodding formally.

Edie felt that she should offer an equivalent, but 'lover of his bed' did not seem calculated to delight her hostess.

'Lady Deverell's maid,' she mumbled instead.

'What happened to Sylvie?' asked Susie sharply of Charles.

He shrugged. 'You'll hear the gossip when your friends visit, no doubt.'

He made a movement towards the threshold, which Susie, with a sigh, ushered them over.

'How may I be of service?' asked Susie sourly.

Charles, who seemed to make a practice of ignoring her nuances of tone, said, 'A pot of tea would be ripping, Susan, if you would be so kind.'

She clattered fiercely about her range while Charles and Edie took seats at the kitchen table. Charlotte sat down in the chimney corner and played with a pair of kittens who had been sleeping there.

'Charlotte's looking well,' remarked Charles. 'She's a credit to you.'

'She is,' said Susie. 'It ain't no small thing to bring a child up alone.'

Edie observed that the cottage was well furnished and its copper and plate were of good quality, gleaming on the chimney breast and the dresser.

'She will be talking in no time, I suppose.'

'She says "mama" already,' said Susie proudly. 'Whether she'll ever be able to say the other thing, who can tell.'

'She knows me well enough,' said Charles, who had lifted her on to his knee once the kittens lost their appeal. 'Don't you, angel?'

The child reached up and stroked his cheek, still muted by her mouthful of sticky sweetness.

'She knows what you bring her.' Susie turned away from the range and gave him a sour look. 'I'll be warning her about that when the time comes. Beware of blokes bearing gifts. Either they want something from you, or there's a guilty conscience behind it.'

'You're going to bring my daughter up to be a cynic? Oh, I don't know if I approve of that.'

Edie looked away from the challenging shaft of eye contact that held the two former lovers locked, uncomfortable at what she witnessed. Susie might be well provided for, but she bore a whole nest of grudges, it was plain to see.

'So, what do you want from me today?' she said.

Charles put a roll of banknotes on the kitchen table.

'Get Charlotte something pretty. Take her to the fair at the weekend. Whatever you want.'

'Whatever I want? Maybe I'll spend it on gin.'

'Susan.' His voice was low, half reproach, half rebuke.

'What do you think?' Susie had turned to Edie, who started, having been absorbed by the wriggling of the child.

'I? Oh, it is your money. You must do as you see fit with it.'

'No, not about the money. About this – a visit by Lord Skirt-Chaser to the child who'll never inherit from him. How kind of you to call. You're his new piece, I take it.'

'I'm ...'

'Edith is my friend,' said Charles icily. 'She wants to hear our story. I'd like her to hear it from you.'

Susan set the tea tray on the table with a clatter.

'Oh, no,' she said, sitting down. 'You've been cruel enough in your time, but parading your new fancy piece in front of your old one and then asking her to humiliate herself into the bargain – no. It ain't fair and I won't do it.'

Charles nodded. 'I can understand that. In that case, would you object if I told her the story in your presence, so that you can interject if you feel I'm misrepresenting any aspect of it?'

'I'd rather not.'

232

Charles put a finger on the bankroll.

'All right,' she said. 'All right. But if I don't agree with what you say …'

'Of course you can put your side of things. Of course. That's why I came here. And to see you, of course.' This last to Charlotte, who was insisting on being bounced on his knee. 'Horsey needs a rest, darling. Down with you now.'

He put her on the floor, amidst much complaining, and took his teacup.

'The common perception, which I have done nothing to dispel, is that I seduced Susie here, got her pregnant and then abandoned her. I've never denied any of it, because the proofs are pretty clear in the shape of my lovely daughter and because my reputation isn't important. I'm rich, I'm male and I'm eligible, no matter what. For Susie, however, this isn't the case.'

'It's terrible, the stigma that's attached to the women who are abandoned by men who get off scot-free,' said Edie passionately, and Susie granted her a smile.

'Funny, but it's often the women who treat you the worst,' she said. 'I get my share of name-calling and whispering in the street, but they know that my little girl's a Deverell so they don't dare say anything to her. And they'd better not do, either.'

'I won't allow it,' said Charles. 'You must come to me if anything of the sort ever happens.'

'Oh, I will.'

'Susie here,' continued Charles, 'was a parlourmaid at the Hall when I came back from the war. Tom had preceded me by a year or so after the business with his leg but I stuck it out to the bitter end. Susie won't deny that I wasn't quite the man you see now when I came back to Deverell Hall.'

Susie hesitated, coloured, then shook her head.

'I suffered a kind of breakdown. Obviously it was hushed up, as these things are, but I was quite ill. Terrible nightmares, sleeplessness, a hopeless feeling of horror and despair – I won't dwell on it, because it's passed, but …'

He paused, swallowing, a haunted look flitting across his face before he composed it once more.

'I used to spend my afternoons sitting in the garden. I tried to read but I had no concentration. My sketching is poor, so I soon abandoned all such efforts. I took to sitting out there with strip cartoons. I became quite addicted to them. They were something my mind could encompass – one of very few things. Susie here was detailed to wait on me on those afternoons. She would go and fetch blankets, drinks, that sort of thing. It was easy enough work and I wasn't up to conversation so at first we spent our afternoons in silence. She was good and attentive. She knew when I needed things before I did. I appreciated her care.'

'I had no idea,' said Edie softly, her heart pierced by

this new knowledge of him. She found herself wishing she could have nursed him, tended to him, brought him back to life.

'Well, you know. It's all in the past now,' he said, trying an insouciant wave that didn't quite come off. 'This is accurate so far, would you say, Sue?'

She nodded. She looked dreadful, grey in the face, as if she might burst into tears at any minute. Charlotte had wandered off to the garden with one of the kittens, perhaps driven out by the sombre atmosphere.

'After a while, she started talking to me. Silly bits of conversation about the weather and so on. I was bothered by it at first and I'm afraid I probably wasn't very polite. But she persevered and eventually our relations became more cordial. Not long after that, things started to change. She would linger around me, tucking in the blanket, leaning over me, putting her hand on my thigh, that kind of thing. I almost wasn't aware of it at first, but it began to become obvious. She's a beautiful girl. I'm a man. I'd been wondering ...'

'You make me sound like ...'

'What do you want me to make you sound like? You did these things, Susie. You brought your banquet right to my table. I'd felt nothing ... no feelings of any kind ... for months, and now desire was back. I *was* still a man, after all. The first stirrings of recovery, and they had to come from my loins. It was inconvenient, but it was exciting. I didn't do anything to dissuade you, that much is true. I let you go on leaning over me and lifting your skirts over your ankles and pushing yourself against me until that day came and I had to grab hold of your waist. You remember that day?'

'Of course,' she whispered.

'That kiss,' he said. 'A drink of water in the desert.'

'Enough,' said Edie. 'I think I understand. You don't have to go on.'

'It was once,' said Charles, 'and it was wrong, but we both wanted it. I didn't seduce her. Tell her I didn't seduce you.'

'He didn't,' said Susie, and tears splashed from her eyes into the milky tea.

'I'm eternally grateful to you, though, love,' he said to her, putting his hand on hers. 'You gave my life back to me. When you told me you were pregnant, it was like a high-voltage electric shock. Everything that had been so blurred and confused was clear again. I had made a new life and I had to provide for it. I gave up the crosswords and took an interest in the day-to-day working of the estate again. And I learned to drive.' He smiled, as if to signal that any sympathy for him might now be put away.

'But it must have been so hard for you,' said Edie to Susie. 'When you found out about the baby.'

Susie shook her head, then nodded, then shook it again. She mopped her damp eyes with a handkerchief and drew a breath.

'I had hopes,' she said. 'I won't lie. I thought we could be married. Everyone knew Lord Deverell had married an actress – so why couldn't his son marry a parlourmaid?'

'He wouldn't allow it. I asked – no dice. It won't reflect well on me, but I was relieved. I was fond of her, but that was about it. It wasn't love. I'm sorry. If it was, I'd have told him to go to hell, gone to Gretna Green, whatever it took. But it wasn't love.'

'For me neither,' said Susie, as if she needed to assert her dignity. 'But it might have been. It might have grown.' She sighed. 'We'll never know.'

'I wouldn't have made you happy,' he asserted. 'It would have been a miserable yoke for us both.'

'But her.' Susie jerked a thumb in Edie's direction. 'You can make her happy, can you?'

Charles was quiet for a little while. Edie had never felt so horribly, sickeningly close to breaking down.

'I hope so,' he said. 'I mean to give it a bloody good try.'

'And your pa'll change his mind about marrying maids, will he?' said Susie scornfully.

'No, probably not,' he said. 'But that doesn't really apply in this case.'

He did not furnish Susie with any of the further details her open mouth seemed to show she was angling for, but stood up abruptly.

'Would you mind awfully if we took Charlotte out for the afternoon? Perhaps she'd like a splash in the lake?'

'Oh.' Susie looked around, putting a hand through her tumble of dark hair. 'I suppose so. I've enough to be doing, that's for sure.'

'She'll be back for tea,' he promised.

***

They drove, Charlotte excited and squealing between them, to the shores of a lake in the area. Edie sat by its shores while Charles, trousers rolled up to his knees, splashed in the shallows with his toddling daughter.

She had so much to think about now. Charles was not quite what she had thought him, and to have found this out on the very day that she already felt light-headed and fatally vulnerable from the morning spent in bed was devastating.

Watching him with Charlotte was like inviting the destruction of her heart. Pang after pang assaulted her senses, every time he laughed, every time he teased, every time a look of pensive affection passed over his face.

Please don't let me be in love with him.

But she felt quite strongly that her plea was too late. Her treacherous mind kept whispering to her. *That could be our child; I could be his wife; this could be our garden.*

She stood up, needing solitude so urgently that she ran to the shelter of some nearby trees, leant against the bark of one and put her hands to her face, sobbing out the multifaceted emotions of her day.

She only stopped when she heard him call for her, his shouts accompanied by little childish imitations. She dried her face, wiped her nose and set a course back to the shores of the lake, where she smiled at Charlotte and took her in her arms in order to avoid meeting Charles's eyes.

'Have you been crying?' he asked curiously, opening the car door for her. 'Where did you go?'

'Just the sun,' she said vaguely, putting Charlotte down on the seat beside her. 'So strong – hurt my eyes, you know.'

They drove back to Kingsreach and left Charlotte, after many farewells and tears and cuddles, with her mother.

***

'She's taken a shine to you,' said Charles, setting off again for the Hall.

'She's a little dear,' said Edie, her voice catching again. Why couldn't she seem to moderate her feelings today? 'Poor little darling.'

'Now look, there's nothing poor about Charlotte. She's the best provided for child in Kingsreach. And her mother doesn't go short of attention either. She has suitors by the dozen – she's a beautiful woman and plenty of men want to play stepfather to a Deverell child. They know they'll be set up for life. Don't go wasting your pity where it isn't needed.'

'She's hurt. You hurt her.'

Charles reached over to squeeze her knee.

'I never intended to,' he said. 'I had a reputation, which she knew of – and, before the war, it was well-deserved. But I'm not that man now.'

'Except where I'm concerned.'

'Everything's different where you're concerned, Edie. All bets are off.'

'You sound as if you see a future in this.'

He looked startled.

'Well, I do,' he said, as if it were self-evident. 'Don't you?'

'I …' She shook her head, looking away from him, not wanting to see what lay behind the wall of suave reserve she had broken down. This was impossible, utterly impossible. Her mother's stepson, the man she had confessed to loving. It did not fit into her design at all.

But she did not want to talk about that, not today. Tomorrow, when everyone was back and Deverell Hall fell into its routine, there was time enough to fret. Today was a holiday from all that.

* * *

She scurried back into the house through a side door, leaving Charles to park the car. In her East Wing bedroom, she threw herself back on the bed and stared

240

raptly at the ceiling. Now she had a moment to herself to contemplate how her post-virginal state felt, and she meant to use it to the full.

She was an experienced woman. It did not feel as different as she had expected it to, apart from the obvious physical side-effects between her thighs. The tenderness seemed to spread through her body, infecting her with a tremulous vulnerability that she must make sure Charles never saw. Charles, her deflowerer, the man who had taken her across that bridge – now there would always be a bond between them. She simultaneously thrilled at and recoiled from the idea. It was all so complicated, and yet it was so dangerously addictive – she could see that now. To fall once was to keep falling; there was no end to it.

Even the sound of his boots on the gravel far below made her heart speed up and her stomach convulse.

Damn it, Edie Crossland, you can't fall in love with him, you simply can't. It's your body playing tricks on you, making you think that, because he's had you once, you want him always. It's a biological ploy, Edie, that's all.

However much sense she tried to talk into her nerves, they would persist in tautening and bursting into fountains of excitement every two minutes, so she gave up trying to be calm and fell into a glorious reliving of the morning's activities.

She was still trying to remember the exact sensation of him upon her when he entered the room, laughing to find her laid out on the bed with her arms up and her cheek to the pillow.

'I've forgotten what I came say to you now,' he said in a low voice, coming to sit on the bed beside her, his hand drifting over her light cotton blouse.

'Words,' she said, still blissfully abstracted, arching her spine slightly to encourage his touch. 'Mmm.'

'Don't make me take you in this mean little room when we have the entire Hall at our disposal,' he said. 'Come on, get up. You need to dress for dinner.'

'What?'

Edie forced herself into an upright position and blinked at her lover.

'An intimate dinner, my love: just you, me, Tom and Giles. The servants have their instructions – we are to be attended to by only you and footman Giles. Except you won't be serving us. You will be our honoured guests. Do you see?'

'I ... don't think I do. The servants ...?'

'They'll be safely downstairs. Giles will bring all the dishes up.'

'But if the servants are guests, who is going to be the ...?'

'Servants? Darling, Tom and I have fought in the trenches. We don't need to be waited on hand and foot. We can fend for ourselves, you know.'

'Won't they think it odd?'

'"They"?'

'The servants.'

'They aren't paid to question what we do, Edie. They might gossip but they can't take their gossip out of the Hall. And do you care about a bit of gossip, anyway? You are above that.'

'I'm not,' she said. 'I'm one of them.'

'No, you aren't,' he insisted. 'You're mine. That puts you in an entirely different position.'

'I am not yours,' she said hotly, but he put a finger to her lips and shook his head.

'Don't argue with me, Edie. Whether you know it yet or not, you are. Now come on downstairs and we'll find you something suitable for cocktails.'

Chapter Nine

She almost ran back up the back stairs when he led her into Lady Deverell's chambers.

'I can't,' she whispered in a panic, but he pulled her onwards.

'Yes, you can. You're about her size and shape. Her gowns will fit you like gloves. Come into her dressing room and I'll choose one for you.'

'I can't,' she repeated, even more urgently, but they were in the sumptuously filled closet before she even finished speaking.

'You can. I'll be your maid. I'll dress you. On the strict condition that I can undress you again later.'

'Charles –' She was flustered, but he was so resolute that she ceased trying to move him and stood like a mannequin in the centre of the room while he cast his eye over racks and racks of gorgeous evening gowns.

'I don't think black,' he said, rejecting a jet-beaded number in midnight lace. 'A fresh little rosebud like you doesn't wear it well. And white isn't appropriate any more, is it, my dear?'

He turned and gave her a wicked smile. Her cheeks flamed.

'We can't,' she said, in a final attempt to steer his course away from her mother's wardrobe. 'What if I spoil the gown? What if we are found out?'

'That day will come eventually,' he said equably.

The words terrified her. This was all galloping away from her, much too fast.

'Don't,' she muttered.

'Don't what? Prepare for the inevitable?' He turned back to the rail, fingering exquisite gowns whose price tags would pay for a year of good dinners for her friends in Holborn. 'Now this –' he said, taking a dress of a peacock-blue silk with a chiffon train attached to the shoulders. At the embonpoint, sapphires and diamonds glittered in an eye-catching knot and the skirt was overlaid with glittering lace, tiny seed pearls sewn into the pattern.

'It's beautiful. I haven't seen her wear it.'

'It suits the shade of your hair.' He held it up to her. 'I'm sure it will fit you. Come on. Take off those drab parlourmaid's-day-out things and let's see you in your full glory. Not that you need any clothes for that.'

'Stop it. Look, I'm really not sure about this ...'

'I am. Slice a bit off my certainty and use it for yourself, if you like. Chop chop, get those buttons undone now.'

Edie's fingers fumbled but she undid the blouse and then the hobble skirt, relieved to be out of it, for its material was too thick for the summer heat and it had made a chafing band around her waist.

'That dreary underwear can go too,' said Charles lightly, already ransacking the drawers for corsets and silk stockings. 'What are you waiting for?'

She knew he had seen it all before, but she still blushed to denude herself entirely before him. When he turned around, holding a pile of impossibly frilly wisps of material, he smiled like a thirsty man who has caught sight of an oasis.

Swallowing first, he said, 'That's the girl. Now, I'm going to put these on you.'

'I can't wear her underthings. Surely it's not ... quite ... well, you know ...'

'They'll be washed,' he said offhandedly. 'I'll put them in the laundry hamper.'

'Not today,' exclaimed Edie. 'The servants!'

He laughed wholeheartedly at that. 'Oh, you sound like your dear mama sometimes, you know.'

'You're not to tease me about it,' she said, sticking out a rebellious lower lip. 'It isn't fair.'

'All right. I'm sorry. God, I could have you right here and now, you gorgeous little puzzle. But I'm going to make myself wait. Going to force myself. Dinner will be all the more piquant for it.'

246

Edie, tired of being naked, urged him to make a start. 'Can I at least put some drawers on?'

'I suppose so,' he said dolefully, handing over a frothy, frilly pair in black lace. Edie had never worn such an article and she felt peculiarly exotic as the lace tickled at her skin and quivered over her bottom.

Charles seemed fascinated by it too, laying his palm over her cheeks and cupping them, then stroking the flounce-covered curves. He moved his hand lower until his skin connected with the backs of her thighs, then his fingers massaged the soft, vulnerable skin at the very top, right by the elasticated border of the drawers.

Edie could feel the blood rushing around her body and a resulting sultry heaviness between her legs. He could let his fingers creep under the elastic, he could let them push between her lips …

But he did not.

Instead he helped her on with her silk stockings, nominally black but so sheer they were the faintest dark sheen on her pale legs.

Next came the corset, and he laced her in tightly, almost too tightly. She held on to the clothes rail for support, gasping and coughing.

'I'm not as slender as all that,' she protested. 'You'll cut me in half.'

'I'm sorry,' he said, loosening them a little. 'It does make your behind swell so deliciously. I got a little carried away. But look at yourself in the mirror. You're a perfect hourglass.'

She was, and she stared, unused to seeing herself on such voluptuous display. She never wore corsets ordinarily, believing, along with her father's women friends, that they were constricting to the health and happiness of females. But they certainly made one look astonishing.

The garment was made of sleek satin, and was black with red velvet swirls and red ribbons. It was cut necessarily low and did not cover the bust, so as not to show over the neckline of the gown. Edie's breasts were bared, their nipples swollen and red with excitement, while beneath them her waist was perfectly nipped in, giving her a wickedly wanton appearance.

'Gosh, I look like something from a brothel,' she said.

'Hmm,' said Charles approvingly. He stood at her shoulder and put his hands over her breasts, watching the pair of them in the mirror as he kissed her neck.

'Even more so now,' she breathed, lost in sensation, despairing of ever being fully dressed, but finding the despair not at all unpleasant.

'I want to keep you chained to the wall,' he said, kissing her ear. 'Dressed like this. My own little private slave girl, to have whenever and however I like. What would you think of that?'

'Oh, no,' she gasped, feeling she really ought to object

to the notion, but it was so appealing at that moment that she hadn't the heart. 'I couldn't ... do that ...'

'You'd have no choice. I'm going to do it later. I'm going to tie you to the bed. I promise you.'

'Charles.' But her legs couldn't support her and she had collapsed backwards into his chest, swimming in sensual rapture. The feel of his thumbs on her nipples undid her every resolve, as did his lips and teeth on her delicate skin. He could make her his whore. He could do it.

'Can't we stay here?' she whispered. 'I've no idea what I'll say to your brother. I can't face it, Charles.'

'Nonsense. He'll adore you. Come on.'

He gave her one last kiss, brisk and businesslike, then returned her to her feet, hands firmly on her shoulders.

'The gown,' he said, picking it up from the footstool over which it lay draped like a cold, blue waterfall. 'I'm putting it on you while I still have the will.'

She stepped into it, shivering at its delicious coolness as Charles guided it up her legs and over her hips. It was constructed so as to require no buttons or other fastenings and it clung snugly, holding her breasts in place better than any foundation garment could.

'Oh, I thought it might not fit but ...'

She could say no more, but gaped at her reflection. She looked so elegant, another woman in another world. This was not Edie the bluestocking with the bitten-down nails. This was, beyond a shadow of a doubt, the daughter of Ruby Redford.

'Bloody hell,' murmured Charles, his palms on her chiffon-covered upper arms. 'This is what she must have looked like twenty years ago.'

'Oh, take it off,' she cried impulsively. 'Your brother will guess my secret.'

'Well, I was rather thinking along the lines of telling him, actually.'

'What?'

'Why not?'

'Charles, no! Until I am able to tell her myself, it's terribly unfair to have a house full of people who know something she doesn't. Something with the power to ruin her.'

'As you wish,' he said, shrugging. 'But he'll notice the resemblance, I can promise you that.'

'So perhaps let me take it off? Wear something plainer, less … her.'

'No,' he said. 'That dress was made for you.'

'But it wasn't.'

'But it should have been. Come into the bedroom. I know just the necklace to wear with it.'

'I feel like a thief,' she said shakily, glorying, despite her reservations, in the way the skirt whispered around her as she walked. She also felt like a goddess. A thief-goddess – was there one?

'You don't look like one,' remarked Charles, glancing up from Lady Deverell's jewellery box. 'I don't think Fagin would accept you into his gang wearing *that*. Here, this is the one.'

Between his fingers diamonds glittered.

Edie put her hands to her throat, suddenly afraid.

'It's too much, Charles,' she said. 'I can't.'

'You can. Turn around.'

She hesitated.

'Turn around,' he repeated, with soft but unyielding pressure.

She obeyed, shuddering at the weight of them. They seemed to imprint themselves into her skin in their setting of loops and teardrops and she wondered how any lady of fashion could forget she was wearing them. The point, presumably, was to be constantly aware of her value.

It struck Edie, quite suddenly, as a little disturbing – a display intended to reflect glory on the man who kept one, who bought one the diamonds. They felt like a collar.

'Lord Deverell gave these to her?' she asked, fingering them.

'A wedding gift,' replied Charles, fastening the clasp.

'Why did she marry him?'

Charles laughed. 'I think the answer is upon you, sweet one.'

'I cannot believe that she is so mercenary.'

'You do not want to believe it.'

'No,' Edie agreed, her voice low. 'No, I don't.'

'What size shoe do you wear?'

'A five.'

'So does she. Let me find you some slippers.'

'Charles,' she said, stopping him en route to the dressing room.

He turned around, waiting for her question.

'Do you hate her so much?'

His cheeks flamed and he gazed at her almost abstractedly, as if it were not really her that he saw.

'I'm jealous of her,' he said. 'I suppose that's it. And angry at her.'

Edie waited for him to say more, but he did not, ducking instead into the dressing room and returning with a pair of dark-blue satin slippers.

'Put these on,' he said blandly, 'and we'll go. Tom will be waiting for us. I ought to do something with your hair, but I'm no coiffeur. I can brush it and pin it, but no more. It'll have to do. Put a feather in it or something.'

He pinned a decorative jewel-clipped peacock feather into her neat housemaid's bun and took her arm.

'Now, shall we?'

'I don't know,' she said, pleading for respite with her eyes. 'I feel that this is wrong. I'm terribly nervous of dining with your brother and his ... friend.'

'I've told you. You've nothing to fear from Tom.'

He put his arm around her waist and compelled her towards the door.

'What if Giles talks?'

'Do you think Giles wants the details of his real relationship with Tom uncovered?'

'No, but all the same ...'

'But all the same nothing,' said Charles resolutely. 'We're taking cocktails in the Blue Drawing Room. Giles will do the honours. He mixes a sensational highball.'

'How long have you known?' asked Edie, tripping down the stairs on Charles's arm. 'About Sir Thomas, I mean. And Giles.'

'Ages. Before the end of the war. They were in the same unit, you know, at Wipers.'

'Ypres?'

'Yes, yes, Ypres.'

'I see. Were you there?'

'Yes. He left after getting his leg shot to pieces at the Somme. I stayed out there until '18.'

'You were lucky to survive.'

'I don't need you to tell me that.'

'No, of course. I'm sorry.'

'When Tom was invalided out, he asked me to look after Giles for him. I kept an eye out for him for the next two years, made sure he was never to the fore of the front line. So you see, you have nothing to fear from Giles. Nothing whatsoever. He's absolutely to be trusted.'

'Yes.' Edie felt sobered and foolish, trying once more to imagine what these men had suffered during the horror of war. She had heard stories, mainly from her friend Patrick McCullen, for few of her father's circle had been anywhere near the trenches. Patrick himself had gone to sea, but he had lost many of his boyhood pals to that barbed-wired patch of hell, and been told the brutal truth of things by those that survived. 'I do see that.'

'Good.'

* * *

They halted before the drawing room door, Charles putting a hand on Edie's shoulder and sweeping a gaze of approval from her crown to her toes.

'They'll wonder whom I've invited,' he murmured, pulling her in for a kiss.

Edie, too nervous of being seen by a stray member of staff, wriggled out of his embrace.

'Let's go in,' she suggested.

She tried to keep a step or two behind Charles but he steered her forwards on his arm, towards the two dinner-jacketed men sitting at the far end of the room beneath an astonishingly huge depiction of a hunt.

Sir Thomas stood immediately and made a formal bow, Giles scrambling up in his wake and copying him.

'May I present Miss Prior?' drawled Charles.

'I say, it's Edie, the new girl,' said Giles, but he was silenced by uncompromising glares from both Deverell brothers.

'Miss Prior,' repeated Charles. 'Meet Mr Salter, Sir Thomas Deverell.'

'Oh, I do beg your pardon,' mumbled Giles, shame-faced. 'How do you do, Miss Prior?'

Sir Thomas echoed the greeting, adding a 'Charmed, I'm sure.'

Edie allowed each man to kiss her fingers, horribly aware of how they tried not to stare. It was clear that they were noting the resemblance between her and Lady Deverell.

'What a beautiful gown,' said Thomas faintly, backing away towards the drinks cabinet. 'What would you like to drink?'

'Whiskey sour for me,' said Charles. 'Edie?'

'Oh, just … I don't know. Something with orange juice, perhaps?'

'A screwdriver?'

'Lovely.'

She sat beside Charles on a deep leather sofa, oppo-site the other pair of lovers, sipping at the cocktail Sir Thomas had handed her.

'Do you like Dublin Bay prawns, Miss Prior?' asked Sir Thomas. 'I believe a fresh catch was delivered this morning.'

'I hardly know,' she said. 'I don't eat much fish as a rule.'

The heaviness of the atmosphere pressed like a weight against Edie's chest. A mass of unasked questions and unspoken assumptions thickened the air into an awkward soup.

Charles broke the silence, throwing back the last of his cocktail and replacing his glass on a solid mahogany occasional table.

'Shall we speak freely?' he said. 'Miss Prior and I are both aware of the nature of your relations, and I daresay you could hazard an accurate enough guess as to the state of ours. Let us be a duet of respectable married couples for the evening, shall we? Or, preferably, bohemian lovers who have run away to Italy or somewhere of that kind.'

'Suits me,' said Giles, taking one of Sir Thomas's hands and squeezing it. 'It's so tiring, all the bloody secrecy – pardon my French, Miss Prior.'

'It must be,' she said sympathetically. 'And do call me Edie.'

'How long has this little *tendresse* been going on?' asked Thomas of his brother. 'I did think something was in the wind, but did not care enough to enquire.'

'Edie and I have an understanding,' said Charles, getting up to mix himself another cocktail.

'Oh, don't say that, it makes me sound like a –'

Edie stopped short. What did it make her sound like?

Somebody bought and paid for, somebody no better than she should be. Was that not, after all, what she was?

'I don't mean to insult you, my love,' he said, returning with his second cocktail and lighting up a cigarette. 'The understanding is that you tolerate my attentions because you're an angel. And I give them because I can't help myself. That's right, isn't it?'

He gave her a smouldering glance to match the glowing end of his cigarette.

'Something like that, perhaps,' she admitted. 'But I'd make a very poor angel.'

'Your hair's like a halo,' said Giles gallantly. 'Such a colour. It's just like –'

Sir Thomas patted his hand rather sharply, interrupting him.

'Oh, don't worry,' said Charles. 'Mere mention of Lady Deverell isn't enough to induce a choleric fit any more. I won't say I've accepted her as papa's wife quite yet, but I have other concerns with which to occupy myself now.'

'Your objection to her was always more about having your nose put out of joint, anyway,' said Thomas with an edge of malice.

'Shut up, Tom.'

'Well, it's true, isn't it?'

'Talk about lousy timing,' said Charles with a sigh. 'I get back from the Front with a broken head and an infected graze wound and instead of parental sympathy and attention I'm left to my own devices while papa wines and dines actresses about town.'

'Poor ickle Charley,' said Thomas.

'Did you not hear me when I told you to shut up?' Charles's words, though aggressive in themselves, were spoken with a weariness that took out much of the sting.

'Well, I think Ruby Redford is good for pa,' said Thomas, smiling slightly at the shaking of Charles's head. 'You've forgotten how he was after mama died. You were busy gadding about town, I know, but for those of us who stayed here at the Hall … well. He needed female company. He pined for it.'

'There's female company and there's female company, Tom. Why couldn't he have kept her in a little place in St John's Wood, like any sane man would?'

Edie inhaled sharply.

'Perhaps she had more pride than to accept such an arrangement,' she said.

'Yes, I daresay that was it. Pride. She had too much and pa didn't have any.'

'Perhaps you might try living her life before you condemn her.'

'Yes, Edie, yes,' he said, his cheeks flushed as he turned to her. 'And perhaps you might try living mine.'

'I can't think of too many people who wouldn't kill to swap places with you, actually, Charles,' she said.

'Damn them to hell if they would,' he said. 'Damn them if they'd kill. I've had my fill of killing.'

Dinner was a repressed affair, too much mannered passing of salt cellars and offers to pour wine, when what really needed pouring was oil on to the troubled waters. Edie felt ridiculous in the gown, hardly able to connect with her own self and thoughts. She certainly had not inherited her mother's easy talent for slipping into alternative identities, even if she was closer, in her own life, to a lady than to a parlourmaid.

'I suppose we can't make Edie go out while the gentlemen remain for brandy,' remarked Charles, giving her a languid flicker of a glance. He had barely spoken to her since the little spat over cocktails. 'So you'll have to tolerate the cigarette smoke and brandy. Perhaps we'll have to tone down the off-colour anecdotes, eh, chaps?'

Giles laughed but Tom looked exasperated.

'I think perhaps both of you should leave the room,' he said. 'And talk to each other.'

'Oh, do you? Well, then, I'm taking the brandy with me.'

He picked up the decanter and stalked out towards the terrace.

Edie, tempted for a moment not to follow him in this mood, looked at the other two men, as if begging them for their advice.

'He's a spoiled child,' said Tom. 'Let him sulk.'

'You don't half look like her,' blurted Giles suddenly. 'In that get-up. Lady Deverell, I mean.'

'Giles …' demurred Tom.

'I, er …' Not knowing how to respond, Edie got up and swept away after Charles. At least, she intended to sweep, but she tripped on the hem of the gown and ended up staggering.

As she put her hand on the door, she heard Tom castigating his lover in a low tone, saying something about being more tactful. Of course, they would think that Charles's relationship with her was some sort of obscure revenge against Lady Deverell. And why would they not, everything being as messy and complicated as it was?

He had put the decanter on the balustrade beside him. He did not turn around to greet Edie but remained in morose silence, gazing out at the darkened park and woods beyond.

'Look,' said Edie. 'I didn't mean to make light of your experiences at war. That was the last thing I would ever intend to do. I just think – and I'm clearly not alone – you should get over this bitterness you have towards my … towards *her*. It's futile.'

He turned his face to her as she came alongside him.

'They think this is about revenge,' he said. 'I should have realised they would.'

'Isn't it then?'

'Edie,' he said, sounding anguished. 'If only it could be that simple. If only.'

'That was what you wanted?'

'At first. I admit it. I thought it would make me feel better.'

'You callous bastard.' Edie flared up with rage.

'Yes, yes, I know. You looked so like her, like a younger, fresher, innocent version of her, and I knew it would wound her ego to see that she'd been put aside for you.'

'It wounded more than her ego. She loves you. And I was to be a pawn in a twisted game. Well, thank you very much.'

Charles unstoppered the decanter and took a swig directly from the Waterford crystal neck.

'You can hate me if you like, but it won't come close to how much I hate myself. I hate myself and now I love you and it's too much, too much, much too fucking much.'

He laid his head on the flat stone of the balustrade and covered his ears with his hands.

'And you're her daughter,' he howled, muffled but still perfectly audible. 'Dear God, help me.'

Edie, all her rage dissipated by his frank distress, put her hand on his back and rubbed it.

'You really think you love me?' she whispered.

He raised his head at that, and his eyes were bleary and a little bloodshot.

'I know it,' he said. 'It's the only thing I *do* know. You needn't think you can make me give you up. I can give up anything else, but you have bagged me like a bloody grouse. The bullet's in me, Edie, and it won't come out.'

'I'm sorry,' she said, floundering.

'Sorry, are you? Then get it out of me, Edie. Get the bullet out. Take it out. Do whatever you have to.'

'I can't,' she said, alarmed now at his vehemence and in no doubt as to his sincerity.

He laughed, a little wildly.

'In that case,' he said, taking her wrist. 'You'd better come with me.'

He dragged her, brandy in the other hand, back through the dining room where Giles and Tom were sitting close to one another and smoking cigars.

They looked up and Tom said, 'I say, Charlie,' but they were out of the room before his remonstrance could be made more explicit.

***

Edie whirled in her lover's wake along deserted corridors and up the stairs to the East Wing bedrooms.

'Charles, you're frightening me. Slow down,' she entreated, but he seemed not to have heard, opening the door to his bedroom and propelling her inside with a force that almost had her falling on to the floor.

She managed instead to stumble to the bed.

He stood over her, shadowing her, when she twisted herself around to face him.

'Take off the dress,' he whispered.

262

'Charles, I don't think we ought ...'

'Take it off,' he said with more volume.

Despite feeling cold with fear, Edie sat up and tried to maintain a cool, level demeanour.

'Not until you calm down,' she said. 'I'm not doing anything for you until then.'

He inhaled deeply and stared at the ceiling for a minute.

When he looked down, the breath released, he said in a softer tone, 'All right. All right. I'm calm. Now take off the dress.'

She put a hand to the diamonds at her throat, still watching him as a stoat might watch a snake.

'You won't hurt me,' she said, enquiring.

'Only if you want me to.'

She shook her head, unable to comprehend what he might mean by that.

'You're still wearing that dress.'

She stood on shaky legs and began to lower it down her arms. Charles watched her intently, every bit the glittering-eyed predator.

Once it lay in ripples of midnight by her feet, he took a step forward and she made an instinctive retreat, falling back on the bed in her haste.

'I said I'd make you love me.'

She looked up into his darkened face. He did not know how she felt. Well, that was one saving grace, perhaps.

'You can't make a person ...' she whispered, conscious of her exposure in this expensive but revealing underwear.

'Perhaps not, but I can make you want me. The distance between wanting and love isn't that far.'

He bent low over her until their lips were close enough to touch. She felt his breath and expected to be kissed, shutting her eyes in readiness.

But instead he spoke. 'You are going to beg for me,' he said.

Then he stood straight again and disappeared into his dressing room.

Edie, heart racing, legs like water, could do no more than wait for him.

When he returned, he held two lengths of plaited, tasselled cord, such as one might use for a bell pull, golden in colour.

'You don't mean to –?'

'Yes, I do. Lie down. Further up the bed. Put your head on the pillow.'

Edie did not register the commands, staring instead at the way he ran the cord through his fingers, caressingly.

'Look, I'm not going to do anything you won't like,' he said, with a touch of impatience. 'Just do as I say. You will be rewarded, trust me.'

Trust him?

Would that be a mistake? Edie could not decide. In the meantime, she did as he asked and laid herself down

264

on her back, looking up at the canopy of the bed, seeing Charles from the corner of her eye as he knelt at the side of the bed and began wrapping one of the cords around the left-hand post.

When it was securely knotted, he crossed to the other side and repeated the procedure there.

'Now,' he said softly, holding the right rope in his hand. 'Give me your wrist.'

'You don't need to tie me.'

'No, I don't need to. I want to. Give it to me.'

'What are you going to do to me?'

'I've told you. Nothing you won't enjoy. You don't trust me, do you?'

She caught a breath.

'I'm not sure,' she said.

'You should. I want you to know, to learn, that you can. I promise you nothing but pleasure. I am, despite what anybody says, a man of my word.'

She knew enough of him to feel that he spoke sincerely, and she offered her hand, which he took, and bound the wrist just tightly enough to make her feel tied without digging in uncomfortably. When both wrists were restrained in this manner, she tugged at the cords, assessing their strength. He had tied them well and she would not be able to release herself without his help.

'How's that, poor, helpless Edie?' he asked, smiling down at her. The flash of his teeth made her feel momentarily afraid, but when he reached out to stroke her brow she calmed.

'Why do you want to do this?' she asked.

'Because you won't keep still. I need to keep you still, to make you stay and listen and understand me. I don't want you running away. You're too good at that.'

She felt the justice of his remark. An impulse to run coursed through her at that very moment. It was a constant motif in her emotions.

'Now, your ankles,' he muttered, making his way back to the dressing room.

Edie tried to pull herself upright but she couldn't. All she was capable of was lying there, waiting for him to return.

He tied her feet as he had her hands, leaving her spread-eagled as a starfish. At least the frilly lace drawers preserved some semblance of modesty between her splayed thighs, but her breasts were uncovered and she had no chance of concealing the state of her nipples. Above them, lying like dead weights on her collarbone, were the diamonds.

'Now then,' said Charles, taking off his shoes. 'I have you where I want you at last. Don't move, will you?'

He laughed and knelt down on the bed, between her spread legs.

'Tell me when you want me to stop,' he whispered, then he braced himself above her and kissed her long and deeply, his tongue claiming her mouth. She wanted to clasp her arms around his neck, put her fingers in his hair, but she could do nothing but accept what he chose to give her.

His hands pressed against the sides of her head, holding it just as captive as the rest of her body. She felt the expensive cloth of his dinner jacket brush and scrape her nipples, while his pelvis lay just above hers, their hipbones occasionally grinding together, faster and harder as the kiss deepened.

By the time he released her mouth, her lips were stinging and her chin sore, but she could have taken more, she could have drowned inside the sensations and lost consciousness. She was no longer equipped to resist the effect he had on her. If there had been a fight or a war or anything of that sort, it was long lost.

He moved to her neck, laying little kisses as light as breaths beneath her earlobes. He lingered especially in the places where the sensitivity of her skin made her shiver. She knew where his hands were heading and it was a kind of relief when his palms cupped her breasts and gently kneaded them.

The sense of having no way of getting him off her was unsettling at first and she struggled in her bonds. The unfamiliarity soon wore off, though, and she found, to her surprise, that the panic was replaced by exhilaration. She arched her spine and tried to kick her legs, because the feeling of captivity was exciting and different, an emotional boundary to be tested.

He laughed softly into her shoulder, which his itinerary of kisses had now reached.

'You can't free yourself,' he reminded her.

She felt her nipples bloom beneath the pads of his thumbs, which swept tingles across their rosy surface.

'I know,' she replied in a whisper.

'Do you want to?'

He paused in his ministrations, looking her seriously in the eye.

She shook her head.

'Not yet.'

'Good.'

He lowered his mouth over the obscenely swollen buds and kissed each in turn, using his tongue to bathe them in warmth. It was almost too much and her breath hitched chaotically as she wrestled with the cords.

'Oh, please,' she whispered, soaked in the sensation. The frilly drawers felt teasing and ticklish against her damp and swelling core.

Charles, his hands on her hips, raised his head from her shining wet nipple and cocked an eyebrow.

'Please?' he enquired.

She couldn't voice her desires, though, and she turned her face away.

'Don't be shy,' he said. When he received no answer,

he resumed his feasting on her breasts, holding her hips more firmly when she attempted to wriggle aside.

'I could do this all night, you know,' he said, surfacing again after a few more minutes.

Edie, deep in an agony of desire, was not pleased to hear it.

'I'm sure you could,' she gasped. 'But please don't.'

'No?' He gave one nipple a delicate little lick.

'Oh,' she moaned.

'Well, perhaps it is time to move on,' he said consideringly. He dashed her hopes by sucking on the other nipple. 'Or perhaps not.'

All she could do was squirm, and she made the most of it, trying to throw him off course by undulating beneath him. It did not work. He was sealed on like a limpet, or a vampire bat draining her life blood.

'All right,' he said, rising with a triumphant laugh. 'I said I'd make you beg. This is just the start, my love.'

He took off his jacket and threw it across the room, then loosened his bow tie and unbuttoned his collar.

'It was starting to feel more than a little tight,' he said. 'I like to be unrestrained. How about you? Oh. I forgot.' His grin was demonic on the way back down to her poor oversensitised nipples for one final lap.

With his jacket gone, Edie was able to absorb and enjoy Charles's body heat through the fine cotton of his shirt. She thought he was hotter than fever and might burn her, but perhaps it was her own delirium giving this impression.

When would he …? Oh, yes.

The elastic waistband of the drawers was breached, long fingers sliding inside.

'I can't pull these down,' he said. 'Not with your legs tied like that. But I can work around it.'

His fingers came out again, then she felt his knuckles pressing at the gusset. He must feel the warmth and wetness seeping through. She tried to dismiss the mortifying knowledge, but she shut her eyes all the same in an effort to defend herself from the worst of the embarrassment.

He spared her his remarks on the subject, using his mouth to better effect by planting kisses along the top of the waistband, where a tiny strip of bare flesh was exposed between her corset and drawers. She squealed when the tip of his tongue invaded her navel, causing a lightning bolt of sensation to flash directly to her core.

At the same time, he pressed his knuckles harder, finding the outline of her lips and the hungry bud between them before commencing a slow rubbing.

The whispery-thin fabric of the drawers slipped and slid along with his manipulations. Delicate as the lace was, there was still a tiny drag against her vulnerable flesh that made it both more pleasurable and at times a little painful.

She couldn't strain her legs against the cords now if she tried. They were losing their force, lapsing into trembling incapacity. Everything of her was concentrated between her legs, while her stomach was tight, fighting against the slow unravelling of her self-control.

'Tell me,' said Charles, coming back up to kiss her nipples again. 'When you're close.'

She knew it wouldn't be long but she didn't want to tell him so. Little spasms jolted through her, directed downwards, preparing her against being overwhelmed.

It was near, so near now, and the drawers were drenched, soaking through to Charles's fingers.

'You must be close,' he said. 'Don't you dare forget to tell me. Don't you dare, Edie.'

Her helplessness, together with his lordly tone, sparked rebellion. She would not tell him. She would take her pleasure without giving him the satisfaction of knowing it.

'No,' she said tightly.

He withdrew his fingers immediately and lifted his head to stare.

'What did you say?'

Her clit fluttered, wanting his touch back rather desperately. She ground her bottom against the mattress, trying to replicate the feeling of contact, but it was useless.

'You stopped,' she wailed.

'Yes, I stopped. You said no. Why?'

'I don't have to do as I'm told. I'm not your maid,'

she said, but it came out in wide-eyed gasps, not in the dignified manner she intended.

'No,' he said. 'You aren't. So you aren't enjoying this? I'm sorry. I'll untie you.'

'No,' she said. 'No, I don't mean ...'

His lips curved slowly upwards.

'What? What do you mean? Tell me.'

'Just ... can't we carry on? Just carry on?'

He laughed. 'Just carry on, you say. Well, I think you'll have to ask me more nicely than that.'

'Please ... do what you were doing. I did enjoy it.'

'And you'll tell me when that moment is near?'

'All right,' she huffed.

This time his fingers crept inside the saturated lacy fabric, found her parted lips and rubbed against the smoothness within.

She knew it couldn't be long. The fire, having cooled for an instant only, was building rapidly.

'Yes,' she said in a panic, fearing she might be too late.

'Yes?' he repeated, using his free hand to hold her face. 'Open your eyes. Look at me.'

She tried to toss her head away but his grip was fast and she almost wrenched her neck muscles. Reluctantly, just at the moment of climax, she forced her eyelids apart and saw his face, dimly, in a colourful blur, watching her as she spent on his fingers. He looked all-powerful, like a god.

She almost hated him for it, or herself, for letting this happen. But there was nothing to be done. He was able to bring her to this point so easily.

'I could have stopped you,' he said, bending to kiss her.

'You think so?' She wanted to wipe her mouth or mop her brow, but she could do neither.

'I could have taken my fingers away and made you wait. What would you have done then?'

'What *could* I have done?'

'Nothing.'

'I suppose you want me to believe you have some kind of control over me. You don't.'

He sighed and laid his head on her chest.

'Not control,' he said. 'Just honesty.'

'Honesty?'

'Come out from your hiding place and show me who you are. I want to be kind to you, that's all, so you'll be kind to me, instead of fighting me every inch of the way.'

'I think it's rather kind of me to let you tie me up, actually,' said Edie. 'I can't think of too many girls who would.'

He burrowed his head between her breasts and kissed the spot.

'That's true,' he conceded. 'There is hope for me yet.'

'I just don't see how this can be anything more than … what it is now. You play up all this love talk, but you don't mean it. You're the heir to this estate. You'll have to marry one day, and it'll probably have to be to an heiress with enough in the bank to keep this pile going. No?'

He raised his head, his eyes troubled.

'You sound like pa,' he said.

'I'm being realistic.'

'It doesn't suit you. I'd prefer it if you'd aim for romantic.'

'Romance is all flim-flam. A way of dressing up the fact that life for women is thankless drudgery.'

'Good God, Edie.'

'You can afford romance because you're a rich, handsome man.'

He was silent for a moment.

'I turn to romance because I've seen the alternative,' he said quietly, putting his head back down.

Momentary guilt splintered her heart. It was all very well to accuse him of being pampered and privileged but he had, after all, been to war and seen horrors from which she had been shielded. Perhaps, as he said, kindness was best.

'I'm sorry,' she said. 'I don't know why I'm being so argumentative. I think it's just a reflex, you know? Fear. Something of that sort.'

'You're hard work,' he said with a sigh. 'But I think you're worth it.'

'Thank you. Are you?'

'That's something you must judge for yourself,' he said, rearing up again. 'I'll give you a clue.'

Without warning, he was between her thighs again and this time he wrenched aside her drawers and put his face where they had been.

Edie inhaled sharply and tried to shuffle away but, of course, to no avail.

Charles' hot breath filled the space, steaming up her skin until it was damp. He kissed and licked her bud back to fullness, quickly reviving it from its previous enervation. She squirmed like fury, tugging at the bonds, desperate to save herself from this overload of sensation. Charles laughed and made enthusiastic noises, his voice sending vibrations through her from her core outwards.

'It's too much,' she gasped, but he held her thighs and feasted all the more.

She gave up her resistance and lay, bonelessly compliant, under his control. He parted her buttocks with eager hands and plunged deeper, pushing his tongue up inside her, his face impressing itself upon her most intimate places.

It felt shameful and so exposing but it built a tremendous tension inside her. It took longer this time, so soon after her first climax, but Charles was diligent and thorough and she knew that he would not stop until he had her thrashing and wailing, a prisoner of his tongue.

'Oh, I can't,' she whispered, 'I can't.'

But she could, and she did, and he was more ravenous than ever, robbing her of the orgasm as if he needed it for vital sustenance.

All the life was sapped from her and given to him, for he seemed more powerful and alive than ever, his eyes shining when he knelt up to grin down at her.

'Twice,' he said. 'But what's the magic number? The one in all the fairytales?'

'Oh, no, you can't …'

'I think I can,' he said. 'I think I will.'

The third orgasm was a weaker affair, but it was a miracle to Edie that she had it in her at all. Wherever it hid, though, Charles was sure to find it and tease it out. He knew every trick, every erogenous zone. He crooked his fingers up inside her and worked on one little spot, rubbing and stroking until she thought she would faint away.

'I can't fight you,' she said. 'I give up. Please. Truce. Pax. Whatever you want.'

He kissed her hairline, so gentle now. Her head was spinning and she was out in space somewhere, in a strange place between peace and sleep and perfect happiness.

'Whatever I want? That's a very wide remit,' he said.

'Hmm,' was all she could say, her eyes shut, her mind far away.

'I'll untie you now,' he said, 'and let you rest. But I haven't finished with you. Not yet.'

Edie's limbs trembled with each unknotting of the cords and she curled up into an exhausted ball, spooned by Charles, before drifting swiftly into a doze.

When she awoke, he wasn't there, and she sat up, disorientated and squinting around the unfamiliar room.

He stood by the window, sipping at the brandy he'd brought up from the terrace, looking out.

He had taken off his clothes and put on a bathrobe instead.

'Charles,' she said, and he turned around.

'I'm afraid I wore you out,' he said with a tender smile.

'I'm afraid so too,' she said. 'Gosh, my arms ache. I can barely move them.'

'Too much struggling,' he said. 'Next time you'll remember to just lie back and let me at you.'

'Next time?' A flutter of pleasurable fear.

'Of course. How are you feeling?'

He put down the brandy, came to sit beside her and put his palm to her forehead as if assessing her temperature.

'I'm not ill,' she said with a little laugh. 'I do feel as if I've had some kind of surgical procedure, though. A removal of some kind. Of my energy, perhaps.'

'I was hoping it might be your hard shell.'

She looked away, swallowing.

'I need that,' she said.

'I'll wear it down in the end.' He brought her lips back to his and kissed them. 'Now it's your turn,' he whispered.

'My turn for what?'

277

'Your turn to do whatever you like to me. Revenge.'

'Oh, I say.' Perhaps she hadn't lost every scrap of her energy after all. 'I could tie you up.'

'You could.'

He tugged at one of the cords, still attached to the bedpost.

'It's only fair,' she said, taking it from him. 'All right. I'm looking forward to this.'

'I'm regretting the offer already,' he said.

'Take off that robe. You're naked underneath, I take it?'

He demonstrated as much, shrugging the robe off and dropping it over the side of the bed.

'You certainly are.' Her eyes drank in his unclothed form, enjoying its lean perfection. 'Good. Now lie down. Just the way I did. Yes.'

He made his arms quite limp when she picked them up. They were heavier than she thought, but she was able to fasten the cord around his wrists without too much trouble. He was not, of course, putting up a fight. Had he chosen to resist her, she doubted there would have been much she could have done about it.

She had not expected to find him so attractive with his wrists tied. She stopped and contemplated him for a moment, enjoying the feeling that he was unable to stop her doing anything at all now.

He must trust her, she thought. Or was this a test? A dangerous one, if so.

'Do you like it?' she asked, stroking his cheek. 'Being tied?'

'So far,' he said. 'It's a new experience for me.'

'Is it?'

He nodded, swallowing. Something about this intelligence moved Edie more than she could say.

'You're a brave man,' she told him.

'Thanks.'

She paused to balance her emotions before tying his ankles. How hairy men's legs were. She had never really had cause to notice before, but she found herself fascinated by the dark down that covered his shins. She stroked it all the way to his ankles, where it thinned before disappearing. His feet were bare and rather soft. If she tickled his insole – oh, but that would be cruel.

All the same, she was tempted.

'Don't tickle,' he exclaimed, reading her mind.

She laughed.

'I was thinking about it.'

'I know. You looked quite diabolical for a minute there.'

She diverted her attention from his feet to the rest of his body. He was in a perfect X-shaped cross with his head lolling on one shoulder, eyes watchful. Looking further down, she could see that he was semi-hard and a little twitchy.

What could one do with that appendage? A great many things, probably.

But they could wait. First things first.

She turned her back to him and bent to kiss his ankle, just above the cord. From there, she proceeded all the way up his calf, very slowly. When she kissed the back of his knee, or as much of it as she could get at, she heard his breath grow heavier.

'Edie ...'

'Yes?'

'Faster, please.'

'I'll go at my own pace, thank you.'

The curve of her bottom brushed in this position against his groin area and she felt that it was hot and slightly damp. She gave a little wiggle, just to tease, then set to the lower portion of his other leg, repeating her earlier actions.

'Higher,' he begged.

'I could do this all day,' she said, feigning a return to the first leg, causing him to groan outright.

She turned to face him, smiling sympathetically. His brow was beaded and his face flushed. Power was rather nice, she reflected.

'You're doing very well,' she consoled, patting his thigh. 'You'll get your reward soon. But not yet.'

Her attentions turned to his inner thighs this time. She made her kisses deeper, pressing her tongue into the firm flesh, sometimes sucking and nipping as she came closer to his groin. His chaotic gasps and whimpers persuaded her that she was doing a good job of driving him wild, just as she intended.

She lingered a little longer than she had at first planned, purely to enjoy all the more the spectacle of her lover losing his habitual suavity in such an unabashed manner. He pulled the most extraordinary faces. They made her simultaneously crueller and more tender towards him. Was this how she made him feel?

'I will make you beg,' she said, but she spoke the words more self-consciously than she wished and then laughed at herself. 'Oh, dear.'

'I beg you,' he said. 'If that is what you want. I beg you.'

'What do you beg for?'

'Relief. You.'

'You beg for me?'

'Always.'

'Oh, Charlie.' She stroked his cheek, too touched to be able to continue in this cruel-mistress vein.

'I like it when you call me that. Say it again, won't you?'

'Charlie,' she said softly, then she kissed his lips. 'Poor misunderstood Charlie.'

'You think I'm misunderstood?'

'Perhaps.'

'You must tell me why. But perhaps –' he paused, glancing delicately down at his erection '– later.'

Taking pity on him, she took it in her hand, her grip loose enough to run her fingers up and down the shaft.

'Mmm, yes,' he whispered.

She crouched over him, drawn to his nipples, which looked fuller than she would expect. How would they taste? She circled them with her tongue, trying to avoid the rogue chest hairs that strayed into the area. They were little pips but so sweet she couldn't stop herself sucking at them. He seemed to appreciate this, but not when her absorption in the act caused her to neglect her handling of his manhood.

'You're killing me,' he claimed.

She looked up at him and laughed.

'Such a death,' she said.

'Have you ever wondered how a man would taste?' he prompted.

'Ah, now you are trying to take control. I thought you'd relinquished it to me, remember?'

She prodded his chest with a finger, but now he had made the suggestion, she had to admit she was curious. Perhaps she would indulge him in this. But only in her own time.

Instead, she fell to kissing and sucking at his neck while her wet parted lower lips ground against his helpless member, making it even harder than before.

'Jesus, Edie,' he gasped, which made her redouble her efforts.

She rubbed herself against his slick length, using it as a toy to bring her back to a state of panting desire. He wanted her to amuse herself with him and he was getting what he had bargained for.

She felt herself rise and fall in rhythm with his heaving chest, her breasts dangling over his pectoral muscles, their nipples brushing together.

If he had his arms free, she thought, he would grab her now and make her sit on him, taking him inside. But his arms were helpless and she could tease until he burst into flame, if she wanted.

She tensed her pelvic floor, testing it for soreness. It was still raw after her deflowering. She would not be able to take him in without discomfort.

Perhaps instead ...

'You think I should taste you?' she said, plunging her fingers into his disordered hair.

'Would you like that?' he panted.

'I don't know. I haven't tried it.'

'Well, don't let me stop you.'

'No. I won't. You couldn't anyway.'

Grinning up at him, she slid back down his body until she knelt upright between his spread thighs. She bent over his erection and breathed on it, slowly and gently, wondering if the little bead of white on its tip would have any flavour.

His answering moan was exquisite. She cupped his testicles in one reverent hand and gave them a gentle squeeze, which brought forth more little breathy moans.

Should she start at the top and move down or vice versa?

She decided to view the little white bead as the pinnacle and began a slow trail of kisses around the base of the stalk, enjoying its warmth and firmness against her lips.

She moved her mouth upwards in tiny increments. He rolled his hips and bucked underneath her, plainly urging her to make haste, but she patted his flank in reproof and kept to her own pace. A good explorer did not rush, she told herself, but took time to make a thorough inventory of her territory.

She tried to humour him with little darts of her tongue and light squeezes of his sac. She was halfway to her summit when he spoke in a strangled voice.

'You are torturing me, Edie.'

'Mmm,' was all she said, extending her tongue for a luscious lick around the perimeter of her target. For no reason that she could have articulated, she moved her fingers behind his testicles and pushed at the hot skin there. He almost shot in the air, momentarily dislodging her.

'Oh,' she said, astonished.

'That's ... good,' he whispered, his eyes shut after a rather dramatic roll.

'I must bear it in mind.'

She decided he had been teased enough, wrapping her lips around the tip and licking off that strange little pearl.

284

It did have a taste, salty and strong. She could not quite describe it, she thought, but perhaps more familiarity would lend the vocabulary she lacked.

He was trembling, she noticed, and his thighs were lightly sheened with perspiration. She felt in possession of the biggest and most ridiculous power on earth, bringing him to such subjection. This was why kingdoms fell and the greatest of men risked ruin. It had always seemed absurd to her but now she began to understand it.

She lowered her mouth, inch by inch, stopping at regular intervals to lick and suck at the newly enclosed flesh. It was rather comforting to do so, in a way, which surprised her. Down she went, further and further, until she was close to having all of him in her mouth. She couldn't quite manage it, though, which was a little disappointing. She wondered if it would disappoint him.

She kept him there for half a minute, sucking gently, then she released him entirely, kneeling up to look at his face.

It was in piteous disarray, his expression flickering from confusion to dismay to other emotions, never able to settle on one.

'Don't you like it?' he croaked.

'Oh, yes, it's lovely,' she said. 'Do you deserve it, though?'

'After everything I did for you!'

She laughed at his outrage and took pity.

'You do. But ... what should I do? Am I doing the right thing?'

He relaxed and smiled at her anxiety.

'Absolutely,' he said. 'Just keep doing what you were doing.'

'Until when?'

'You'll know when.'

She supposed she should take him at his word and returned to her mission, sucking happily and using her fingers to prod at that area that had caused him so much consternation before.

His pained rapture was so very gratifying that she did not lose one iota of motivation, even when her jaw began to ache and she started fearing that the mysterious 'when' might be a long time distant.

But, just as she was about to take her mouth from him to give her protesting mandibles some respite, the moment came. She felt him still for an instant, then begin to thrust in her mouth, his pelvis in a blur of motion. Before she understood what had passed, a slightly bitter liquid, the close cousin of that she had tasted earlier, spurted to the back of her throat, causing her to retreat with an exclamation of shock.

'Swallow it,' he shouted, as if he commanded her.

In her state of surprise and consternation, she did not hesitate to obey, and the liquid slid down her throat. Not entirely pleasant to taste, but certainly no poison either – this must be what had gone into the prophylactic before.

'You did not warn me,' she said, once she had finished grimacing.

He said nothing for a while, basking in the ebbing remains of his bliss.

When eventually he opened his eyes, he said, 'I assumed you would know. Oh.' He blinked and looked concerned. 'Have I disgusted you?'

She shook her head. 'Not disgusted. I just ... I daresay I am terribly naïve, but I didn't expect you to ... But please, don't fret on that account. Really. Don't look so crestfallen. Oh, dear.'

She kissed his lips, wondering if he tasted himself on her.

'I shall remember it for the future,' she whispered.

He brightened at that. 'The future? This is promising. Unless you mean the future with some dull husband in London. Is that what you mean?'

'Charles.'

The sadness in his tone took her aback. She untied his wrists and he wrapped his arms around her as she lay beside him on the bed.

'Well?' he sighed.

'I don't know what I meant,' she said. 'I don't know at all. I can't explain how I feel even to myself.'

'You might try,' he said, pulling her tighter and kissing

her forehead. 'Thank you, by the way, for being so utterly ravishingly marvellous.'

'Did I do it well?'

'You did it perfectly. Now tell me how you feel.'

'When you said no woman could go to bed with a man without falling for him, well, I thought, what nonsense. And I still do, actually. But I do seem to feel something for you. I don't think it's to do with going to bed with you. I think it's more to do with spending time with you and ... finding things out about you. Unexpected things.'

'I'm not the man you thought I was?'

'No.'

'And my exceptional prowess as a lover hasn't swayed you even slightly?'

She giggled and snuggled closer.

'You're not modest, are you? But you are ...' She broke off and sighed expressively. 'Yes, damn you, you are very good.'

'Damnably good,' he said. 'Yes, I like that as an endorsement. And you're probably right. Most men couldn't earn a woman's love by taking her to bed. But I'm not most men. I know how to give pleasure. I think that's rather a big point in my favour, don't you?'

'I don't know any other men to compare,' she said.

'That bloody chauffeur would like to change that,' said Charles with a sniff.

'Oh.'

'What?'

'I said I'd go to the village dance with him.'

'I forbid it.'

'Oh, Charles, of course you don't.' She sat up, frowning at him.

He frowned back, in double measure.

'I can't have you gallivanting with other men, Edie. I'll go mad with jealousy.'

'But you know it's you ...' She twisted her fingers, looking away from him.

'Do I?' He sat up beside her, his still tethered ankles straining at their bonds. 'What do I know it's me? Tell me. Say it.'

'I can't,' she whispered. 'Don't make me.'

He took hold of her upper arm and made her face him again, then cupped her cheek in one hand.

'I'm in love with you, Edie,' he said. 'I didn't think I knew what love was, but I do now.'

'You say that ...'

'I say it because I mean it.'

'But it's just not possible,' she cried, covering her face with her hands.

'It's more than possible, it's happening. It has us, Edie, don't you see? It has us and we can't shake it off. We can only go where it takes us.'

'I didn't want this,' she said, pushing her fists into her eyes. 'I don't know what to do about it.'

'You can stop this silly game with your mother. Tell her who you are. Tell her the moment she returns from London.'

'Oh, God, Charles, I can't. I'm scared.'

'You? You're brave, Edie. You're the bravest girl I ever met. Of course you can.'

'But it feels too soon, and if she rejects me ...'

'If she rejects you she's a cold-hearted bitch and you're better off without her. I'll stand with you, Edie. Whatever strength you need, I'll be here to give.'

'Really?' Through the tears she tried to gauge his expression. Could she rely on him, trust him to see her through this crisis? It seemed too much to hope, but she was well and truly hooked now, horribly and inconveniently in love with him and her foolish heart was starting to believe there might be some future to be had with him too.

'Really,' he said. 'I know how to fight and I'll fight for you, Edie whatever-your-name-is, to the last drop of my bad blue blood.'

'It's Crossland,' she said, half-laughing, half-crying. 'Edie Crossland.'

'Crossland,' he said with a nod of satisfaction. He took her hand in his and stroked the ring finger. 'Perhaps Deverell one day.'

'Oh, don't,' she said, trying to pull free without success. 'Don't tempt fate.'

'You believe in that, do you? Fate?'

'Not really.'

'Well, then.' He put her fingers to his lips and kissed them. 'You're exhausted, my girl. Untie my feet and let's get some sleep. But tomorrow ... Tomorrow there are serious discussions to be had.'

Chapter Ten

There was rain when Edie awoke. She slipped out of bed, looked back at Charles's peaceful sleeping face, and then gazed out of the window. It was early but the gardeners were about, hurrying along in their green gumboots, pushing their wheelbarrows with heads well down.

Soon Lord and Lady Deverell would be home and she would have to ... what? Could she really do it? Perhaps she should leave, get out of here and get the train back to London before Charles had even stirred from his bed. She could write a letter. It would be easier, kinder to all concerned.

But it would mean leaving Charles and never again sliding between those sheets with him, lying beside his warm male body, clasped in his arms. It was more than she could give up now.

She could, however, return to her room and avoid the 'serious discussion' he had mentioned last night. Yes.

She tiptoed past the bed and had one hand on the

door handle when she jumped at the sound of his voice, slurred and heavy with yawns.

'And just where do you think you're going?'

She turned and flattened her back against the door, her face warm with guilt.

'I don't know what time they'll be back. I thought I'd better –'

'It's the crack of dawn, girl. Come back to bed.'

It might be the last time.

She wavered, torn between her desires and her good sense.

'Are you going to make me come over there and get you?'

'I'm just worried in case ...'

He sat up and pushed the covers aside, his face a picture of wicked determination.

'All right, all right,' she said.

She climbed back into the bed and found herself straightaway wrestled onto her back and pinned down beneath him.

'You know there's no escape from me, don't you?' he said, all predatory teeth and glittering eyes. He was definitely awake now.

'So you say,' she said, but she was allowed to speak no more, her mouth given over to kisses.

The minute he was near her, she was lost again. Something in his scent, in the transmission of warmth from his skin to hers, sent her over a precipice into giddy addiction. To break it, she would have to get a long way away from him. But not now. Not while he pressed himself against her and whispered in her ear.

'I want to do things to you that aren't even legal,' he said, grinding his pelvis against her. 'If I could keep you here for the rest of the day, I would.'

She wrapped her leg around his hip, opening herself to him. Was she ready to take him again? The soreness had dulled and she was only aware of the lightest twinge now. If he wanted her …

'Oh, you'd like that, would you?' he teased, his lips on her earlobe. 'Well, I'll just have to do as much as I can while I can.'

He put his hand between their lower bodies, pushing two fingers gently inside her lips.

'How is it?' he whispered.

'Fine,' she whispered back.

He began rubbing and stroking, augmenting the sensation by kissing and nipping at her neck and shoulders, then moving down to her breasts.

He scarcely needed to do anything to make her want him, she thought. The merest touch made her flood with desire for more. She was like a magnet, helplessly driven to connect with him. *Opposites attract*.

She almost forgot about the French letter until he knelt up and retrieved one from the bedside table. How could she be so stupid? Did love make one lose one's mind? It certainly seemed that way.

When he drove into her she cried out with pleasure. The feeling of having him inside her was enough to override entirely any residual pain. She spread herself wide for him and pushed her bottom up to meet his plunging length. They were one being, fused at their roots, belonging that way.

They rocked back and forth, slowly at first, Charles taking care to stoke the fire he had laid with even strokes. Edie clung to his neck, covering his face with kisses and allowing him to cover hers in return. The languid pace allowed her to feel the stretching of her inner walls and enjoy the continuing work of his fingers on her bud. Step by step, she climbed towards her peak, but she wanted it to last for ever, to lie there underneath Charles, made breathless by his weight on her, warm and wanted and loved, until everything went dark.

She tried to hold out but his fingers would not allow it and she soon felt the quiver of approaching climax. Now there was nothing she could do to stop it, she let it take her. Charles thrust deeper and harder – he must *know* – and she clasped her legs tight around him, ready for the moment.

It spilled out of her, in her voice, in the spasms of her muscles, in the trembling of her limbs, in so many ways. He kissed her through it and kept up his rapid pistoning until he was able to join her.

It was almost as good as her own throes of ecstasy to watch him in his. How astonished he looked, as if he had not expected to feel this, and how touchingly alarmed. She laid his head on her breast afterwards and unplastered the hairs from his damp skin.

She felt too much for him. Without knowing quite how, she had waded into dangerous waters. But there was nothing she could do about it except try to keep afloat.

'Are you going to speak to her?' he said at last. 'When she gets back?'

'I hardly know. I keep rehearsing opening lines in my head and then … I can't continue.'

'I will be with you.'

'Perhaps I should do it alone. Perhaps I should wait. Oh, perhaps I should just go.'

He raised his head and levelled his eyes with hers, saying nothing while her agitation increased.

'You couldn't,' he said. 'You wouldn't just go.'

'It is too late,' she said. 'Too many years have passed … I must accept that I don't have a mother. I was happy enough before I knew of her.'

'No, Edie. No.'

'Why not? Do you care what's best for me, or can't you bear the thought that perhaps your father is happy with her, and might remain so?'

His face contorted with what looked like pain but was probably anger.

'The truth is always best,' he said.

'Not always.'

'If you don't tell her, I will.'

Edie sat up sharply.

'You will not! It is not your truth to tell. Do not pretend this is all about honesty and clarity and truthfulness when it is about your personal vendetta.'

His eyes were painful to look into. She shut hers.

'That is what you think of me,' he said.

'Charles, you admit yourself that you carried on an affair with her out of revenge. What am I meant to think of that?'

She waited for an angry outburst, the tilting of the mattress, even perhaps a slap on the cheek, but there was only silence for a long, long moment.

'No, I see,' he said quietly. 'I do see.'

She opened her eyes. 'You regret it?'

'Yes.'

He got off the bed, pulled on his bathrobe, moved over to the window and drew aside the curtain.

'Rain,' he said.

He turned around.

'Edie, can we start this again? Can we rub out the past?'

'The affair? The hatred? It's not the Charles I know and ...' She swallowed.

'What was that?' The tiniest hint of a smile twitched at the corners of his mouth. 'You know and ...?'

'You could be such a lovely man. You *are*, with me.'

'You make me better than I am.'

'No, I don't. Not at all.'

'You think there is hope for me, then?' He laughed, somewhat desperately.

'Oh, Charles.' She held out her hands, bringing him back to her.

They lay down in each other's arms and held each other in silence.

'If I tell her,' said Edie softly, 'and she chooses to say nothing to anybody about it, what will you do?'

'I couldn't share this house with her. I couldn't keep that secret. Not from my own father.'

'So you would tell him?'

'Not if it meant losing you.'

They looked at each other, trying to make sense of the decision that lay ahead.

'Would it mean losing you?' he asked in a whisper.

'I'm lost already,' she said. 'Oh, dear. So very lost.'

A knock on the door.

'Coffee, sir.'

'Tom's valet,' he whispered, covering Edie with the sheets and drawing the curtains around the bed. 'Bring it in,' he ordered aloud. 'Just put it on the table, would you? There's a good fellow.'

'I trust sir is feeling himself this morning?'

'A tad under the weather, that's all. Thank you. You may go.'

'I was intending to lay out your clothes, sir.'

'There's no need. I'll do it later. Thank you.'

'Perhaps a bath?'

'I can run a bath. I'm perfectly capable. Good morning.'

'Good morning, sir.'

The puzzlement in his voice made Edie want to giggle despite her fear of being found out. Mind you, there would be talk below stairs now and perhaps her name would come into it. She couldn't blame people for working out what was going on – it must be obvious by now.

'Bath's not a bad idea, is it?' said Charles, releasing Edie from her sheet-bound hiding place. 'I'll go and run one. Help yourself to coffee.'

'It should be my job,' she said. 'I do it for … Her Ladyship.'

He had no comment to make about that. He kissed the top of her head and wandered off to the splendidly modern en suite bathroom.

She poured a cup of coffee and took it to him. He sat on the lip of the bath and motioned her to put the drink down.

'How hot do you like it?' he asked.

'Coffee?' She was confused.

'No, the water, silly. Come here. Test the temperature.'

She put a finger into the swirling depths.

'You have hot-water pipes up here on this floor,'

she said. 'Everyone else gets hot water from the kitchen. It takes so long to organise. It's ridiculously old-fashioned.'

'We'll install more of these in due course,' said Charles. 'I got the first one. A coming-home present after the war, of sorts. That kind of alteration takes time in a great place like this, though.'

'It must do. Expensive, too, I imagine.'

'You haven't told me if it's too hot.'

'It's lovely and warm.'

'Then what's stopping you? Jump in.'

'I wish I'd brought my toothbrush down,' she said shyly.

'I have an unused one in the cabinet. Use it, by all means.'

It felt wildly indecent to be brushing her teeth in front of a man – in a way, strangely more so than the physical act of coupling. She thought she must be breaking all kinds of rules, but Charles had no qualms, sitting sipping his coffee while she scrubbed.

'You haven't smoked a cigarette this morning,' she noted, rinsing the brush and putting it away.

'Don't remind me,' he said, teeth gritted.

'Why not?'

'I don't have any. I need to get to the village as soon as I've had breakfast. Before I've had breakfast.'

'Oh, dear. You're on edge.'

'I'd be a lot worse if it weren't for you. I find that waking up with a beautiful girl in my bed rather dulls the pain of tobacco withdrawal.'

She laughed, blushing. 'Warm water is said to have analgesic properties too,' she said. 'Why don't you get into the bath?'

'Only if you'll get in with me.'

'Oh! Well. All right then.' Sharing a bath couldn't be any more indecent than sharing a bed, surely.

She watched Charles drop his robe and lower himself into the water until he lay submerged to his chest, his face already sheened with steam.

'Well?' He blew a strand of hair from his eyes and treated Edie to his most seductive smile. 'Aren't you joining me?'

There was a peaceful quality to lying in the hot water in Charles's arms that made Edie wish they could stay there, careless of wrinkling skin and the ever-cooling temperature, for as long as possible.

Charles, however, was in a rush to find his next cigarette, so he kept proceedings brisk, scrubbing Edie all over and lathering up her hair before rinsing it clean.

He dressed quickly, telling her that he was going to the shop for cigarettes.

'If they get back before me, hold fire, won't you? Wait for me before you say anything to the – I mean, your mother.'

Securing her consent, he kissed her brow and ushered her out of his room.

***

From her window she watched him drive away, insouciant in white linen and a striped blazer, although his face was shadowed and thoughtful.

Was she really going to tell Lady Deverell her story today?

If so, the time was coming very close indeed. Almost as soon as Charles's vehicle disappeared into the cover of the long wooded drive, Lord Deverell's Rolls Royce emerged.

They were back.

302

Chapter Eleven

Edie stepped away from the window and hurried to don her uniform, expecting that Lady Deverell would call for her as soon as she was back in her rooms. Quite some time passed, though, before the knock at the door came, and in the interim she could hear a lot of raised voices in the corridors and rooms on the floor below.

Charles was back from the tobacconists and he stood lounging against the wall outside Lady Deverell's bedchamber, smoking moodily, when Edie came down.

'Just to warn you,' he said in a low voice, checking that they were not observed. 'There's a most fearful row. Pa's still in London.'

'What?' Edie gripped the doorknob tightly, terrified that her story might have come out already, without her, unlikely as this was. 'Why?'

'She'll tell you herself, no doubt. I think we'd better postpone any further revelations for the time being.'

'Come in then, if you're coming.' Lady Deverell's voice from the other side of the door was querulous.

Edie nodded at Charles and left him outside in his cloud of smoke.

'Edie,' she said, looking her up and down dispassionately. 'Unpack my cases, would you?'

Edie was surprised and a little disquieted to see that Lady Deverell was smoking as well, something she had never before seen her do. She stood at the window, using a long, varnished cigarette holder.

'I hope you had a pleasant trip,' ventured Edie, opening the case and sorting through the crumpled contents.

An expostulation that could have been disgust or irritation was her only reply.

'Did you buy any new gowns?'

'Never mind new gowns,' she said. 'We're going to have to cancel this damn weekend party. I'll have to write and put everyone off. I only hope it's not too late.'

'What? Oh, but that was your whole reason for going to London, wasn't it? To buy new clothes for the weekend.'

Lady Deverell crossed to her bedside table and stubbed out the cigarette in a pretty china ashtray.

'We can't very well host a party when the host isn't here, can we?'

'Lord Deverell ...?'

'Still in London. And there he'll stay until he finds that perishing girl.'

'Perishing girl?'

'Mary, of course. Silly bitch has run off and nobody knows where to find her.'

Edie paused in the act of unravelling a ball of bunched-up stockings and stared at her mistress and mother.

'Mary has run away?'

'That's what I said, isn't it?'

'You must be terribly worried.'

'If you have nothing more helpful to say than that, perhaps it is best you hold your tongue.'

Charles was right. It was not a day for further upset. It was with some relief that Edie determined to postpone her unburdening. She offered silent thanks to Mary, at the same time hoping fervently that the girl was somewhere safe and well.

She was desperate to get away and ask Ted exactly what had gone on, Lady Deverell having reverted to monosyllables and terse commands after her initial explanation. Once the mistress was seated at her writing desk in preparation for composing many dreary letters to invited guests, Edie was free to make her investigations.

***

She found Ted in the garage, buffing the Rolls with an oily cloth.

He looked up as she came in.

'Aye aye,' he said. 'Look what the wind's blown in.'

'Lady Deverell's busy writing letters. She's released me for an hour or so. Ted, what happened in London?'

'I'm sure you've heard. Lady Mary's gone AWOL.'

'But why? Doesn't anyone have any idea where she is?'

He stopped his buffing for a moment and stood, shirt-sleeves rolled up to the elbow, passing his rag from one hand to the other.

'She was in Bond Street with Lady D, getting fitted for frocks. Lady D goes into the back room to try something on. When she comes out, Mary ain't there. And that's all I know.'

'Were you in the car, waiting outside for them? Did you see anything?'

'I was parked up round the corner, and no, I didn't see a thing.'

'What if she was kidnapped? Have they called the police?'

'She weren't kidnapped,' said Ted with a shake of his head and a smile. 'They'd been rowing non-stop all the way up to town and they were still at it when I drove them to Bond Street. Mary wanted to stay and go to some party her friends were throwing. His Lordship said no dice.'

'Then I suppose she may be with those friends?'

'His Lordship's up there looking for her. I expect you're right. It's nothing to worry about, leastways. That's my estimation.'

'Not everyone is as sanguine as you.'

'As what-guine?'

'It doesn't matter.'

'Just between you, me and that garage door,' said Ted, lowering his voice and moving closer to her. 'I think it might all be up between His Lordship and our Ruby Redford too.'

Edie sucked in a breath. 'Really?'

'Fierce row, they had, over whether he should have allowed Lady Mary to stay in London or not. Lady D took Mary's side; he was having none of it. I didn't hear all that was said but I picked up a few choice words. Let's see what happens when he gets back.'

'Oh dear,' said Edie, meaning it. If the edifice of the Deverell marriage was already crumbling, could she be the one to strike its death blow?

'Perhaps she'll go back to the stage and you can be her dresser, eh?' he said with a wink. 'It's a glamorous life, I've heard. Though I don't suppose you can beat being a lord's little bit of crumpet for glamour.' The smile was gone and his expression was stony, the rag bundled up tight in his fist.

'What do you mean?'

'I mean, my dear, that there's a lot of talk about you

307

below stairs. A *lot* of talk. Some reckon your bed wasn't slept in last night.'

'Some can keep their disgusting opinions to themselves,' shot back Edie, trembling all over. 'And while they're at it, they can keep their beaks out of other people's business.'

'So it's true, then? You and Charlie boy?'

She made to storm out of the garage but Ted caught her by the wrist and held her back.

'Never mind,' he said quietly, once she had worn herself out with struggling. 'It don't signify, not any more.'

'The village dance is off,' she said.

'Yes. Yes, I daresay it is. Go on, then. His bed'll be getting cold.'

'Don't you dare go spreading scurrilous gossip through the kitchens. Don't you dare.'

He stopped her again, grabbing her shoulder as firmly as he had taken her wrist.

'Scurrilous gossip,' he repeated. 'You do have a nice turn of phrase, Edie. I've always thought so. Just out of interest, who the bleeding hell *are* you?'

'You know who I am.'

'No. I don't, because you haven't told me. Tell me now, while you still can.'

'While I still can?'

'Times are changing for Deverell Hall, love. You can see that. Who knows if and when we'll meet again?'

'Stop it. You're frightening me. Tell me what you mean.'

He half-laughed and released her shoulder.

'Sorry. Take no notice of me. I'm a bit rattled by what's gone on, that's all. And I'm disappointed in you, falling for that plummy-voiced bastard, if you'll pardon my French. I don't know why. I shouldn't be surprised, should I? You're pretty, and he can seduce anything that moves. It was always going to happen. But I did think for a moment there …'

'Ted,' she said gently, putting her hand on his. 'Nothing is as it seems. Nothing is what you think it is.'

'Well,' he said after a pause during which he stroked her fingers. 'You're right there, girl. You ain't far wrong. Now, if you don't mind, I've got to get on. Back to London to ferry His Lordship up and down the City Road and in and out the Eagle.'

'That's the way the money goes,' said Edie absently.

'Pop goes the weasel,' they both chorused, then they laughed, the tension between them dissolving for that one sweet moment.

'Take care, eh?' he said, patting her hand. 'Don't get caught out like Susie.'

Edie did not have the strength to deny it any more.

'I won't,' she said. 'I promise. Drive safely, won't you?'

'Don't I always?'

* * *

She left the garage, pondering on the conversation. It was well-known, it seemed, that she and Charles had an ... attachment. The very thought of their being linked in people's minds made her both fearful and delighted. She felt ridiculously lucky and privileged. He had said that he loved her. Either she loved him or he had cast a very potent spell on her. He had made her reckless, caused her to forget her caution and drop her customary defences. Now she would pay the price for it. But what was the price?

Without quite knowing how she had gotten there, Edie found herself walking on the shores of the lake. The sun was high in the sky again and the grasses dry and scratchy. Edie took off her shoes and walked in her stocking feet around the water's edge, thinking constantly of Charles and Lady Deverell and how on earth it could all work out for the best.

So preoccupied was she that she did not hear the crackling and rustling behind her. She was aware of nothing but her own thoughts until, in a heady rush, she was caught around the waist, pinned to the trunk of a weeping willow and kissed until her breath ran out.

'Charles,' she protested, trying to fill her lungs with air again. 'Are you trying to frighten me out of my wits?'

'I saw you go into Kempe's garage,' he said, in a low, dangerous voice. 'What did you want with him?'

'You are so jealous,' she exclaimed.

'Of course I am. I'm jealous of that grass you walk upon. I'm jealous of that pair of shoes in your hand. I'm jealous of everything and everybody that gets closer to you than I do.'

'Nothing is closer to me than you at this moment,' she pointed out.

'Your clothes are. I want to take them off you.'

'Charles, we are in the open air.' But his words thrilled her and she pictured herself, thighs wrapped around his hips, being taken against the tree.

'I know,' he said. 'Warm, isn't it?' He pressed himself into her.

'A bit too warm,' she replied with a nervous laugh.

'Especially in those black-and-whites of yours. So neat and sweet, crying out to be rumpled and messed up.'

'You're insatiable.'

'I know. But let's stick to the matter at hand, just for the moment. What were you doing with Kempe?'

'I wanted to ask him about what happened in London, that's all.'

'What did he say?'

'Nothing much. Mary was with Lady Deverell in an outfitters in Bond Street and she disappeared while nobody was looking. She might be with friends who were throwing a party. Are you worried about her?'

'Mary? No. She's no trembling ingénue. She can take

care of herself. She *wants* to take care of herself, if only pa would let her. I expect she'll write to me in a day or so, tell us we're all fussing about nothing.'

'What about her reputation, though?'

'Oh, her reputation.' Charles smiled and shook his head. 'It really rather depends what's she's doing up there, doesn't it?'

'She could be with a man.'

'Like you are, you mean?'

'I don't mean to censure her. But I know how important reputation is, to people of your class and station. If Mary loses hers ...'

'Mary's got a decent enough head on her shoulders. Besides, there's no reason why anyone should know.'

'I don't suppose Lady Deverell is giving people the real reason for the cancellation of this weekend party.'

'No, she's pretending to be ill.'

'You've spoken to her?'

'Briefly.' He looked away.

Edie was surprised by the sharpness of the pang in her chest. She should not be afraid that he and Lady Deverell would recommence their affair. It wasn't at all likely now. But she still held that fear deep in her heart.

'How is she?'

'Put out, mainly. And raging against pa. Why am I talking about her when I have this highly ravishable maid up against a willow tree?'

All discussion melted into the sultry air as Charles fastened his lips upon Edie's and kissed away the speculation.

She let herself be carried beyond her workaday concerns and into the magical world of erotic sensation. The heat made her tight dress cling uncomfortably and there was bark scratching and tickling her, but it all seemed secondary to what was being done to her. Charles kissed her with hungry passion, his tongue searching inside her mouth. He pushed one of his knees between her legs and moved it up and down inside her thighs. Her petticoat chafed at the sticky, damp flesh until she longed for it to be gone.

Her most intimate parts felt heavy and overused, but they could not seem to stop themselves bursting into eager bloom, begging for more of what they had already thoroughly taken.

Charles removed one of his hands from her pinioned wrists and used it to raise her skirt, then her petticoat. He bunched them behind her and stroked her hip through her drawers before finding the elasticated top and slipping his palm inside.

She tried to gasp, to exclaim, but he had her deep in the kiss and there was no way she could break it. All she could do was keep her eyes shut and revel in the exquisite danger of having her lover's hand inside her underwear while she stood in broad sunlight.

His fingers soon located the heat of her parted lower lips and he pushed them inside, to rub gently and slowly at her fattened bud.

She twisted against him, tiny mewls caught up in her throat. He kept her words stoppered up with his sealed lips on hers, scouring her with his tongue.

Once his fingers were slick with her juices, he pushed them inside her. She raised her leg to grant him deeper access and he took full advantage of it, spearing her and grinding his hips against hers at the same time, so that she felt the bulge of his erection.

'Got to have you,' he panted, breaking off.

In a moment, his trousers were down and so were her drawers. Their groins mashed together and she held on tight while he lifted her up, cradling her bottom in his hands, and placed her astride him.

'We can't,' she whispered. 'We mustn't.'

'We can,' he said, with an urgent thrust. 'We will.'

Edie clung to his neck and let him grind her to a sweaty pulp against the tree. It shed its bark continuously as they rutted, but she was aware of nothing but their primitive connection and her need to be taken by him, regardless of where or when or how. She forgot to care if they were seen or what any consequences might be.

And when it was done and she streamed with her own perspiration and his seed, only then did she remember another important concern.

'Oh, no,' she said, staring at him while he mopped his brow and leant on the trunk for support.

He kissed her head.

'You didn't like that?'

'No, I mean, I did, but … that's not it.' She looked down at her dripping thighs.

'Ah.' He fell to his knees and lay down on the grass, one hand over his face.

Edie, irritated by his lack of response, went to the edge of the lake and dipped her handkerchief in the water. She was dabbing at the mess when he sat up, corrected his dress and spoke.

'Would it matter so much?' he said.

She turned, outraged.

'Would it matter? No, not to you, I daresay. But it would ruin my life, if that means anything at all to you.'

'I'd marry you like a shot.'

She turned away from him and continued her frantic efforts to remove all evidence of him from her.

'Charles,' she said levelly, unable to face him. 'Did you do that deliberately?'

'No, of course not. I was carried away in the moment just as you were. All I'm saying is that it needn't be the end of the world if you … if it led to something.'

'But how could it?' she said, wiping the last traces and dipping her handkerchief back in the tepid waters. 'Charles, how can we ever …? Oh, why did I come here?

It's the worst mistake of my life. Several of the worst mistakes, in fact, all at once.'

'Well, if that's how you feel.'

Charles stood and she turned to see him stride off through the glade and away towards the house.

'I don't mean you ... I don't mean ...' She broke off. He was out of earshot. 'You,' she whispered, watching his back recede.

She pulled up her drawers, sat down with her back to the willow tree that had supported them through their frantic coupling and burst into tears.

It was a horrible mess, that was for sure, and she couldn't sustain it any longer. She would have to go, just take the next train to London and try to pick up her life where she had left it off. In Deverell Hall and its inhabitants she had bitten off very much more than she could chew.

Perhaps, in time, she could write to Lady Deverell. And as for Charles, well ... He only said these things about their future to sweeten her, probably. She couldn't marry the man whose stepmother was her natural mother. There was bound to be a law against it. All the same, her body and soul conspired against her, making the thought of leaving him almost physically painful and impossible.

'It's best for him if I do,' she said out loud. 'He'll meet someone more suitable and, and, perhaps so will I in time.

No,' she continued after a moment's reflection. 'I'll never meet anybody else. But that's fine. More time to read.'

She wobbled to her feet, dashing the tears from her cheeks with her sleeve, her handkerchief being out of commission. Was there a chance she could get back to the house, pack, change and leave without attracting any unwanted attention?

She was not sure, but she meant to try it.

* * *

A movement in the trees, a flash of scarlet, diverted her from her path. She stopped dead, wondering who it could be, and how long they had been there.

'Hello,' she said uncertainly.

The figure stepped out from the greenery, revealing Lady Deverell in a bright red skirt and silk blouse. Her lips were the same shade and she parted them in a wide smile.

'Edie,' she said, more effusively than she might in the ordinary way of things. 'Taking a little walk by the lake?'

Edie nodded and smiled weakly back. Her flight would have to be postponed.

'Whatever have you been doing? You're absolutely filthy. Look at your uniform. The apron's streaked with … what is that? A grass stain?'

'Oh … I …'

'And your hair.' Lady Deverell was close enough now

to reach out and put a hand over Edie's half-uncoiled bun. 'Full of bits of bark. And leaves.'

'I'm sorry,' she stammered. 'I'll go and get changed.'

'Yes, I think you should. And bathed.' Lady Deverell put up a finger as if a marvellous idea had just occurred to her. 'But there's no need for a bath,' she said. 'Look at what we have, right here in front of us.'

'I'm sorry?' Edie was stupid with dread. She was sure Lady Deverell had seen Charles, or – even worse – seen the pair of them together, at it.

'The lake,' elucidated Lady Deverell, her smile wider than ever. 'There's a marvellous spot, just a little further on, where I like to come to bathe. Nobody can see it from the shores – it's quite sheltered. On a hot day like this, it's bliss. Come on. Why don't we?'

'Oh.'

'What? Goodness me, you look absolutely awful, Edie. Are you ill?'

'No, but –'

'Come on then.'

'I can't swim.'

Lady Deverell turned back round, cocking her head to one side.

'Of course. London girl, aren't you? Well, never mind. I'll teach you. Quickly, then. It isn't far.'

Edie's heart was tight and so was her throat as she followed Lady Deverell's back along the shore. She knew.

318

She had to know. Or were Edie's fears causing her to project things that were not there on to Lady Deverell's manner? Was she, in fact, just being her usual self?

She hardly knew what to do. Was Lady Deverell inviting her to confess before she performed a humiliating unmasking? Was she supposed to seize the chance to come clean? Would it be better for her if she did? Or should she play it safe and assume that Lady Deverell's skittish manner was a product of her stressful trip to London? Yes, yes, it could so easily be that. It must be that.

She would go along with her mistress's whim and then try to get away as soon as she could after that. And a dip in the lake would actually be rather nice. She felt as seedy as she had ever done in her life.

'Here, now,' said Lady Deverell, coming to a halt in a little inlet, overhung with weeping willows so that the waters beneath looked quite green. 'It's beautifully private and the water will be cool, out of the brightest part of the sunlight.'

'Yes, it's lovely,' said Edie.

Lady Deverell removed her hatpin and, for the briefest of moments, pointed the sharp end in Edie's direction before putting it, and her straw hat, on the ground. She shook her head, releasing long snakes of rich auburn hair. Here and there, a silver thread broke the glorious colour, but they were scarce enough and, unless the sun was glaring, one would hardly notice them.

'Help me with my clothes, then,' she said. 'Honestly, what kind of lady's maid *are* you, Edie?'

Edie stumbled over to her mistress, unsure where to start.

'My blouse,' hinted Lady Deverell, and Edie set to the buttons with clumsy fingers. 'How did you get into that state? You smell awful. Never mind,' she said, apparently taking pity on her mute maid. 'It'll all come out in the wash, as they say rather vulgarly.'

Edie removed the delicate blouse and folded it as carefully as she was able. Lady Deverell's upper body was revealed in a camisole of silver-grey silk, trimmed with cream lace. Beneath it, her girdle accentuated her full breasts, the rounded flesh spilling from the cups.

Edie removed Lady Deverell's skirt next. When she stepped out, Edie was reminded of some magnificent piece of statuary. She could pose for Britannia, she thought, or grace the prow of a ship.

'Are these the legs that launched a thousand pricks?' said Lady Deverell idly, stretching her long limbs in their silk stockings. 'Oh.' She smiled at Edie, the expression never reaching her eyes. 'I've shocked you.'

'Not at all,' mumbled Edie, placing the skirt beside the blouse on the grass.

'One of my lovers said it, back in the days when I was permitted a little vulgarity. Back in my theatrical days. I had a great many lovers, Edie. Doesn't *that* shock you?'

'It is none of my business,' said Edie.

'Tell me – you're very pretty. Are you a virgin?'

Edie's look of outrage was not feigned. The question was extremely rude and unexpected.

'Surely not,' continued Lady Deverell. 'I don't believe you can be. Tell me about your lover.'

'Your Ladyship,' said Edie in a low, pleading voice. 'I am going back to the house now.'

'You are not.' Lady Deverell's easy, teasing manner changed in an instant. 'Get your clothes off. I'll deal with my own underwear. You're coming swimming with me.'

'I've told you, I can't swim.'

'And I've told you, I can teach you. Chop chop.' She clapped her hands, then lifted her camisole over her head.

Edie's fingers moved reluctantly to her apron strings, then the buttons of her dress.

'Are you sure nobody can see us?' she asked, looking around her through the thick greenery.

'Not a soul. I've often bathed here naked, especially when I needed to get away from stuffy old Hughie. Which is most of the time.'

Edie felt a pang of sympathy for Lord Deverell. Try as she might to feel charitable towards her mother, she could not find her likeable. Of course, there were reasons for it – there had to be. She must have been ill-used indeed to have constructed such a hard shell around herself. All the same, Edie could wish that she might try to break through it.

'There now,' said Lady Deverell, beaming upon Edie's nudity with a look both benevolent and rapacious. 'Let's dip our toes in.'

Her Ladyship was even more splendid unclothed. Her flesh, dappled by sunlight, was generous and beautifully unmarked by time. She was a little broader about the hips than she might have been in her youth, but she was none the worse for it. Her stature and poise made her seem larger than she was, an Amazon goddess in her natural surroundings. Beside her, Edie felt meagre and plain. It was hardly surprising Charles had wanted to start an affair with her, whatever his motivations. She was simply the most stunning woman Edie had ever seen.

She followed her mother into the green-tinged water. It was deliciously warm, despite the shade, and the river weed brushed sensuously against her toes, winding its way around them.

Lady Deverell turned to face her and spread her arms wide, displaying her breasts to their best advantage.

'Isn't this heaven?' she exclaimed. 'The lake, the sun, just you and me, no men to spoil it all.'

'Will Lord Deverell be back today?' asked Edie.

Lady Deverell lowered her arms and fidgeted with her hair.

'I don't think it likely,' she said.

'I hope Mary will be found.'

'I don't think that very likely either.'

The way in which she spoke the words cast a sudden chill over Edie.

'Why … not?' she asked.

Lady Deverell's answering smile twitched at the corners.

'We have quarrelled,' she said. She waded forward and took Edie's elbow. 'Come on. Let's go deeper.'

The water lapped around Edie's knees, then her thighs, finally submerging her to the waist.

'I hope the quarrel was not too serious,' said Edie in a small, fearful voice.

'Oh, I'm afraid it was. Very serious. I know you're too polite to ask me what it was about; would you like me to tell you?'

Edie was not sure. Her heart was pounding wildly and she felt sick. Suddenly it seemed very important that she should get back to the shore.

'Would you?' Lady Deverell prompted. 'Perhaps you might like to guess. Go on. Guess.'

'I … can't.'

'I'm sure you can.' She wrapped her hand tightly around Edie's wrist, tightly enough to bruise. 'Go on.'

'Ow! Charles. Sir Charles,' she blurted.

'That's right. Sir Charles. It seems somebody had left my husband an anonymous note in his valise. I wonder if you'd know anything about that?'

Lady Deverell bent, pushing her face close to Edie's.

323

'Heavens, no! I know nothing about a note. I wouldn't, truly, I would never ...'

'Such a little innocent. Such a little slut.'

A heavy slap landed on Edie's cheek, stunning her so that she staggered backwards. But Lady Deverell still held on tight with her other hand, making escape impossible.

Edie looked desperately towards the shore, but the unearthly peace and stillness prevailed.

'I know what you and he have been up to,' she snarled. 'Everyone knows.'

'I didn't mean it,' said Edie, the words rushing out, wrenched from her by fear. 'I didn't mean to. It just happened.'

'It just happened. But you knew what he meant to me, and I suppose you wanted him all to yourself, you little bitch.'

'No,' sobbed Edie. 'I didn't write any note. Please believe me. You must believe me. I wouldn't do anything to hurt you. I made him break it off with you because I didn't want you to get hurt ...'

'What?' Lady Deverell almost released her grasp, tightening it at the last minute, just as Edie thought she might slip free. 'You made him break it off with me? You made him?'

'I was scared Lord Deverell would find out,' said Edie, and then she could say no more as Lady Deverell kicked her viciously off her feet and assisted the work of gravity by pushing her down beneath the surface of the water.

She breathed in water and weed, her ears rushing, her vision black with panic. She did everything she could to fight against the other woman's superior strength, eventually succeeding in cresting the water again, coughing and spluttering so that she thought her lungs might burst.

'You don't understand,' she gasped. 'You're my mother.'

At that, Lady Deverell released her grip and fell to her knees on the lakebed. The water was now around her collarbones and she pressed wet hands to her face and moaned.

'No, no, no, it isn't true. It isn't true. It can't be true.'

'It is true,' said Edie, trying to sound gentle, but she had no control over anything now. 'My father is Angus Crossland.'

Slowly, Lady Deverell removed her hands from her face, peeking out at Edie. She looked terrified, like a cornered animal seeking a way out.

'And you have come here to punish me? You have come for your revenge?'

'No. Oh, dear God, no.'

'He sent you? Your father?'

'He does not know I am here.'

Lady Deverell took several deep breaths, her eyes fixed on the willow canopy above, and Edie seized her opportunity to edge out of her reach.

'I had wondered,' said Lady Deverell at last. 'But I did not dare ... you do have such a look of me. I did wonder ... but I didn't dare ...' She continued in this vein for a few moments more, as if trying to fix the sense of the words in her head.

'I only wanted to see you,' said Edie, her eyes filling with tears that she couldn't check. 'I only wanted to know you. I never meant you any harm or ... anything but goodwill.'

'Your father doesn't know you're here?' repeated Lady Deverell, seeming to be out of her wits and rambling. Edie worried that her latest revelation had tipped her mother's already fragile mental state over a precipice. Should she have kept quiet? But no! Her life had been threatened.

'Who knows this?' demanded Lady Deverell. 'Who have you told?'

'N-nobody,' said Edie, not wanting to bring the subject of Charles back up.

'But you mean to tell? You mean to tell Lord Deverell, perhaps? You have come here to ruin me.'

'I swear, I have not.' The tears were falling fast now.

'I will not be ruined. I have everything I came here for – except Charles, and I'll have him again. He and I, and the Hall, and everything I have lived for. I won't have it taken from me. I won't.'

She advanced upon Edie, who turned to the shore and tried to run through the thick, resistant waters. She stumbled and fell forward into the rich green warmth.

She felt a strong hand on her shoulder, pushing her down, then the same hand on her head, holding it under the water. She had seen, just for a second, just when she opened her mouth to scream, the flicker of movement in the trees ahead of her, but now all was dark. Roaring darkness, a body that would not work in the way she needed, everything closing in on her, entering her, roaring darkness.

Chapter Twelve

She came to and she was not in heaven, nor was she in hell.

She was lying in some grass, still naked, wet and weed-covered, with a shadow over her. When she opened her eyes, she saw that the shadow belonged to Charles, whose own eyes were wide and face pale. His clothes clung to him, sodden, and his hair was plastered in weeds.

'I did not drown,' she whispered.

'Not quite,' he said.

'Where is …?' Edie tried to sit up and look around her, but Charles hushed her and laid her back down.

'Not terribly gentlemanly but I had to knock her out.' He nodded a little way further over in the glade. Lady Deverell lay sprawled nearer the lake's edge.

'Did she mean to …?'

'Kill you? It certainly looked that way from where I was standing.'

'Charles, I think she has gone mad.'

'I don't care what's happened to her. Let's get you somewhere safe.'

He lifted her into his arms and carried her away from the lake, across the grounds of the Hall.

Edie was hazily aware of her nudity but too shell-shocked to let it trouble her. She buried her face in Charles's chest and tried to shut the world out.

* * *

Once inside the Hall, he gave brusque instructions to one of the footmen to find Kempe and have him drive to fetch the police, then he took Edie to his rooms and laid her on his bed.

When he seemed to be leaving the room she propped herself up and called after him in dismay, but he had only gone to run her a bath.

'What happened?' he asked once he had returned and seated himself on the edge of the bed. 'Why did she do it?'

'I told her she was my mother. She thought I had come here for some kind of revenge. Oh, Charles. What will happen to us all?'

Charles took her hands.

'I don't know,' he said, squeezing them. 'But I will be by your side, whatever it might be. I love you and I think you love me and that will give us what strength we need. Yes?'

She nodded, her eyes leaking tears again.

'You're going to have her arrested,' she whispered.

'She tried to kill you.'

'But did she? Do you really think? Or was she just trying to warn me?'

There was sympathetic pain in Charles's eyes as he answered, 'Darling, you are still trying to make excuses for her. I understand that you desperately want her to be something else – a loving mother, a wronged woman. But she is who she is. Unscrupulous and self-centred beyond your comprehension.'

'It can't be that way. It just can't.'

'Come and lie in the bath, my love. Try not to think of it. I need a bath too – that pond weed clings to everything.'

He helped her to her feet and led her into the bath-room, where he shut off the taps and found towels in the linen cupboard.

For the second time that day, they sat in the bath together, but this time there were no lazy caresses or teasing kisses, just a profound, silent connection between them as they tried to manage their galloping thoughts.

'I didn't die,' said Edie, speaking into the steam. 'So they wouldn't hang her. They wouldn't, would they?'

'Of course not.'

'Can't we put the police off?' She twisted around to

face Charles, pleading. 'Your family name will be dragged through the mud. Wouldn't you rather …?'

'Keep it a secret?' finished Charles with bitter relish. 'That's what this whole mess is about, isn't it? Secrets. Lies. Pa will hate me for it, but I've had enough of secrecy. From now on, everything in my life is going to be decent and above board.'

'The perfect revenge,' she said.

'No.' He clamped his hands over her upper arms. 'No, Edie. No. She hurt you. That's what this is about. She hurt you and I can't have her doing it again. You can think the worst of me if you like, and, if what I'm doing now drives you away, then so be it. At least you'll be safe. That's all that matters.'

Edie searched his face for any signs of bluster or insincerity and found none.

There were no more questions to ask herself. He loved her, beyond doubt.

She laid her head back on his shoulder and started again the work of collecting her emotions. A loud knock at the door interrupted her.

'Sir, please, sir.' It was the voice of the footman Charles had detailed to find Kempe to fetch the Kingsreach police.

'What is it, Rivers?'

'May I come in, sir?'

'I'm afraid I'm in the bath.'

'But it's rather important, sir. I could stand outside the bathroom door.'

'All right, come in. What's happened?'

Edie sat upright in the bath, dreading that Lady Deverell had come to and done something awful. She gripped Charles's wrist as if it might spare her the worst of what might be.

'I went to find Kempe in the garage, sir.' The footman's voice was nearer now, just beyond the bathroom door. 'But he had already gone with the car.'

'Damn,' said Charles. 'Well, there's nothing for it but for you to go to Kingsreach on horseback.' Under his breath, he added, 'Why wouldn't pa have telephones installed, the ridiculous old dinosaur? I'll make him do it.' Raising his voice again, he said, 'Tell them there's been a serious incident and Sir Charles must see a senior man immediately. Or – oh, hang it, I'll go myself.'

He rose from the bath, shedding water all over Edie.

'No, no, sir, that's not all of it,' said the footman anxiously. 'He left a note on his workbench, sir. He didn't put it in an envelope or anything, so I'm afraid I read it …'

Charles wrapped himself in a towel and peered out through a crack in the door.

'What? Give it here.'

He snatched the piece of paper and read it, brow darkening as his eyes darted downwards.

'Jesus Christ,' he exclaimed, crumpling it in his fist.

'What's the matter?' whispered Edie, mindful of the footman's continuing presence just beyond the door.

'The man's gone and eloped with my sister,' he said, staring at Edie as if half out of his wits. 'She's run to some ferry port and he's meeting her there. They mean to go to France.'

'Ted?' Edie forgot to whisper, the word exploding from her. 'And Mary?'

'Yes. Good God. Poor pa. This will finish him. I need to … dear God. Look, Edie, let's get dressed and drive to Kingsreach. I need to telegram pa and see the police.'

'Is there anything I can do, sir?' ventured the footman.

'Yes, you can get down to the lake and look for Lady Deverell. See that she doesn't leave the estate. Take some of the other men with you. If you have to restrain her, then so be it.'

'Sir?' It was clear from his tone that he thought Charles might have gone mad.

'She's dangerous, Rivers. Those are my orders – do as you're told. Now go.'

'Yes, sir.'

***

They dressed quickly and ran out to the garage, a hastily constructed adjunct to the stables. Charles's car was the only vehicle in there, reminding them of Kempe's whereabouts – and his company.

'Did you have the slightest inkling?' asked Edie, as Charles hauled her into the passenger seat.

'Not the faintest,' he replied. 'I wonder how long it had been going on?'

'Was all that flirting with me some kind of cover?' mused Edie. 'Gosh. Is anybody in this house what they seem?'

'Apparently not.'

Charles revved the engine and reversed slowly out of the garage.

Edie looked at the house, from which a band of male servants emerged through the side door. Off to hunt down Lady Deverell.

Deverell Hall stood as majestic as ever, emblematic of an unchanging order in society. And yet so much upheaval was at hand. It hardly seemed possible that those respectable old grey stones could house such intrigue.

It should not happen here, she thought. These are London events.

Charles was in too much of a hurry even to put on his driving gloves, she noted. His hands were tight on the wheel, his knuckles white.

'Too fast,' cautioned Edie. They were barely a hundred yards from the house and already his speedometer was veering up to its maximum.

'This is important,' he said, and that was the last thing she heard before the car skidded sharply to the left, raced off the road and lurched on to its side, throwing her from her seat.

* * *

She lay on the ground for a minute or two, dazed and feeling that she had wrenched her heart right out of her chest. When she was able to move her aching neck, she turned to see that Charles was unconscious, his leg trapped beneath the body of the car.

She tried to crawl towards him but she could barely move.

'Charles,' she panted urgently. 'Darling. Please wake up. Please.'

But he would not, and she couldn't somehow get to her feet.

It might have been hours before Giles ran up, yelling Charles's name, but it was probably minutes.

'Please,' she said weakly. 'Help him.'

'Edie!' Giles cradled her and tried to lift her to her feet, but one of her legs was too injured and he had to let her sit back down on the ground. 'What the hell happened? Thomas is on his way but, as you know, he can't move as quickly ...' He had knelt to take Charles's pulse and put a hand to his brow.

'Is he alive? He is alive, isn't he?'

Giles nodded. 'What happened? Did he lose control of the steering wheel?'

'No, I don't think so. He was going too fast, though.'

'Slashed tyres.' Giles put a finger over a tiny puncture in the rubber. 'But who would ...?'

'Lady Deverell.'

'What?'

Shouts from the direction of the lake distracted him from his investigations.

'Look, don't stop here chatting. Please get him some help. Saddle up and get over to Kingsreach, as fast as you can.'

'Right, yes, you're right. No time to lose.'

Giles ran back to where Sir Thomas was just limping into view around the bend, spoke to him briefly then ran on.

Edie took her place by Charles's side, stroking his forehead and whispering entreaties to him to please be all right, to please live, to please keep breathing. His pallor and limpness terrified her so that she could barely think, let alone pray.

When Sir Thomas drew nigh, she let him take her in his arms and soothe her, understanding instinctively that it was not a time for interrogations or recriminations but for wordless human comfort.

Perhaps he had learned that in the trenches, she thought. Perhaps, like Charles, he had gone to war one man and come back another.

This thought dispersed in her mind, shattered by a blast of pain in her head so intense that, after a few moments, she slipped out of consciousness.

* * *

Cause of death: drowning.

That was what the certificate said. Edie looked out to the lake from her bedroom window and tied the ribbon of her new black hat. It was a rainy day. Autumn was halfway here and the pane streamed just as it had done when she first arrived at Deverell Hall.

She felt leaden, her heart weighted down, but the day had to be faced and endured. She turned and set off for the little chapel at the side of the house. A Deverell funeral would usually be held at the large parish church in Kingsreach, but Lord Deverell's orders were for a small and intimate burial with the minimum of fuss, and that was what would take place.

The tiny chapel was full. Edie took her place with the staff at the back of the room, but Charles, hearing the susurration of whispers that had started up at her appearance, hobbled over on his stick and made her come to sit at the front, between him and …

'Oh,' she exclaimed, clapping her hand over her mouth.

The man on the other side of her was her father.

'Edie,' he said, his voice thick with emotion. They

embraced tightly, then recalled their surroundings and reverted to quietness and solemnity.

In front of them, Lord Deverell's back was straight and stiff, his collar high. Sir Thomas was beside him. Ever since Charles had returned from having his bones set at the hospital, he and his brother had been nicknamed 'The Hopalong Twins'. Charles was fortunate, though, in that he would recover. Thomas's limp was for life.

Mary and Kempe had not returned for the funeral, although they had sent their condolences by telegram, having presumably seen the news in the papers.

Nobody else was present – not a single representative of Lady Deverell's theatrical past. But then again, Lord Deverell had not had funeral details published and had positively discouraged any attendance by those not connected to the family.

He had returned from London grey-faced and tight-lipped, with little to say about the events preceding Lady Deverell's return and her untimely end. Whether this was due to grief or shock, nobody could say.

The funeral proceeded as grimly as could be expected. The loudest sobs came from Sylvie, who stood in the row behind Edie, swathed in black lace from mantilla to skirt hem. Mrs Munn beside her looked mortified and tried to distance herself from the undignified display, but Sylvie wept on, oblivious to the unwritten rule that servants were not meant to draw attention to themselves.

Edie had written the eulogy and, as the vicar delivered it, she felt her own grief rise to the surface. A curious grief, more for what she had never known than for what she had, but no less real for that. Her father and Charles both laid their hands on hers, willing her through the difficult words.

That awful struggle in the lake seemed surreal to her now, almost a scene from a story. She had tried to excise it from her memory and see only the vibrant, laughing woman she had known. A woman who could have been a mother to her, in another time and place. A woman who had not deserved to die.

As nobody knew if her death by drowning was accidental or self-inflicted, she was interred in the family vault with the other deceased Deverells, in a small crypt below the level of the chapel.

* * *

Afterwards, tea and light refreshments were taken in the morning room while the rain swept across the parklands outside.

Edie stayed close to her father while Charles rallied around his own parent, with Thomas.

'Thank you so much for coming,' she said. It was all she could think of.

'Edie,' he said, contemplating his teacup, shaking his

head. 'Dearest girl, I don't know what possessed you to do this …'

'I'm sorry,' she blurted. 'But if you are going to castigate me –'

'No, no, not in the least. It is you who are owed the apology. I should never have kept the truth from you. It was at her request, you know. She thought it best.'

'She disowned me.'

'She felt the least painful way of proceeding was to pretend to herself that you had never happened. It was the only way she could continue with her life – and her career was just at its most promising stage. To have kept you would have ruined that. I tried not to judge her for it. I know what a hard face the world presents towards an unmarried woman with a child.'

'Yes,' said Edie, thinking of Susie and her little Charlotte. 'That is unfortunately true.'

'She knew you would be safe with me, and happy.'

'She was right,' said Edie, tears in her eyes again. 'But I wish she had not felt that she had to cut me out of her heart. Just a letter now and again … the difference it would have made.'

'She did what she thought best.'

'I know. That's what makes it seem so cruel. Papa, it must have affected her mind. It must have twisted it in some way. I'm sure she wasn't a bad person … or she didn't need to be. The world failed her.'

'She made a very fine marriage,' observed Mr Crossland. 'Not many people would agree with you about the world failing her if they came and took a good look at what she had here.'

'Spiritually, I mean, not materially.'

'Ah, yes. You were never a materialistic girl, were you, my dear? All the same, I struggle to picture you as a housemaid. Did you really set these fires and wax these floors?'

'Yes, but not terribly well.' Edie turned a rueful face to her father, grateful for the moment of light relief. 'It must have been a great shock to you, when you read of her marriage.'

'I almost mentioned it to you,' he admitted, taking off his glasses and polishing them. 'But what good would it have done? You'd have come haring up here. My instincts proved correct.'

'I'm sorry,' said Edie. 'You must have been frantic with worry.'

'Well, there was a little of that, yes. But your friend, young Patrick, put my mind at rest.'

'He told you?'

'He has a heart, Edith. He made me promise not to follow you, though.'

'How is Pat?'

'He is well. Languishing for want of you, I rather fear.'

'What? Pat? Oh, don't be silly.'

341

'You never could see what was under your nose. Patrick has had his heart set on you for years.' Mr Crossland chuckled, genuinely surprised. 'I thought you must know.'

'Oh dear.' Edie chewed her lip. 'I really hoped his interest in me was as a fellow idealist, a meeting of political minds.'

At that, Mr Crossland laughed out loud, subduing his amusement when all eyes turned sharply in his direction.

'Forgive me,' he said to the room in general, then to Edie, 'I think a meeting of more than *minds* was hoped for.'

Edie sighed and swished her tea in its cup.

'Well' was all she could think of to say.

'I suppose you are coming back to London with me? By the afternoon train?'

She looked up at him, blinking, for a few moments.

'I don't know,' she said. 'There's something … someone I need to talk to. Would you mind awfully …?'

She did not wait for his reply, but put down her teacup and made a tentative approach to Charles.

To say that she was not Lord Deverell's favourite person at this moment was to understate matters, but he continued to treat her with patrician civility even now he knew her true provenance. All the same, she preferred to remain beyond his notice whenever possible. Unfortunately, it wasn't possible now.

342

'Excuse me,' she said nervously, breaking into the little conference of father and sons. 'Charles, might I have a word, please?'

'Of course,' he said, bowing his head to his father and taking her arm with the hand that didn't grip the stick, as they walked towards the quietest corner of the room.

'Charles, I need to get out of here for a few moments. I feel I might – oh, dear, it's hard to breathe. Do you understand?'

'Yes, yes, come on. Don't worry. They don't need us here.'

***

Emerging into the hallway, Charles put his stick down, selected a huge golfing umbrella from the stand and opened it over the pair of them before limping out into the rain.

'Yes, I needed to get outside,' said Edie. 'This is just the thing. Thank you.'

They walked slowly over the gravel towards the formal gardens at the side of the house. How lovely they looked, even in the teeming rain. But soon the rhododendrons would be brown and dry and all the beds would be bare.

'How are you?' asked Charles.

'Oh, I don't know. Everything came so thick and fast.

It still seems like three weeks ago, in my head. I can't catch up with myself.'

'Your father seems like a good sort.'

'Yes, he is. The best.' She turned and smiled, warmed by his recognition of her father's priceless qualities.

'You haven't told him about us?'

She clutched his arm.

'Oh, Charles. What should I tell him? What could I tell him?'

'What do you want to tell him?'

She thought about this, pressed into his mourning-suited body, hearing fat drops of rain thump on to the umbrella above them. He smelled comforting and blissful and she appreciated his not lighting his usual cigarette yet.

'Well?' he said, a little less gently, and the cigarette box came out of his pocket, as did the lighter.

'Smoking again.'

'Do you want one?'

'No, thanks.'

'Don't look at me like that. I'm nervous. Any minute now you're going to tell me that you're jumping on to that London train with your governor and that's the last I'll see of you.'

'Charles –'

'But it won't be, you know,' he said fervently after taking a deep drag. 'You'll never see the back of me. I'll pursue you until I wear you down.'

'Charles,' she said, pinching his arm to shut him up. 'Stop it. Don't presume to speak for me. Give me a minute to straighten my thoughts.'

'All right,' he muttered. 'I'm sorry. I told you – I'm nervous.'

He smoked on, Edie pressed into his side, holding on to his arm for dear life, until the cigarette was spent. He threw it into a wet flower-bed, causing Edie to tut slightly, then they walked on.

'I wish things had been different for my mother,' said Edie.

'So do I.'

'She had to rely on men, and their good opinion, all her life. She had no way around it. Her world was ruled by them and she had to subject herself to its strictures. Be glamorous, be beautiful, be fascinating to men. Those were her commandments. If she'd only been born twenty years later ...'

'Things aren't so different now,' said Charles.

'Not as much as they should be, no. But the war changed things. Women's voices are being heard at last. We are starting to assert ourselves and to insist on being seen as people. That's all we really want, Charles. To have our humanity acknowledged as being parallel to that of men. Not the same as men, but capable of many of the same things, and certainly no less important to the world.'

Charles held up his hands. 'You don't need to preach to me, Edie. I'm with you. Votes for women, etcetera.'

'Good. So you'll understand that I don't want the life my mother wanted. She knew she wouldn't be truly secure unless she had the patronage of a very rich and powerful man. Once she had it, though, she realised how short it fell of what she really needed.'

'You don't know what she really needed. Pa loved her. She did not love him. She wasn't some suffering victim.'

'They both were. Victims of a world that accepts it as natural that a rich man will want a beautiful woman. An adornment. It's all so false, Charles, and so damaging. Don't you see?'

He shrugged. 'Perhaps, a little.'

'It isn't what I want for myself.'

'What? So because I'm rich and you're beautiful, we can't truly love each other? That's wrong, Edie. Quite wrong.'

'That's not what I mean. I want the freedom she never had. The freedom to be flawed and to make mistakes and to love whom I want, how I want. She was imprisoned by society's expectations of how women should be – I refuse to live in a prison.'

Charles smiled and kissed her forehead.

'Bravo,' he said. 'They should put you on a soapbox at Speakers' Corner. You'd be very good.'

'Don't tease me.'

'I'm sorry. I don't mean to. But, much as I agree with

your lofty sentiments, my love, I'd like to know how you mean to apply them to *me*.'

'I won't ever be Lady Deverell,' she said, looking him straight in the eye.

He winced.

'I can't live that life, Charles. I'm sorry. I've seen it and it's not for me. But ... don't look so crushed. It doesn't mean I won't love you and be loved by you.'

'I don't understand. If you won't marry me ...'

'"Come live with me and be my love,"' she quoted, closing her hand over the one that held the umbrella's crook.

'Like a shot, darling. But how is that possible?'

'I mean to go back to London, if not today then within the week. It is for you to choose whether or not you will come with me. We can live as man and wife – we can even marry, if you must – but I don't want that title and I don't want to come back here. Ever.'

'Good God,' said Charles, feeling reflexively in his pocket for another cigarette. 'That's quite an ultimatum. Pa ...'

'I know. It's not really fair to ask it of you. And if you can't bring yourself to give up all of this – your birthright and all that – then of course I'll understand. And I'll miss you terribly and love you always but I'll know that it can never be.' Her voice jolted, the tears forming rapidly.

'Edie, think about this. We needn't live here, of course. We have a place in London, you know that. We can stay there, all the year round. Tom can manage the Hall in the event of pa's death.'

'Your father won't be happy.'

'He never is. Let me speak to him.'

'All right. If there's a compromise we can reach, then so much the better. I don't want your title, though, and I don't want your riches. Make quite sure he understands that.'

Charles looked at his unlit cigarette and put it back in the box, rejecting it in favour of a tight embrace.

'You're like nobody else I've ever met,' he said, stroking her hair with his free hand. 'What's the opposite of a gold-digger?'

She laughed, huddled happily in his arms. Perhaps, after all, something could be salvaged from this terrible tragic mess.

'I know you've been groomed for this all your life,' said Edie, waving to indicate the Hall and its surroundings. 'If you can't give it up ... but I won't say any more. It's really up to you.'

She tried to disengage, bent on running full pelt back to the funeral party, but he would not let her go. Instead, he held the back of her neck and kissed her, through her tears and the rain, until the sound of footsteps on gravel interrupted them.

'Young lovers.'

They looked at the source of the words.

'Sylvie,' said Charles with a polite bow.

'You are dancing on her grave,' she replied, her face twisted with disgust.

Edie felt the force of the accusation. Perhaps it was not proper to be kissing her mother's stepson at her funeral after all. Embarrassed and ashamed, she crossed her arms and stepped away from Charles.

'No, don't,' he said, pulling her back into his side. 'I don't think we have anything to hide. Sylvie, on the other hand ... It was you, wasn't it? Who wrote that anonymous letter to papa?'

'Charles, this isn't the time or place,' urged Edie, but Sylvie had already answered with a sneer and a nod.

'Thus,' he persisted, 'setting a chain of events in motion that led to her death. Whether by accident or suicide I don't suppose we shall ever know. Why did you do it?'

'Why do you think? It's obvious, surely. She gave my place to this ... girl. I was angry. Furious.'

'So you betrayed her to my father.'

'You were going to do it anyway.'

Charles flinched and Edie turned swiftly to him. The accusation was just. He could not deny it.

'There was a time,' he admitted. 'But I'd changed my mind. Besides, I wouldn't have told pa she did anything with *me*. That's not the tack I would have taken, for pretty obvious reasons.'

'You wanted to get rid of her.'

He shrugged.

'It's not my finest hour,' he said. 'But at least I held back in the end. Whereas your little stunt has left us with one person dead and another devastated. Pa's just about made up his mind that the accusation was a spiteful lie, but I don't think he'll ever look at me in quite the same way again, all the same. The wedge has been driven in between us, Sylvie, and it's all thanks to you.'

Sylvie's face changed from a mask of vengeance to tired and grey. She went to sit on a garden bench, apparently insensible to its wetness, and put her head in her hands.

Edie, recognising utter desolation when she saw it, went to sit beside her.

'No, go away. You have taken everything from me.' Sylvie's voice was hard and tight. 'I wish you had died, not her. I loved her. I loved her and now she is dead.'

'Whether you hate me or not, I am sorry. So sorry,' said Edie. 'I hope you will find peace.'

'*Putain, va-t'en!*'

Edie got up and ran back to the house, knowing she would easily outpace Charles, whose feet she could hear, crunch crunch crunch, behind her.

'Don't go,' he cried. 'Edie. Don't go.'

She had gone to her room and packed her belongings within the hour.

* * *

Alighting from the train at Paddington, Edie leant heavily on her father's arm. She was quite light-headed and wobbly from the tempest of weeping that had kept any other passengers from joining them in their compartment during the journey.

And now, even dear old London could not soothe her, with its sooty air and its solemn station clock and its eddying tides of people everywhere.

It just seemed grey and noisy and firmly unsympathetic. Where was the space for the finer feelings? Where was the respect for grief and tender-heartedness when a gang of yahoos elbowed one out of the way, cheroots in the corners of their mouths, with a cheery 'Is your face long enough, love?'?

Her experiment had been the very worst kind of failure. Instead of gaining a mother, she had lost one. And that was not all. Her heart seemed to be somewhere out of her keeping too.

'I shall invite the McCullens for supper,' declared her father. 'They will be delighted to see you. It'll do you good.'

'Oh, please, don't,' said Edie. 'Let me have the evening alone. I cannot bear company just yet.'

She staggered and he helped her regain her balance.

'You seem terribly weak, Edie. Come to the station buffet. I'll get you some coffee and sandwiches.'

Ensconced by the window, looking out on to the busy

351

concourse, Edie tried to address herself to potted-meat sandwiches but they were too hard to stomach and she concentrated instead on the coffee.

'Have you eaten at all, since it happened?' asked her father.

'Barely. Or slept.'

He shook his head.

'I wish you had felt you could have told me your plans. I would have written to her. Perhaps she might have visited us.'

'At least I knew her. However briefly.'

'Yes. At least you knew her.' Her father gave her hand a sympathetic squeeze.

'Did you love her?'

'When we were together? Not that it was ever a conventional kind of romance. Yes, I did. Of course I did, Edie. Especially when you were the result of that union.'

'Did she love you?'

He smiled sadly. 'Not enough,' he said.

'Some people are better at loving than others.'

'Yes.' He watched her toy with the crusts of her sand-wich for a few moments, then said, 'Edie. I couldn't help noticing at the funeral ...'

She looked up.

'Yes?'

'There seems to be ... something, a little something,

352

I don't know what … between you and Lord Deverell's elder son.'

She escaped into the coffee cup, avoiding his eye.

'I've never seen you look at a chap like that,' her father persisted. 'Tell me he hasn't …'

'Hasn't what? Made me fall in love with him? Because I can't tell you that.'

'Oh, my poor child.'

'But never mind,' she said, putting her coffee cup down with a decisive thump. 'He has to stay and be a lord and all that. There's no alternative. I have to find a way to do without him.'

Without him.

'For what it's worth,' said her father gently, 'the way he looked at you was no less remarkable than the way you looked at him. He cares for you, I think.'

'Well, he shouldn't. I don't even like him.'

Edie laughed, a little hysterically, then tears stung her eyes. *Not again.*

She took out her handkerchief, but it already needed wringing out.

Amongst the milling crowds she saw in the corner of her eye, something moved with greater urgency, drawing her gaze towards it. A well-dressed man with a stick, hurrying as best he could, but seemingly with no destination in mind, for he stopped and doubled back and went to the edge of the platform and peered along it a dozen times. Their train still stood in the station and it was not until he broke free of the throng and began opening and closing carriage doors, looking into each compartment, that she realised who it was that she watched.

'Oh,' she said, half-standing.

She looked at her father, and uttered another 'Oh!' before running out of the buffet without further explanation.

He was still opening and shutting doors when she stood at the end of the platform and called his name.

'Edie!' He closed the final door and limped along the platform towards her. 'I thought you must have caught another train or got off somewhere else or ...'

'We were in the buffet.'

'I had to drive like a maniac to get here before you – no easy task with a gammy leg like mine. Nearly got myself killed. And then you didn't come out ... oh. Come here.'

He grabbed her and swung her into his arms, kissing her face all over while people passed them, tutting or murmuring with nostalgic sympathy.

'I had to leave,' she said through tears and kisses. 'I couldn't stay another minute. I'm sorry.'

'You didn't say goodbye.'

'I know.'

'I wouldn't have let you. Perhaps you knew that.'

'But Charles, I can't come between you and your birthright, so –'

'Hush. So nothing. Birthright nothing. I don't want all that – any of it. All right, a little private income doesn't go amiss, but as for the Hall and the name ... hang it. I asked pa to write me out of the succession. Told him to give it to Tom.'

'Oh, you didn't. What on earth did he say?'

'I don't know. I didn't hang around to listen. Too intent on chasing you to London.'

'He won't agree.'

'Whether he agrees or not is neither here nor there. Perhaps I'll have to keep the title and Tom can manage the Hall. Whatever works best for everyone. The important thing is that you and I are together. Don't you think?'

'Yes. I do.'

'Then everything else can settle itself.'

They kissed again, oblivious to all the bustle and drone and roar and clank and hiss. Nothing existed for them but their love. There would be no more secrets now.

9 780007 553396